VERMIN

2.0

HUNGER PAINS

Lee Gabel

FRANKENSCRIPT

Frankenscript Press
Box 717, #105 - 1497 Admirals Road
Victoria, BC, Canada   V9A 2P8

VERMIN 2.0

Cover illustration and design by Lee Gabel

Cover images supplied by Shutterstock
Rat icon supplied by Vector Portal

Cover font (Benguiat) by Bitstream Inc.
Body font (ITC Galliard Pro) by International Typeface Corporation
Folios, heads and caps (Zapf Humanist 601) by Bitstream Inc.

ISBN: 978-0-9918498-3-3 (ebook)
ISBN: 978-0-9918498-4-0 (paperback)

Want to join Lee's Reader Group or find out more about Lee and the books he writes? Please go to:
LeeGabel.com
LeeGabel.com/facebook
LeeGabel.com/twitter
Or follow Lee on BookBub at LeeGabel.com/bookbub

VERMIN 2.0

HUNGER PAINS

Titles by Lee Gabel

Detest-A-Pest Series
Molerat 2.0
Arachnid 2.0
Vermin 2.0

Standalone
Snipped
David's Summer
Tied

For Ken, who always remembered to ask
"How are the rats doing?"

Airport

Four o'clock in the morning. The cloudless skies over Hunts Point twinkled with stars and the new moon made the Point just a little darker. New moons are an active time for rats at night. The cover of darkness paired with the lack of moonlight brought the rats out of their burrows in droves. From deep under the streets, rats scuttled through the dirt and slime-covered sewer walls, past rusting access ladders and grimy concrete conduits. Trash, long since forgotten, lined the old sewer walls as rats made their way to the streets in search of food.

Sam slept a fitful sleep in his ground floor apartment on Casanova. He tossed and turned in his bed, as if he could sense the rising tide of rats beneath him. He could hear their teeth forever gnawing, chewing through anything, his apartment door, his mattress, his legs and arms.

Sam's scream woke him up in a cold sweat. His chest heaved like he had just run a marathon. He sat amongst his strewn sheets, and kept his body as still as possible. Sam listened and watched for movement. The air was still and all he could hear was his own breath.

He noticed that he had left his bedroom window open again. The past week had been uncomfortably warm, and Sam had opened his bedroom window during the day in an attempt to air out the place, but he kept forgetting to close it. But the sunshine and warmth sure beat the ice, snow and sub-zero temperatures of last January when Sam had moved in.

After five months a free man, he wasn't used to the smells of normal life. Instead, he still preferred the antiseptic institutional smell of a prison cell. At least he didn't have to deal with the body odor of other inmates any more.

He rolled off the bed, walked to the window, and paused to scan the alley. Sam's sleep-weary eyes couldn't spot any movement. He could smell Kingsley Fried Chicken & Pizza from one block over, his go-to joint, mixed with the funk of garbage from the overflowing dumpster in the alley. Fried chicken was one thing, but mixed with rancid garbage was quite another.

Sam closed the window and collapsed back into bed.

There are no rats here. It's all in my head. Sam repeated his mantra and closed his eyes. He was desperate to relax. In twelve hours he would leave to meet the son he'd never known.

But there were rats here, outside, and they bubbled up all over Hunts Point. One rat emerged from a sewer grate and almost looked adorable if it weren't for its wet, matted fur and long, greasy gray tail.

Rats are omnivores and opportunists. They're intelligent and go where the food and water are plentiful. They used the interconnected sewers and catch basins of the Hunts Point Pollution Control Plant as their travel conduits. It was the perfect breeding ground. Rats multiply rapidly and produce a new litter of up to a dozen pups every three weeks. Many believe that there is a rat for every person who lives in New York City. Eight point five million. One of those rats was perched below Sam's window.

The rodent caught a scent in the air, and scurried along the sidewalk's curb and over to the alley beside Sam's building. It was a familiar path for the rats in this area. Anyone who looked close enough would see the grimy paths painted onto the sidewalk from nightly food runs.

Up on its haunches, the rat paused, sniffed, and reassessed its chosen route. There was a different smell in the air, one that wasn't entirely foreign to this rat, but also one that signaled caution.

Out of the darkness, a new, different rat emerged to block the other rat's path. This newcomer was leaner but bigger, with clearly defined muscles and a white-tipped tail that flicked and seemed to glow, even in the moonless dark.

Being social animals, the first rat stretched its head forward. The rat's cautious whiskers twitched madly, and it sniffed the new rat in a rodent greeting. The new rat remained motionless and held its ground. Its whiskers vibrated as it gnawed its own incisors down into sharpened points.

Chomp!

In a matter of seconds, the first rat's head was clamped in the jaws of the second. The first rat began to squeal and struggle in a desperate attempt to break free. It curled its back around to try and kick the new rat, but the aggressor's jaws remained locked in a death grip.

The screeching sounds of struggle lured new rats out of their dark hiding spots, new rats with white-tipped tails that flipped wildly. The swarm descended on the first rat with vicious intensity. They worked together to eviscerate the first rat's body with quick precision.

The killers with white-tipped tails, provoked into a feeding frenzy by their blood lust, fought over the remaining carcass. Their snouts, soaked in sticky crimson, sniped at each other in order to win the ultimate prize of the last bite. The battle for the remains pulled what was left of the first rat onto the sidewalk and left behind a messy red smear, like the first stroke of a plein-air painting. The blood feast was cut short when headlights from a passing vehicle washed the sidewalk with light. The rats with the white-tipped tails and gory muzzles scattered and disappeared into the shadows. What was left of the carcass remained on the sidewalk, abandoned.

SAM WAS NERVOUS. He had every right to be. Apart from the one photograph he had been allowed to keep during his fifteen years behind bars, Sam had no idea what his son Bradley looked like.

He pulled his wallet out of his front pocket and ran his hand across it. Black, smooth and thin, made of genuine leather. Unblemished, just like new from being stored in the property room for all those years. Claire had given the wallet to him on his twenty-fourth birthday. Now, he held onto it like an anchor, as if without it he'd float away, back into a life owned by the State of New York.

Sam flipped it open. The wallet contained a small amount of cash, his driver's license (five months old), and his only picture of Bradley framed in one of its windowed pockets. Bradley had been one at the time the picture was taken. Sam remembered the day with ease. Bradley smiled on the kitchen floor as he played with a Tupperware Shape-

O-Toy. Sam began and ended each day memorizing that smile. The photo was faded and worn on the edges from years of exposure on his cell wall, but intact, even after guards had tossed his cell, moved him to other cell blocks or thrown him in solitary. That photo was Sam's only tangible link to the life he had known. He had received no updates or letters. Claire had seen to that.

After Sam was convicted Claire had wasted no time. She packed up and moved across the country to California and left no forwarding address. She had always hated New York. "Too crowded and dirty," she had said.

The conversations were all the same: short-tempered, intolerant, and unforgiving. They all melted together in his memory, but as with all memories, bits and pieces would forever stand out. With Claire, it was the bad memories that floated to the top.

"You don't deserve to know him," she would say. "Once a drunk, always a drunk." That was the death knell of the calls. After that, there would be no convincing her, even though he knew he would never touch a drop of alcohol again for the rest of his life. He knew this as surely as he knew his own name, but Claire would never understand.

Sam would protest anyway. He would claim to be a changed man, a better man (he was). Even after all these years, Sam could still picture Claire on the other end of the phone, as she shook her head and fumed silently. He used to find her reaction endearing, back when their marriage was young and he still had a life that resembled something close to normal, but now it just frustrated him. He just wanted to see his son, and maybe, if he was lucky, update his old and bleached photo of Bradley. From the little snippets of dialog he heard in the background, it sounded like Bradley's interest in seeing him was mutual, but he couldn't be sure. Claire would have none of it.

"Send him out for a week," Sam remembered saying. "Let me hang with him for a while."

"I'm not going through this again." Predictably, Claire hung up the phone and that was that. It was the last time Sam would speak to her. When he was released five months ago, he had tried to call her, but the number was out of service. Not even Sara Armstrong, his parole officer, was able to track down Claire's new phone number this time.

It was all a great unknown. When Sam got the unexpected news that Bradley would be visiting, his brain started tick-tocking in all the wrong places. It didn't help his mood, either. The idea that Sam found himself falling back on and the only answer that made sense, was that Claire had gotten tired of Bradley's questions about him and relented.

Sara had called Sam last week to let him know that Bradley would be visiting for the summer.

"For the entire summer?" Sam remembered feeling happy, stunned, and mostly scared.

"That's what Claire said."

"I said a week. I don't know if I can handle an entire summer," Sam's mind raced. "What am I going to do?"

"Try being a dad," Sara said.

"Yeah. Easy for you to say. By any chance did she leave a phone number?" Sam knew it was a long shot.

"What do you think?" Sara flipped through her file on Sam. "I already checked. She used a pay phone. That woman's got serious hate going on for you."

Serious hate. How can I fight that?

Sam pushed Claire and her bad energy to the back of his

mind. He had other worries now, like how to entertain a sixteen year old boy for ten weeks.

Sam found himself at John F. Kennedy International Airport three hours early. He stood and waited in Arrivals, close to gate C38 in Terminal 8. He had looked forward to meeting his son all week and didn't want to make a bad first impression by being late.

J.F.K. was a massive, busy complex and served more than fifty million passengers per year. He hadn't set foot in an airport for the better part of two decades and Sam found the sheer number of people in one place amped his feelings of insecurity. Most days he longed for the solitude of a prison cell.

But three hours early? What am I, nuts?

Bradley was due to arrive on American Airlines flight AA-288, 4:35 pm. His flight had been on schedule for the past two hours, every time Sam checked the vertical display screens that listed arrivals. For the first hour of Sam's wait, Bradley's flight didn't even show up on the display screen. He thought he got the day wrong but a woman at the information desk assured him that flight AA-288 was on its way and on time.

Sam checked his watch, then checked the arrivals display screen. His watch was two minutes fast every time he looked. As the time of Bradley's arrival approached, Sam's heart pounded harder in his chest. Even though he hadn't drunk a drop for fifteen years, he would forever feel the pull of alcohol. A beer would take the edge off.

Sam distracted himself by checking his watch, then the arrivals screen, and back to his watch. He noticed a barely perceptible tremor in his arm. He raised his other hand up to confirm his shakes, then balled his fists.

Relax. Any time now.

Sam shifted his gaze to the sliding doors that separated arriving passengers from waiting loved ones, or in his case, an absent ex-con father who had no idea what his son looked like.

A deadbeat. Claire was fond of that title.

Fucking Claire. How else have you poisoned Bradley against me?

Cold sweat collected on the hairline of Sam's closely cropped buzz cut. His long-sleeved flannel shirt had become damp from his soaked t-shirt underneath. He wiped his brow with his sleeve and his hand brushed against his coarse five o'clock shadow. He had forgotten to shave.

Great. I look like a god damned bum.

The first passengers began to trickle out of the arrivals gate. The sliding doors opened and closed with an audible *shhhik*. Sam scanned their faces looking for something, anything familiar. Soon the trickle became a mad crush. People flowed out and made a beeline for the luggage carousel. The sliding doors never had a chance to close.

Is it the kid with the USC t-shirt? Or the one wearing the Cincinnati Reds ball cap? Or the fat one there?

Sam couldn't keep up. He watched the unknown faces move and squeeze past him. He was sure he had missed some, but didn't dare check to look behind for fear of missing more people exiting the arrivals door. He felt his knees weaken under his anxious weight and had to sit down on a nearby row of seats. His lower seated position wasn't optimal because people further back were more easily obscured.

I haven't missed him, have I? Shit. Wouldn't it be a joke to have to look for Bradley at the Lost and Found?

The numbers of passengers began to thin dramatically. Sam scratched his head.

For fuck's sake, I missed him. Why couldn't Claire have sent me a more recent picture? Bitch.

Sam stood up. He steadied himself on the seat back, and headed towards the sliding doors of arrivals, which were now closed. He looked down the corridor beyond the glass and spotted the pilots and flight attendants approach. The arrivals door slid open.

"Are you from flight AA-288?" Sam's eyes flitted between the pilots and the attendants.

"Yes," the taller pilot said. He shot a glance to his co-workers, then back to Sam. "Are you alright, sir?"

"Is anyone else on the plane?"

"The crew is always the last off," the pilot said. "Do you need assistance?"

Sam shook his head and let out a sigh.

"You sure?"

Sam nodded, and walked toward the open arrival doors.

"Sir, I'm afraid you can't go in that way." The other pilot held Sam back as the doors slid shut.

Sam's shoulders slumped, defeated.

Fuck.

BRADLEY'S FLIGHT WAS just over five hours. He hadn't eaten enough before takeoff and was famished by the time the flight attendant came to take his order. The only meal options left were a Chicken Apple Sausage Skillet or a Kid's Snack Pack.

"I'm not a kid, so I'll take the skillet." Bradley was

curious what sausage made from chicken and apples tasted like. It couldn't be all bad.

The flight attendant took the crumpled ball of bills from Bradley and handed him his meal.

The picture in the brochure always looked better than the real thing. His skillet was light on the sausage and heavy on the potato and scrambled eggs. He counted three pieces of apples. To be fair, the meal tasted fine, but it was hot in the center and cold on the edges. Bradley stirred it to give it an overall lukewarm temperature. For some reason, the flight attendant handed him a fruit cup as well. It was mostly melon. He hated melon.

Bradley had been up since five-thirty in the morning. At this point he didn't care what he shoveled into his stomach. He ate like there was no tomorrow, wolfing down everything, including the melon, plus coffee and orange juice.

The entertainment offerings were lame, and he didn't want to pay for Internet access. He had grown bored of the games on his phone and kicked himself for not downloading something new for the trip. He eased the seat back and managed to get an hour or so of shut-eye.

Claire had ruined his summer and his fitful dreams picked up on his anger and ran with it. He had wanted to get a job after school was out and earn some extra money for a new computer. He wanted to meet his dad, maybe spend a couple weeks with him, but the entire summer?

"I had plans, Mom!"

"Sam's been on my case to meet you, so here's your chance," Claire said. "Maybe now he'll shut up about it."

"But ten weeks?" Bradley said. "I don't even know him. What if I hate him?"

"Then that'll make two of us." Claire kissed Bradley on the forehead. "You'll know for sure by September."

Bradley fumed. "This sucks, Mom."

"Give it a couple weeks," Claire said. "If it sucks as much as you say it will, we can renegotiate."

Bradley awoke in a foul mood, and angry with Claire. There was still two hours left in the flight. He tried to distract himself by watching one of the flight attendants. "Trix" was emblazoned on her lapel pin and he fantasized about getting hot and heavy with her. But Claire's head kept popping in and ruining the scene.

"Do you love her, Brad?" Claire's voice echoed in his head. "She's not good enough for you, Brad."

Jesus Christ, Mom, leave me alone.

He pulled his day pack out from underneath his seat and unzipped one of the pockets. He removed an old photo of Sam and Claire and studied it. The date on the back: May 28, 2000. Claire was kissing Sam's cheek. He was looking up feigning surprise in a playful way. A happier time and a much more useful reference than the baby photo Sam had of him. Bradley pulled out his phone and took a picture of the old photo, just in case. He worked the digital image with his fingers to enlarge the view.

What would my family have been like if you hadn't gone to prison? Would I have been happy like this?

Sam's face in the photo continued to grin his goofy grin, as if he was averting his eyes from any other questions. Bradley shoved the photo back into his day pack without care and pocketed his phone, now pissed at both his parents. The summer was bound to suck, guaranteed.

He was seated beside the wings in the middle of the plane, not even a window seat like he had asked Claire for.

When the plane touched down, he disembarked well-mixed with the rest of the passengers. His little black cloud followed him and kept his mood in a dark funk.

Bradley moved through the arrivals exit door and spotted Sam right away. His hair was shorter than in the old picture and he looked thinner, too. Bradley wasn't ready to meet his dad, so he decided to have some fun.

He pushed his way to the outer edge of the surge of bodies and moved towards the baggage carousels, opposite Sam's position. Bradley hunched down a little and looked to his left, which obscured his face from Sam's view. When he was sure he was clear of the exit, Bradley doubled back and took a wide route. He positioned himself behind a support pillar and kept Sam in view with every step. He felt like a private investigator.

Bradley poked his head out and watched Sam crane his head from side to side, trying to find him in the exodus. The passengers thinned and Sam sat down. It looked like he was in a panic, which gave Bradley a small sense of satisfaction. A little bit of payback. If he had been asked why payback seemed important then, Bradley would have had no answer. As the last passengers streamed past Sam, the arrivals door slid closed with a *shhhik*.

Bradley watched Sam stand up, steady himself on the seat back and walk toward the arrival doors. He looked through the glass.

Sam took a step back as the flight crew exited the arrivals door. They talked but Bradley was too far away to hear their conversation. One of the pilots held Sam back as the arrival door slid shut. Crestfallen, he stepped back from the sliding doors as the flight crew walked away. Sam remained standing, and looked through the glass as if he expected something to change.

Bradley's little escapade had done wonders for getting him out of his bad mood, even if it was at Sam's expense. But it was time to come clean.

He stepped out from behind the pillar and began to walk towards Sam, but something stopped him halfway.

Sam sensed someone behind him and turned. When their eyes met, he knew it was Bradley in an instant. The fact that they were the only two people left in arrivals made no difference. He saw himself, he saw Claire all at once in his son's face and eyes. Bradley's day pack hung off broad, young shoulders.

"Bradley?" Sam's legs went rubbery as he fought to maintain his composure.

Bradley nodded and offered a small wave. "Hi."

Sam took a tentative step forward, then another. Bradley closed the gap between them. Now he stood face to face with his dad, a completely familiar stranger.

Sam didn't know what to do with himself. "Do I hug you now? I'm a little rusty."

"About as rusty as you can get." Bradley offered his right hand to shake.

Sam took his hand and they exchanged a firm handshake. Overwhelmed, Sam pulled Bradley close and gave him a hug anyway.

"I've been waiting fifteen years to do that," he said.

Bradley didn't reciprocate. It was too soon for him. When Sam released him and stepped back, Bradley noticed Sam's eyelids were rimmed with tears. He wiped them away before the tears had a chance to fall.

"It's good to finally meet you…" Sam paused and searched his memory. "Do you prefer Bradley or Brad?"

"Brad. That's what my friends call me."

"Okay, Brad. Let's go get your luggage."

Sam lead Bradley past the entrance and into the luggage carousel area of Terminal 8.

BRADLEY TOOK OUT his phone and tapped something into it. Sam studied his son absorbed by this small electronic device.

"Who are you talking to?"

Bradley looked at Sam like he had asked for his deepest secret. "I'm texting Mom." He turned to hide the screen of his phone from Sam.

Sam nodded. "Cool." He thought about asking Bradley to say hello for him, but the thought evaporated faster than he could say the words. It wouldn't have meant anything anyway.

Bradley wore jeans and a leather jacket over a t-shirt with the words "Guess what?" and an arrow that pointed to a chicken's rear end. A raccoon tail hung from his belt. Sam didn't get it and made a mental note to ask Bradley about it later.

Baggage began to flow down from the ramp in the ceiling and onto the revolving carousel.

"Which bag is yours?" Sam scanned the bags that were already following their perpetual circle route. "What should I be looking for?"

"No worries," Bradley tapped at his phone with his thumbs. "I got it covered."

Weren't kids supposed to respect their elders?

Not today. Bradley was engrossed with his phone. He ignored the baggage making its rounds, as well as Sam who stood by and waited.

"How long does it take to send a message to your mom with one of those things?"

"Mom already knows," Bradley said.

"So who are you texting now?"

"Some friends."

That was it. Sam had had enough, of the crowd, the delays, and the lack of respect. He walked up to Bradley and grabbed his phone out of his hands.

"Hey! What the hell are you doing?" Bradley tried to grab his phone back, but Sam shoved it into his front pocket.

"I'll make you a deal," Sam said. "Get your bags and I'll give it back."

Bradley daggered him with a look that promised revenge. "Uncool." He sulked over to the carousel and started to look for his baggage.

Sam took Bradley's phone out of his pocket and looked at it. One huge difference Sam noticed from fifteen years ago was how much cell phones had changed, and how much people relied on them. When he had began his prison sentence, cell phones could make calls, send texts and had monochrome LCD screens. Now they could do practically everything, but the technology was foreign to him. Not only could he not afford it, he had no interest in it.

Bradley looked back at Sam and saw him with his phone. "Hey!" he yelled back. "Don't touch that."

Sam put the phone back into his pocket. "Cool your jets, Brad."

Bradley's two bags slid into view. He grabbed them and dragged them over to where Sam stood. He held out his hand. "Give me my phone back."

"Didn't Mom teach you any manners?"

The muscles in Bradley's jaws clenched in angry angles. "Give me my phone back, *please*."

Sam dug Bradley's phone out and handed it back to him.

"You better not have done anything to it."

Sam grabbed Bradley's shirt by the collar and pulled him close. "How about a little respect?" As soon as the words were out of Sam's mouth, he knew he'd fucked up.

They exchanged angry gazes, both recognizing themselves in each other's eyes. Sam held his hand out towards one of the bags.

"Let's go."

Bradley relented and handed over one of the bags. He was glad not to have to carry it, but he'd never tell Sam that.

"Follow me," Sam said as he began to walk toward the exit of Terminal 8. Bradley followed a short distance behind, his eyes narrowed and a scowl on his face. The little black cloud was back.

That went well, Sam thought. *Way to alienate your son in two minutes. Fuck, I'm shitty at this.*

Sam found his beat-up old Ford F-250, flipped open the tailgate and hefted Bradley's bag into the truck bed.

Bradley stared at the truck in awe. Its faded orange paint job made the rusted holes in the side panels harder to see.

"Holy shit." Bradley dug his phone out and prepared to take a picture. "Is this thing safe?"

Sam reached towards Bradley's other bag. "Come on. Let's load up. And put that damn thing away."

"Chill." An audible *click* sounded from the phone. "I'm

just documenting your life." Bradley rolled the bag over to Sam, who waited at the back of the truck.

"Who said I wanted my life documented?" The notion of Sam's meager existence recorded for all to see chilled him to the bone.

"I just thought—"

"You thought wrong." Sam threw Bradley's second bag into the back of the truck and closed the tailgate with a slam. "Get in."

Bradley pocketed his phone and grabbed the passenger door handle. It didn't budge. Sam reached over to unlock it from inside the cab. The door groaned and creaked as he pulled its dead weight open. Again, thoughts of safety wandered through his head. Bradley threw his day pack into the footwell and climbed into the truck. He closed the door behind him with a tired, mechanical *clrunk*.

"Aren't you going to tie down my bags?" Bradley locked his seatbelt across his waist. He pulled his raccoon tail out of the way so it wouldn't get caught.

"They'll be fine." Sam jammed his key into the ignition and gave it a turn. The whine of the starter rose up from the front of the truck but the engine failed to turn over. Sam repeated the sequence without success.

"Come on you piece of shit!" Sam turned and held the key's position. The starter released a high-pitched grinding sound that reminded him of the metal lathe in the prison workshop. It was a case of third time lucky. The engine roared to life, then settled into a low rumble. "Know anything about cars?"

Bradley shrugged.

"Damn," Sam said. "Was hoping you could help me with a tune up."

Sam left J.F.K. and headed north on Van Wyck Expressway. Traffic was heavier today and the trip took longer than the usual hour. He chose to take Grand Central Parkway because he thought it was a more scenic route.

Bradley sat, silent and sullen under his black cloud. So far the visit hadn't gone at all like he thought it would.

Sam wished he could have a do-over, but he accepted the consequences of his actions. The drive helped sooth him, and it was something he had missed in prison. But the heavy silence in the cab was overwhelming. Sam couldn't stand it anymore.

He switched on the radio to Nash 94.7 FM. Carrie Underwood's "Heartbeat" crackled over the old speakers.

"Country?" Bradley said. "Are you serious?" He reached forward and turned the radio off.

"What, you don't like country?" Sam said.

Bradley sat and brooded.

They passed the New York State Pavilion. "Hey, remember Men in Black? With Will Smith and Tommy Lee Jones?"

Bradley said nothing, but his eyes crept to look out the passenger window.

"They shot part of the movie there, the first one," Sam said.

"I wasn't born yet."

"Oh. Yeah." Sam did a quick calculation in his head. Bradley was right.

I can't win for losing, he thought. Sam decided to keep his mouth shut for the rest of the drive. If this was how the summer was to begin, he dreaded how it would end.

Bronx

HUNTS POINT WAS divided by a bustling industrial park to the south and poor residential neighborhoods to the north. Once a vibrant and sought-after vacation destination for New York's elite at the turn of the 20th century, the district had became more and more industrialized, pushing residents away and forming one of the most impoverished neighborhoods in the Bronx. More than half of all residents lived below the poverty line.

The building Sam had called home for the past five months sat on the corner of Casanova Street and Spoffard Avenue. The neighborhood housed mostly Hispanics and African Americans and reminded him of prison, but he wasn't one to complain. Sara had helped him secure an apartment and a job upon his release. His situation wasn't optimal, but he wasn't about to look a gift horse in the mouth. Sam was happy to have a roof over his head and didn't mind the riffraff that came with it. The truth was he was riffraff as well.

When Sam moved in, he hadn't expected to play host to Bradley. Otherwise, he may have held out for a less crime-riddled neighborhood. Prostitutes, drug addicts and dealers were within a stone's throw from his apartment, or anywhere in Hunts Point for that matter. If Claire had taken the time to research the neighborhood and discovered that the Point was a red-light district, she would have never approved of Bradley's trip.

It had shaped up to be a perfect June. All week the temperature had hovered in the low nineties.

Bradley hoped Sam lived in the heart of Manhattan. *That was where all the action was.* That would have made up for a lot. But the skyscrapers that shrunk in the truck's rear cab window confirmed his fears as they trundled over the Robert F. Kennedy Triborough Bridge. Ahead, there were no skyscrapers, no excitement. He took out his phone and snapped a picture of Manhattan before it completely disappeared from sight.

"This is the Bronx." Sam turned right onto Leggett Avenue from Bruckner Boulevard.

Bradley watched a 7-Eleven convenience store pass by followed by what seemed to be endless rows of auto glass, tire and body shops, some boarded up and tagged with graffiti. The truck hit a pothole that bounced the rear end. Bradley imagined his bags being flung out of the truck and crashing onto the street. He looked back through the rear window of the cab and was reassured when he saw his bags were still there.

"This isn't what I pictured New York looking like." Bradley framed a photo through the windshield.

"What did you expect?" Sam said. A quick glance revealed Bradley's uneasiness.

"You know, skyscrapers. I saw them back the way we came."

"I can't afford to live in the big city," Sam said. "This is all I can manage at the moment."

"Everything looks so rough." Bradley watched row upon row of warehouse doors pass by. *Click* went the shutter noise on his phone.

"You've got a good eye for detail," Sam said. "Hunts Point is rough, but New York City couldn't survive without it. It's an important food distribution center, one of the largest in the world."

Bradley slunked down in his seat, not interested in the history lesson that had begun to unfold.

Sam cast Bradley a sideways look. "You groan, but just out your window lies the three hundred acres that keeps the entire state of New York alive and eating, every day. All twenty million of us." He looked at Bradley again. "Well, twenty million and one."

Sam turned left onto Casanova Street and passed a woman dressed in a tight white tank-top, red hot pants and heels to match.

"Holy shit. Was that a…" Bradley turned to watch the woman through the rear window and snapped a photo with his phone. She caught his stare and waved.

"A hooker? Probably. They don't call it Casanova Street for nothing." Sam grinned and pictured Claire's reaction upon learning that her son would be living in a red light district. "Don't tell your mom, but Hunts Point has a certain… reputation."

Maybe this won't be so bad, Bradley thought, as he pinch-zoomed the photo on his phone and ogled the prostitute. The phone's camera had caught her mid-wave.

All along Casanova, cars and trucks were parked and double-parked in a haphazard way. Some were even backed up onto the sidewalk. Sam pulled up to the curb and killed the engine.

"This is it." Sam looked through the windshield at the rundown, three-story apartment building. Its red bricks were cracked and crumbling in places and a set of weathered concrete steps led to an arched vestibule. Around the entry steps was a set of locked bars that had the top tips sharpened and bent outward and down, which made climbing over them a dangerous, if not impossible task. Attached to the bars was a sign that read "Rooms for rent" with a phone number underneath. The building was bordered by a set of fire escapes on its right side over a narrow alley, and Spoffard Avenue to the left.

Bradley took a photo through the grubby passenger window of the truck. "Looks like a dump."

"Yeah, well it's my dump. It's all I got." Bradley's words stung a bit. After five months, Sam called it home, even with a little affection. He unfastened his seatbelt and pulled the handle to open the driver side door. It stuck and opened on the second try. "Come on. Grab your bags and I'll show you around." He closed the truck door with a rusty *clrunk*.

"Gee, I can't wait," Bradley said.

Sam dropped the tailgate and pushed Bradley's bags towards the back bumper. Bradley grabbed his day pack and slid off the old vinyl seats that were cracked and polished to a sheen from years of denim-clad asses. As he stepped down to the sidewalk, his foot landed on the sun-baked carcass from the previous night.

"The fuck is that?" Bradley looked down at the rusty smear that lead to his foot. Even though the sun had evaporated most of the moisture from the rodent's ravaged body, its sinewy entrails and bones still stuck to his new Vans.

"Watch the language," Sam said. "Just because you're with me doesn't mean you can spout off like that."

"Whatever." Bradley tried to scrape off the rat gore with the edge of the curb. "These are brand new Classics."

Sam watched Bradley pull out a set of keys and dig chunks of congealed blood from the diamond-textured shoe tread. "We can clean them up inside," Sam said.

Bradley continued to dig at his shoe tread. He was obsessive, just like his mom.

Sam pulled Bradley's two bags out of the back of the truck and slammed the tailgate shut. He looked at Bradley as he worked up a sweat in his leather jacket. "Aren't you hot?"

Bradley stopped and looked at him. "Aren't you? You're dressed like a lumberjack." Bradley refocused his attention back on his shoe tread. "What's with the long sleeves?"

Sam tugged his sleeve's cuff in line with his wrist and ignored the question. "Okay… What's with the tail?" Sam motioned toward the raccoon tail that hung from Bradley's belt. "You a teen wolf?"

"Funny," Bradley shook his head but remained on task. "You wouldn't understand."

Sam grabbed a bag and dragged it toward the front steps.

"Whose stupid idea was this trip anyway?"

"I don't know. Your mom stopped taking my calls," Sam said. "But I'm pretty sure it was her stupid idea to make it ten weeks instead of one."

Content with his cleaning job, Bradley scraped remnants of blood off his keys with a discarded napkin he had found nearby, and placed them back in his pocket. He grabbed his second bag and followed.

"She just wants the summer to herself," Bradley said.

"I guess we're stuck with each other for a while."

Sam pulled a huge collection of keys out of his pocket and picked through them one at a time. A cat appeared at the top of the stairs, alerted by the jangling keys, and sauntered down the steps. It squeezed through the bars in front of the stairs and snaked around Bradley's legs.

"How much does a place like this go for?"

"Five hundred seventy-five a month," Sam said.

"Holy crap," Bradley said.

"It's a steal." Sam sorted through his ball of keys. "Most other places you'll pay two or three times that."

"What's with the bars?" Bradley said. "Trying to keep the rats out?" He remembered the rubber rat in his suitcase that Claire had given him the night before he left.

"Give this to Sam," Claire had said.

"Why?" Bradley had thought it was a strange request.

"It's just a gift." Claire had winked at Bradley. "Tell him it's from me. Surprise him with it. He'll appreciate it."

Sam gave Bradley a grave look, then nodded at the cat. "That's Piper's job. He keeps the rats in line. Don't you, Piper?"

"It's just a dumb cat," Bradley said.

"Maybe to you, but one less rat in this world is good in my books." Sam found the key he was looking for and unlocked the barred iron gate. He carried one of Bradley's bags up the stairs to the front entryway. "Close the gate after you."

Bradley knelt down and gave Piper's head a scratch. He rotated the collar around his neck to get a look at the tags.

The vanity tag read "Piper the Scoundrel" and had a picture of Puss-in-Boots winking. The other tag was heart-shaped brass and had a name and phone number stamped into the metal. Bradley could hear Piper's loud, instant purr as the cat nuzzled his leg. Claire didn't allowed pets at home, so Piper was a nice discovery. However, Bradley kept that detail to himself.

"He should clean up after himself." Bradley thumbed over at the crisping blood stain on the sidewalk before he closed the gate and followed Sam up the steps.

EMBEDDED INTO THE wall just inside the front entrance were the mailboxes for the six apartments in the building. Opposite that and a little further down the hallway was the door to Sam's apartment. The hallway ran the length of the building to the back and was lit by weathered, antique wall sconces that ended on either side of an old elevator. A semicircular brass floor indicator topped the ornately decorated doors.

Sam stopped at the door to his apartment, 102, with "Building Superintendent" spelled out underneath in cobbled together press-and-stick letters of various sizes and styles.

"You're the Super?" Bradley said.

Sam could hear the surprise in Bradley's voice. "I'm not a good for nothing bum, despite what your mom says. Got to work for a living. It's a perfect setup." Sam jangled out his keys and unlocked the door.

Right beside the door was what would best be described as a mud room, without the room. A plastic mat for shoes, and various tools (a rake, a yard stick, a tool belt with a hammer) hung off a row of mismatched and misaligned wall hooks. On the floor next to the mat was a large toolkit and a rolling metal box with various tubes and cords. Bradley wondered why anyone would need a rake here, with no grass to be seen anywhere.

The kitchen was sparsely furnished with just enough to get by. In the center of the room sat a 1950s Formica table with four chairs, matching in both their vinyl covering and their state of disrepair. A single light bulb hovered above, one of those new compact fluorescent ones with the curled glass tubes. The sink had a window on the right wall, which offered a fine view of the alley if one didn't mind turning their head when washing the dishes. On the counter top, right of the sink, sat a Mr. Coffee machine from 1974 and an old push-button telephone. To the left was a rusty hot plate and a tired old Frigidaire.

"Living like a king, huh?" Bradley said.

"You get used to life being a certain way." Sam disappeared down the hallway.

Bradley scanned the drab kitchen, his repulsion seeped into a scowl. He tried not to touch anything. "You steal that table from Grandma?"

"Came with the place." Sam's voice emanated from another room off the hallway.

Bradley dropped his bag and day pack, and began to look through the cupboards above the sink. A few plates and glasses, some chili flakes, and crackers. He grabbed the shaker of chili flakes and looked for the best before date.

Sam returned to the kitchen. "Don't worry, they're fresh. I go through them like shit through a goose."

Bradley returned the chili flakes to the cupboard. "So, where am I crashing?"

"Down the hall, last room on the right." Sam said. "I dropped your other bag on the bed."

Bradley grabbed his day pack and remaining bag and headed down the darkened hallway. He tried what he thought was the light switch before he realized that the light fixtures on the walls had no bulbs in them.

The bedroom was even more sparse than the kitchen, with a bed in the center, headboard against one wall, and an old dresser with a lamp on it. The bed faced the window and overlooked the alley. Bradley dropped his bag and his day pack in the corner and lifted his other bag off the bed. The mattress's noticeable sag in the middle failed to spring back.

I wonder if his prison cell was as barren as this, thought Bradley. He deposited his bag with his other luggage, walked to the window and looked out. The dumpster in the alley overflowed with garbage.

"This sucks," he said to himself.

He knelt down, unzipped one of his suitcases and reached into one of its interior compartments. Bradley's hand brushed against something that felt cold and clammy. At first he didn't know what it was, but remembered once he wrapped his hand around its cold, squishy body and rolled its rigid cord of a tail between his fingers. It was the rubber rat Claire had given him before he left. He turned it around in his hands and examined its realistically painted and textured fur. Its eyes were a bright red. It even had whiskers made of fine fishing line. A subtle and short-lived smile crossed Bradley's lips.

Neighbors

Morning came fast for Bradley, but he hadn't slept well. His back ached and he didn't feel rested. The bed had the support of a hammock stretched to its limits.

Sam poked his head into the bedroom. "I got to run and get some supplies," Sam said. "If you want to come, I'm going now."

"Nah. I'll hang here," Bradley said.

"Suit yourself. Be back in about an hour."

Moments later, Bradley heard the front door to the apartment close. He grabbed his phone, charging on the dresser beside the bed, and checked the time. He laid in bed and looked around the featureless room. All the walls were bare and it wasn't hard to imagine what it would be like to live in a prison cell. Bradley threw off the covers and walked to the window. Apart from the sun and the shadows they cast, the same alley, the same overflowing dumpster stared back at him. He could see the browning blood streak on the sidewalk from yesterday and Sam's truck was gone. Bradley changed into his clothes, pocketed his phone, and headed to the kitchen, drawn by the smell of coffee. He was ravenous.

There was a loaf of bread on the counter and the coffee machine's carafe was half full. Bradley opened the fridge:

ketchup, relish and an open package of hot dogs. That was it.

Does he even know the meaning of breakfast?

He grabbed a couple of slices of bread and, after they received mold-free approval, jammed them in his mouth. Bradley found a clean cup and poured himself a liberal dose of hot black coffee. It smelled better than it tasted, but the dry bread didn't discriminate and soaked up the coffee like a thirsty sponge.

His hunger staved off for the moment, Bradley explored the minimal offerings of Sam's apartment.

The first door on the right after the kitchen was the bathroom. It was narrow, not much wider than the door itself, and provided a tub/shower combo at the end by the window. Beside that was the toilet and a simple, free-standing sink. A mirrored medicine cabinet hung above it.

Bradley opened the cabinet. He expected to find medication, but was disappointed to discover only a tube of toothpaste, a well-used toothbrush and a Bic razor. For an ex-con, it looked like Sam lived a pretty clean life.

Between the bathroom and his bedroom was what Sam called the "TV room."

Should have called it the unentertaining room.

The space was smaller than his bedroom by half, and lodged a ratty old couch and an old tube television. Bradley looked for a remote control, and wasn't surprised when he didn't find one.

He turned the TV on. It took some time for the picture to warm up and fade in. Bradley flipped through the thirteen channels on the analog dial. Ten of them offered hissing snow, and of the three channels the TV could pick up, nothing of interest was on. He turned the TV off in disgust.

A LITTLE LATER Bradley found himself sitting on the stairs leading up to the building entrance as he waited for Sam to return. Locked out, he watched the few people that walked by but spent most of his time playing games on his phone. He hoped to see another prostitute, maybe on the corner of Casanova and Spoffard. Instead, an elderly woman with a cane pulled a wheeled wire cart partially filled with groceries to the wrought iron gate. She unlocked it, stowed her cane in her cart, and began to climb the stairs to the front doors.

The woman shielded her squinting eyes with her free hand and looked up at Bradley. "Good afternoon to you now." The woman spoke with a thick Scottish accent.

Bradley pocketed his phone and prepared to stand up.

"No, no, sit down, child. I'm fine." The old woman waved at Bradley to sit. Her wrinkled hands looked soft and doughy, tipped with thick, milky fingernails that curved to subtle points, like those he'd seen in vampire movies.

"I've been climbing these stairs longer than you've been alive," she said. "Still strong as an ox."

"I'm not a child," Bradley said.

The woman caught Bradley's scowl. "Aye. Right you are."

Bradley watched the woman struggle up the stairs, one step at a time, until she stood next to him with her cart on the top landing. She paused to catch her breath.

"Have you seen a cat around by any chance," the woman said. "A tabby? Piper's his name."

Bradley kept his gaze locked on the street. "Actually yeah. Saw him here yesterday." He pointed at the fading blood streak on the sidewalk. "See that? He killed a rat over there."

"Piper! That blasted cat." The woman pushed her cart to one side of the front entrance and eased herself down next to Bradley on the top step. She turned to look at him. "So, who do you belong to?"

"My dad's the super."

"You're Sam's boy?" The woman's face lit up with recognition. "Now that you mention it, I can see it. You got his eyes."

Bradley didn't care. The woman could see it in his face and in the way he tensed up when she talked about Sam.

"Sam's been through some tough times, I don't care to know what, but he's a good man," the woman said. "He really looks out for us here… even the bad ones."

Bradley knew what the woman was trying to do and part of him wanted to listen and believe, but old hurt won out.

"He's a stranger to me."

"Everyone's a stranger once," the woman said. "Give it some time."

"I got all summer, unfortunately." Bradley sighed.

Piper mewled from around the side of the concrete stairs. He poked his head through the bars in the railing and strolled up to join Bradley and the woman sitting at the top.

"Ah, there he is." The woman smiled and made a *nick-nick* sound with her tongue. "Piper's a regular scoundrel, and a handsome one at that, hey boy?"

Piper pushed his head under the woman's weathered hand and she responded by giving him a head scratch.

"You got a cat at home?" the woman asked.

"No," said Bradley. "My mom won't allow it. She's a bit of a square."

"Maybe when you get home you can convince her to change her mind."

"Maybe." Bradley looked at the woman. She had managed to crack his foul mood, if only slightly.

Piper saw something in the alley, froze for a second, then was off with a start down the stairs.

"There he goes again. Damn cat." The woman began her struggle to stand up. "I'd best be going now."

Bradley stood up and helped the woman to stand.

"Thank you, dear. Say, what's your name?"

"Brad."

"Nice to meet you, Brad. I'm Mrs. Baxter, up in 302." She held her right hand out.

Bradley took it and they shook hands. He was surprised by the strength of her grip. His earlier impression of her hands had been completely wrong.

"Come up and visit any time." Mrs. Baxter grabbed her shopping cart. She located her keys and opened the front door of the building.

Bradley grabbed the door and held it open for her. She lifted her cane from the cart and moved through the door. At the end of the hallway, the elevator doors slid open. Two elderly men in their sixties shuffled out. Mrs. Baxter's eyes narrowed and her demeanor flipped in an instant.

She leaned over to Bradley, as if to whisper, but spoke loud enough for the men to hear. "I'll let you in on a secret," Mrs. Baxter said. "See those two? Gus and Mel. You'd be best to steer clear of those arseholes."

Bradley cracked a smile as the two men approached. Gustavo, the taller of the two, wore moth-eaten clothes and his bushy gray mustache hovered over a permanent scowl. Except for the overwhelming odor of booze and sour sweat, there was nothing memorable about Melvin except Carny, a little bichon frise that trailed at his feet. Reddish-brown stains surrounded the dog's eyes, mouth and paws. At first glance, Bradley thought it was blood.

"Out of my way, Baxter," Melvin said. "Your frozen dinners are melting." As if to join the conversation, the little dog began to growl and bark with a high-pitched *yip-yip*. Bradley thought the dog was a joke.

Mrs. Baxter tapped Bradley's shoulder and gave it a gentle squeeze. "You be alright, now, Brad." She turned to Melvin and said: "Keep your hands to yourself, you bugger. And keep that rat of a dog away from me or I'll string him up."

"Same goes for your old, dirty pussy," said Gustavo. "Oh sorry. I meant your cat."

Mrs. Baxter's eyes went wide like saucers. Melvin and Gustavo enjoyed her reaction and broke into hearty laughter. She swung her cane at Gustavo and missed him by inches.

Carny looked up at Bradley, his little body tensed in an attack pose. Bradley chuckled but it didn't matter how he reacted. The dog took offense to anything he, or anyone, did. Carny began to growl. Bradley growled right back. Carny switched to his annoying *yip-yip* bark and began to lunge at Bradley's feet. Bradley pretended to attack. He thrust his body forward and stomped his feet. The little dog backed up, scared, but maintained his incessant *yip-yipping*.

Melvin poked his head back into the building. "Carny! Move yer ass. Git!"

The little dog responded in an instant, and ran towards

Melvin, *yip-yipping* back at Bradley at the same time. They both disappeared down the front steps.

"Put that thing on a leash!" Bradley said.

"Shut your damn mouth, boy." Melvin's response was muted only slightly through the front doors to the building.

Mrs. Baxter pulled her shopping cart down the hallway towards the elevator. She called back, "His bark is worse than his bite."

"Thanks." Bradley wondered if Carny had the courage to bite anything. The little dog would find out soon enough.

The elevator doors opened with a rusted, scraping sound. Mrs. Baxter stepped in and pulled her cart behind her. She turned and gave Bradley a small wave as the doors swallowed her up.

Eviscerated

3:38 A.M. THE WARM summer air blew bits of debris like tumbleweed into the darkened corners of the alley. The dumpster overflowed with garbage, even though pickup was scheduled weekly on Mondays. For some reason, the sanitation trucks had bypassed Sam's building. He had calls into the Department of Sanitation, going back a few weeks, but nothing had been done. It amazed him how four tenants could produce so much garbage.

Tonight Piper was on the prowl. From the third floor, he had hopped from an open window to the fire escape and made his way down to the alley. Perched atop a box in one corner, Piper surveyed his domain. His normally vertical pupils were stretched open to their maximum, and made his eyes seem bigger and blacker, like inky marbles.

Movement! Piper flicked his head toward the darkness of the alley and what was hidden within it. If anyone had watched Piper and what he was focused on, they would have seen nothing but blackness. But Piper saw it.

A rat skittered out from the shadows and stopped to sniff the air before it continued to his goal, an open frozen dinner package. The rat stuck its head into the corner of the package, and snatched a remnant of crust in its jaws. Up on his haunches, the rat sampled the air once again before it decided it was safe to settle in and eat the crust. Its glistening white-tipped tail lay relaxed on the pavement, except for the very tip, which vibrated like the tail on a rattlesnake.

Piper jumped down behind the box. He switched into silent stealth mode and peered around the back corner. Unblinking, Piper licked his chops and zeroed in on the rat. His intent was clear. Like an episode of Wild Kingdom, the cat crept closer, with slow, quiet steps.

The rat sensed something. Danger? Its evening meal dropped to the ground. Its quivering nose and whiskers caught the subtle breeze. Again convinced of its safety, the rat picked up what was left of the crust and resumed its evening feast.

Piper stopped within striking distance. Hunkered down, he coiled his legs up, like a tiger ready to ambush his prey. Alternating left and right, the muscles in his rear legs tensed and loaded with energy, the pads of his paws seeking traction. Piper locked his black glassy gaze on his prize and waited.

Piper's approach was perfect in every way, except for one thing: the breeze. Rats have a keen sense of smell and it was Piper's own scent carried on the eddies in the alley that betrayed his position.

The rat caught a whiff of his predator and bolted. Piper leaped after him in hot pursuit. The two animals tore around the dumpster. The rat stuck close to the sides and reversed direction. Piper lost sight of the lightning-fast rat for a moment before regaining his target, but the break in visual contact gave the rat the advantage.

The rat sat motionless, except for its wildly flipping tail, centered safely under the dumpster. Unable to fit his body under the dumpster, Piper laid on the ground and worked his paws, claws out, first one then the other as he tried to hook the rat. Piper scrambled to the other side of the dumpster and pawed again madly. It was no use. Under the dumpster, the rat made sure it was out of reach from all directions of attack.

When Piper was back at the front of the dumpster swiping with his extended paw, the rat reversed and shot back toward the shadows where the brownstone and the alley met.

From Piper's point of view, the rat had disappeared into thin air. Piper could still smell the rat and was determined to catch it. He circled the dumpster round and round, back and forth, checking and rechecking. Piper's frantic search yielded no success. Giving in to defeat, Piper stopped and sniffed the frozen dinner box the rat had eaten from. Besides the strong scent of his lost prey, Piper detected the remnants of a chicken pot pie. He nudged the flap of the box open and licked the plastic tray inside.

Behind Piper, a small nose with pulsating whiskers broke through the shadows. The fur around the snout, as well as its grinding yellow incisors, were stained crimson with blood. Roles reversed. The predator became prey.

With no hesitation, the rat leapt three feet through the air and landed on Piper's back. Back in battle mode, Piper rolled and tried to dislodge his attacker, but the rat's claws and its jaws clamped into the loose skin of his back.

Another rat emerged from the darkness to join the fight. Then another and another. In a matter of seconds, swarming rats covered Piper's body, scratching and gnawing at his back, head and neck. Their white-tipped tails flipped and flashed like possessed weed eaters.

Piper screeched and struggled in a desperate losing battle. He was no match for the horde of rats that dug and tore through his skin and into his toned, muscular flesh with their razor-sharp incisors. Their white-tipped tails were soon mottled with maroon clots.

From the darkness of the alley, a new rat appeared, its left ear grizzled from battles long since won. It, too, had a white-tipped tail, and it bared its teeth like a guard dog about to attack. It was easily three times the size of the other rats.

The alpha rat crept toward the current battleground, where the other smaller rats had reduced Piper to a blood-soaked mess. The smaller rats parted to make a path for the alpha rat.

It opened its jaws and latched into Piper's lifeless and unrecognizable body, his collar now entangled with torn, blood-caked fur and muscle. The alpha rat dragged the remains back towards the shadows of the brownstone and the alley, leaving a trail of red-stained fur and bits of torn flesh behind on the pavement. The other smaller rats clamped their jaws into the sides of the carcass and aided its transportation into the depths.

3:51 a.m. Silence returned to the alley on the currents of a mild summer night's wind.

Sam dropped a pizza box on the kitchen table, Kingsley Fried Chicken & Pizza written in bold letters on the top and sides. The word "Pizza" was smaller than the rest of the words in the logo, and looked like an afterthought.

The smell that drifted out of the cracks in the lid caused

Bradley's stomach to growl loudly. He could have eaten the box.

"I'm starving!" Bradley had skipped lunch because what little food existed in the refrigerator wasn't fit for eating.

"I told you to have a hot dog," Sam said.

"Have you seen them?" Bradley opened the fridge and pulled out the package of wieners. "For one thing, they're past the best-before date. But the worst part is they're sticky and slimy, like they've been dipped in honey."

"I can't remember when I bought those. Most of the time I live on take out." Sam nodded at the pizza box on the table.

Bradley took out a wiener and held it up over the sink. Semi-translucent fluid dripped off the hot dog in globs. "That ain't honey. That's nasty."

"Okay, well chuck 'em." Sam grabbed two plastic plates from the cupboard. "Garbage's under the sink. Now go wash up."

Bradley tossed the hot dogs and headed down the hallway toward the bathroom, but made a quick detour to his bedroom. He reached into his suitcase, grabbed the rubber rat, and jammed it into his front pocket. He returned to the bathroom and gave his hands a cursory rinse.

"With soap," Sam's voice echoed from the kitchen. "What are you, five?"

Bradley grumbled at Sam's keen ears, and washed his hands again properly. It was probably a good idea anyway, especially after he had handled that decomposing wiener.

"Who do you think you are?" Bradley said under his breath. "My da—" He stopped short when he realized what he had planned to say and was surprised and angered that he couldn't say it. He dried off his hands and returned to the kitchen.

"How can you afford to order take out the time?" Bradley jammed his right hand into his pocket, cupped the rubber rat, and sat down. Under the cover of the table, he pulled out the rat and held it loosely in his hand.

"That's the cheapest pizza in the Bronx," Sam said. "It's a chain. They're everywhere."

"And I guess it's just coincidence that their initials are K.F.C.?"

"Guess so. Never thought about it."

Bradley opened the lid of the pizza box. "Kingsley's Best" it proudly proclaimed, and revealed a sparsely topped pizza with a crust as thin as the corrugated cardboard it sat on.

"Cheap is right." Bradley sat down, grabbed a slice, and placed it on his plate. "You can practically see through it."

"But it smells good, right?" Sam smiled. "Right?"

It did smell fantastic, but Bradley had no intention of agreeing with him.

"Want a Coke?" Sam said.

"Sure."

Sam opened the fridge and grabbed two cans of Coke. While his back was turned, Bradley placed the rubber rat into the pizza box and closed the lid.

Sam returned to the table and handed one of the Cokes to Bradley.

"Thanks." Bradley watched as Sam spun the box around and opened the lid.

Sam shrieked and retracted his hand. He hooked the pizza box with his thumb and dragged it off the table, dropping his can of Coke as he stumbled backward over his chair. The pizza box hit the floor on one corner and ejected the rubber rat out and towards Sam, now on his back, eyes wide.

Sam's realization: *it's a rubber rat*. He looked up at Bradley, now gazing over the far edge of the table. Sam saw the remorse and guilt on Bradley's face. He knew he was in deep shit.

Sam collected his wits. He stood up, picked up the pizza box and the Coke, and placed them on the table. Bradley watched his every move. He grabbed the rubber rat by the tail and carried it to the sink. Along the way, Sam couldn't help but notice how detailed the decoy was, with its finely painted fur, whiskers, and glistening red eyes. A shiver ripped through his body.

He opened the door under the sink. The hanging garbage bag attached to the door banged against it with a *clunk*. Sam opened the lid, stained from years of food and mold, and released his two-fingered grip on the rubber rat's tail. It fell to the bottom of the garbage bag like it was made of lead.

Sam closed the lid to the garbage and the door under the sink and returned to the table. He righted his chair and sat down. He opened the pizza box. The entire pie had folded over onto itself and stuck together. Sam salvaged a slice and dropped it on his plate. He closed the lid to the box and revealed Bradley sitting across from him with a pathetic, sorrowful look on his face.

"Real funny, you little shit," Sam said.

"Mom said you'd appreciate it."

"Did she? And you believed her." Sam switched his unopened Coke with Bradley's and slammed it down on the table. "Just for that, you're on garbage duty."

"I guess it was supposed to be a joke," Bradley said.

"You mean you don't know?"

Bradley had no words.

"Shut up and eat." Sam ripped into his slice of pizza, working hard to keep his cool.

DINNER WAS EATEN in silence. Bradley found the pizza surprisingly delicious, but he had lost most of his appetite after the rat prank went off the rails. He felt ashamed for scaring Sam so badly, and angry at Claire for suggesting the idea. She had known what would happen. Bradley was sure of it.

After dinner, Sam moved to the TV room. Bradley cleared the table, and washed and dried the plates. The left-over pizza was deposited in the fridge.

Bradley opened the door under the sink. The garbage bag swung back and forth, knocking its wooden supports. He lifted the lid and looked in. Remnants of meals past festered in the bag and a fetid odor drifted up to meet his nose. Bradley considered rescuing the rubber rat, but dismissed the idea. The damage was done. He unhooked the bag and tied it up.

Sam had tuned in an old episode of Starsky and Hutch. Bradley appeared at the door of the TV room and watched him. He wanted to apologize but didn't know how to begin.

"Need something?" Sam kept his eyes on the television.

Bradley held up the bag of garbage. "Where does this go?"

"End of the hall. You can't miss it."

Bradley hesitated at the doorway.

Sam looked at him. "Need something else?"

Bradley took a deep breath. "Sorry about the rat. It was a stupid thing to do."

Sam continued to look at him, expressionless. He was still pissed, but he promised himself that he wouldn't carry a grudge. After a moment, Sam returned his gaze to the television.

BRADLEY STEPPED OUT into the common hallway and wandered toward the elevator. At least the wall sconces lit the way. Without them, the spill of natural light from each end would have left most of the long hallway in shadow. The thought of the same unlit passage at night gave Bradley the creeps.

At the elevator, the common hallway joined a secondary hallway in a T-junction that spanned the width of the building. Windows terminated both ends. The left one looked out onto Spoffard and had steel bars bolted to it. The right one lead out to the fire escape and the alley.

To the left of the elevator was the emergency stairwell. To the right, the hinged garbage chute in the wall that led to the dumpster in the alley. This confused Bradley, since he was on the first floor, but the apartment was built on a slope. Sam's apartment seemed higher off the ground than the apartment across the hall.

The garbage chute was beaten up and dirty from years of abuse. Bradley grabbed the handle and drew it back, repulsed. The handle felt sticky and unclean. In his head, he pictured slime threads forming between the handle and his hand. He hooked his index finger onto the far edge of the handle and pulled the chute door open. The smell of ripe and rancid food rose up to his nose. He fought the gorge that rose in his throat and stuffed the garbage bag into the maw of the chute. The bag slid down part way and stopped just out of reach.

"Shit." Bradley looked into the gaping chute. There was no way he would lean in there to push the garbage further. He wouldn't have been able to reach the bag of garbage anyway.

He poked his head into the hallway. "Dad!" The word just came out. Bradley hadn't planned on addressing Sam as his "Dad" any time soon. He looked down the hallway to where the door to apartment 102 stood ajar, and hoped that Sam hadn't heard him slip up.

There was no response. Bradley heaved a sigh of relief as he made his way back to the apartment. Sam hadn't heard him over the volume of the television.

Bradley leaned back on the door frame to the TV room. Sam watched Hutch being bound and gagged by mobsters.

"It won't go down," he said.

In fading 1970s color, Starsky pulled his gun as he broke through a warehouse door. "What?" Sam said.

"The garbage," Bradley said. "It's stuck." He stared at Sam, getting under his skin.

"Shit. That was a good episode." Sam stood up and flipped off the television. He trudged past Bradley and into the kitchen. Bradley followed. "Can't even do a simple thing right." Sam grabbed the hanging rake from off the wall.

"I did exactly what you said." Bradley rebounded off Sam's angry energy. "It's not my fault."

"We'll see about that."

When they reached the garbage chute, Sam yanked the door open. The bag of garbage sat right where it had been when Bradley left to get help. Sam reached in and tried to push it, but it was a couple of inches beyond his reach.

"Hold the door open." Sam grasped the rake's wooden handle with both fists. Bradley pulled open the chute's door and held it open.

Sam inserted the rake into the chute and pushed. The garbage bag slid a little more, then stopped. He pushed again, but the bag wasn't going to budge.

"It must be blocked on the outside. Come on." Sam extracted the rake and headed for the front entrance.

A MOUNTAIN OF garbage, about ten feet up from where Sam and Bradley stood, flowed out of the chute and into the overflowing dumpster. Something had clogged the chute's exit.

"Hold this." Sam handed the rake to Bradley and heaved himself up onto the lip of the dumpster. Skirting around the edge, Sam managed to reach into the chute's exit opening. The clog was a little further up.

Sam beckoned with his hand. "The rake."

Bradley passed the tool to Sam's extended hand. He inserted the tines into the chute and pushed the rake back and forth. A few pieces of garbage fell past the rake's handle and rolled into the dumpster. Sam rotated the rake and the tines hooked onto something.

"What is it?" Bradley said.

Sam gave another firmer yank. The clogged refuse

popped free and barreled down the chute propelled by the stacks of garbage on top of it. The rake shot out of the chute and deep into the trash heap, its tines sticking up.

A barrage of frozen dinner boxes knocked Sam backward and off the lip of the dumpster. He hit the ground before Bradley could get to him.

Sam grabbed one of the frozen dinner boxes on the ground and tossed it out of his way. "Mrs. Baxter." He grumbled under his breath.

"What?"

"The things I do to keep this building running." Sam sat on the alley pavement to catch his breath.

"You okay?" Bradley said.

"A little help?"

Bradley forced himself to ignore the sticky, rotting garbage juices that covered Sam's hands and grabbed his extended arm.

But some of it wasn't fluid from the dumpster. "You're bleeding," Bradley said.

Sam looked at the palms of his hands. They were covered with chunks of clotted blood and fur. Bradley looked at the hand he had helped Sam up with, and realized with revulsion that some of the blood had transferred to his hand as well. Not wanting to wipe the slurry on his pants, he looked for something to scrape it off with but didn't want to touch anything.

Sam examined his hands, and found no cuts or scrapes. "It's not my blood."

Bradley exchanged a perplexed look with Sam. Bradley's earlier prank seemed to dissolve in the back of Sam's mind as he faced a new mystery, his son on his side this time.

It was almost seven o'clock in the evening. There was

still plenty of light out, but the shadows of the alley around the dumpster prevailed. Sam fished a penlight out of his pocket and focused the beam on the pavement. What he saw was blood and lots of it.

"Then... whose blood is it?" A shudder moved up Bradley's spine.

Sam knelt close to the pavement and shone the penlight around the base of the dumpster. The trail of blood and fur seemed to lead to the apartment building. He followed the light of his flashlight to the base of the building, where it revealed a large, dark hole. Normally, the dumpster sat flush with the wall of the building, which was why he hadn't seen it yet.

Sam crouched low and got his head close to the pavement and the base of the building. An odor of decay began to overtake the essence of blood mixed with rotting garbage. He fought to control his revulsion, and aimed his penlight beam into the hole. A gold flash reflected back at him, and a small sense of recognition twigged his memory.

"Do you see something?" Bradley said. "What is it?"

"I'm going to find out." Sam wanted answers instead of more questions. He thought about rolling up his sleeves, but they were already soaked with dumpster juice. He laid the penlight on the ground. Bradley watched with a mix of fascination and horror as Sam's right arm disappeared past his elbow into the hole. When his hand met the source of the blood, it felt like a rack of ribs. His fingers moved over the bony surfaces held together with cartilage and fleshy connective tissue, and found a flat metal surface with a point on one end.

"Got something." Sam pulled the metal object out of the

hole, and dragged whatever was attached to it out as well. "Feels like a—"

As soon as Sam pulled the object clear of the hole, even though it was covered with blackened blood and fur, he knew what it was. He cleared the surface of the flat heart-shaped metal object with his thumb. The crimson sludge slid off and revealed the word "Piper" on it. He didn't need to see the rest.

"Oh Jesus." Sam pulled the tag further out of the hole. What was left of Piper's body slid out with a sickening *shplop*. The tag and the collar connected to it was entwined with Piper's partially eaten corpse.

"What?" Bradley crouched to get a better look. His question answered itself when he saw Piper's bloodied vanity tag flip out of the hole beside the bloodied collar. "Shit, that's messed up."

Sam unbuckled the collar and pulled it out from around Piper's exposed neck. His small, tightly connected vertebrae was visible, even without the flashlight. The skull and what was left of the skeleton lolled like a rag doll.

Sam examined the collar and sighed.

"Want to help me deliver the bad news?" Sam looked at Bradley. They both were unenthused by the task ahead of them.

BRADLEY STOOD AT the kitchen sink in a daze. He washed the blood off Piper's collar, and his own hands in the process. Even though he had just met Mrs. Baxter and Piper, he felt a connection to them, and now a loss. He blotted the collar with a towel, leaving pink blood stains behind.

Sam entered the kitchen and placed his hand lightly on Bradley's shoulder. "Ready to do this?"

Bradley nodded. They both left the apartment and walked to the elevator at the end of the hallway. Sam pressed the call button and the doors opened in front of them, screeching metal on metal.

"You need to grease these—"

"The doors? Yeah, it's on my to-do list," Sam said. "Not a high priority."

The father-son duo entered the elevator. The doors closed and swallowed them up as it begun its creaky ascent to the third floor.

Bradley held Piper's collar. He turned it around in his hands, stopping to look at the vanity tag once more. There was something about the picture of Puss-in-Boots that made him choke up a bit.

"You going to be okay?" Sam watched him.

Bradley nodded and looked away. "You ever have to do something like this before?"

"No," Sam said. "First time."

"I wish it was that yappy dog instead," Bradley said.

"Carny. Melvin's dog."

"Yeah."

Sam nodded his head in agreement. "True, Carny is damn annoying, but I wouldn't wish what happened to Piper on him, or any other living thing for that matter."

The elevator doors opened to the third floor. Sam and Bradley stepped out and walked to apartment 302, halfway down the hallway. On the door was brass knocker, a ring clasped in a lion's mouth.

Sam looked at Bradley. He nodded back. Even though they were bearers of bad news, the task of informing Mrs.

Baxter of Piper's misfortune had solidified their relationship in a small, but noticeable way.

Sam grabbed the door knocker and rapped it three times. After what felt like a long time, they heard shuffling behind the door, fumbling with the lock. The door swung open and revealed Mrs. Baxter standing in a housecoat.

"Sam, Brad. This is a surprise." Mrs. Baxter worked to blink the sleep out of her eyes.

"Sorry to bother you so late, Mrs. Baxter." Sam held Mrs. Baxter's gaze. Bradley couldn't manage it.

"Nonsense. Come in." Mrs. Baxter beckoned. "I'll put on a pot of tea."

"Maybe another time," Sam said.

"Shot of whiskey?"

"I don't do alcohol anymore, I'm afraid."

Mrs. Baxter shifted her gaze from Sam to Bradley and back. She sensed something wasn't right. Then she spotted the collar in Bradley's hands and recognized it immediately. The color drained from her face.

"What is it?" Mrs. Baxter said.

"Brad and I found this out back." Sam looked at Bradley. He had heard Sam but he was somewhere else in his head. Sam placed his hand on Bradley's shoulder and gave it a light squeeze. This brought him back and he looked at Sam, whose eyes were on the collar in Bradley's hands.

Things clicked and Bradley presented the collar to Mrs. Baxter, still damp from being washed.

Mrs. Baxter took the collar. "Piper, that scoundrel." She tried to maintain a strong front. It was clear to Sam that her coping mechanism was talking. "He's always losing his collar. I'm going to have to give him a talking to when he gets home."

"I don't think Piper's coming back this time," Sam said.

"What do you mean?" Mrs. Baxter tried to avoid the truth. Bradley turned his gaze to the floor.

"Something got to him." Sam held Mrs. Baxter's gaze. "I don't know what. Maybe a dog."

Reality began to crash down around Mrs. Baxter. She looked down at the vanity tag. A wide-eyed Puss-in-Boots stared back.

"Can I see him?"

"There was nothing left." Sam realized the harshness of his words. "I mean nothing you'd want to see."

Mrs. Baxter saw her answer in Sam's eyes.

"I'm sorry," Sam said.

With the collar clutched in her hands, Mrs. Baxter turned to walk back into her apartment. Some of the sparkle in her eyes left her in that moment.

"You going to be okay, Mrs. Baxter?" Sam poked his head into her apartment and watched her disappear down the hallway to her bedroom. Bradley was struck by how warm and inviting her apartment was compared to Sam's.

Sam closed the door. "I don't want to do that again any time soon."

Back in the elevator creaking under their weight, Sam and Bradley descended back to the first floor.

Bradley broke the silence. "Why does bad shit happen to good people?"

"Sometimes they bring it on themselves." Sam recalled his own crime and sentencing fifteen years previous.

"Mrs. Baxter didn't deserve that." Bradley watched the elevator's floor indicator spin back to one as the car bounced on its old, stretched cables.

The doors scraped open and Gustavo pushed his way into the car before Sam and Bradley had a chance to exit.

"Hey, my water pressure's low," Gustavo said. "Been like that for weeks."

Sam was well aware of Gustavo's water pressure issues. "It's on my list," Sam said.

Gustavo scoffed. "How about you put it on the *top* of your list?"

I'm so tired of your shit, Sam thought. "Yeah, I'll get right on that."

"Kill any cats, lately?" Bradley eyed Gustavo as he moved toward the hallway.

Gustavo hooked a thumb at Bradley. "Kid's got a mouth on him." His ever-familiar scowl was back in full force. "Going to get him in trouble one of these days."

"Well, did you?" Bradley wanted an answer.

Gustavo grabbed Bradley's arm and gave him a once-over. He paused a little long on Bradley's raccoon tail. "You accusing me of something, you little shit?"

"Back off," Sam said as the closing elevator doors triggered on his foot and reopened.

Gustavo glared at Bradley and released his arm, then focused back at Sam. "I didn't kill nothing." He pointed at Bradley's raccoon tail. "But it looks like you did."

"Mrs. Baxter's cat is missing." Sam looked for any irregular behavior that might indicate Gustavo's dishonesty, but either he was telling the truth or he was a very good liar.

"So? How is that my problem?" Gustavo stared after Sam and Bradley as they walked down the hallway. "I don't give a rat's ass where that cat is."

Sam leaned close to Bradley. "Don't respond," he said, quiet enough so Gustavo couldn't hear.

"What, are you spreading lies about me now?" The elevator doors began to creak shut. "Don't forget about my water—"

The elevator doors closed tight, and silenced Gustavo's complaints mid-sentence.

Visit

Sam lay on the couch wide awake, still dressed in his soiled work shirt and jeans. He wanted to sleep, but his body would not let it happen. The lumpy sofa combined with the evening's events left him staring at the shadows on the ceiling. Over and over, his mind returned to the dumpster, where he and Bradley had used the rake to collect and deposit what was left of Piper into a black garbage bag. Soon, the cat would be on a truck on his way to his final resting place: a landfill in New Jersey. It all felt wrong to Sam.

Yeah, Piper was just a cat, but he deserved better in the end.

Mrs. Baxter had been denied the opportunity to say goodbye, to give his fur one last stroke. Sam wondered if people would act differently day-to-day if they knew for sure that a loved one was going to die. So many thoughts pushed sleep out the door, and if Sam had known that Mrs. Baxter had cried herself to sleep that night, there would have been no chance at sleep at all.

What he really wanted was a drink: beer, wine, whiskey, anything. By offering him a shot of whiskey, Mrs. Baxter had opened a can of alcoholic worms Sam managed to keep closed most days.

Just to take the edge off, Sam thought, but he knew that

wasn't an option. If word of him drinking ever got back to Claire, she would make sure that Sam would never see Bradley again.

A noise shifted Sam's focus. He sat up and cocked his head to one side and waited. His brain canceled out muted traffic sounds that seeped through the window. The apartment air hung quiet and still.

There it was again, the same noise, followed by similar, smaller sounds of commotion, like pieces of wood clattering against each other. The darkness of the apartment seemed to amplify the noises and the hairs on the back of Sam's neck stood at attention. He dug out his penlight and aimed its beam out the door of the TV room and into the hallway. The little light cut the darkness with its narrow beam. Bradley's bedroom door was closed.

Sam stood in the hallway, stopping to listen and relocate the source of the noise. With each slow, careful step, Sam made his way to the center of the kitchen. The floor creaked with each step. He stopped and scanned the counter tops and baseboards, but was met with nothing but silence. He searched the kitchen one more time, under the table and chairs and along the front of the refrigerator.

As he turned to leave, something rattled close by. He redirected the penlight on the sink, then on the door underneath. Another scratching sound.

Sam approached the door, his hand outreached in front of him. The penlight's beam locked on the door's handle like a target. His periphery fell into dark unknowns, bringing with it rising unease. Sam didn't like the dark. He'd experienced enough darkness from his time in prison to last him a lifetime.

He drew in a deep breath and grabbed the door's handle.

He pulled it open and stepped back at the same time, keeping his penlight aimed on the door as it swung open. The garbage bag that hung on the inside inherited the door's motion and rocked back and forth as the handle struck the front of the counter. Then nothing but silence.

Sam froze. Something was there, inside the bag. He just didn't know what. Sam took a tentative step forward and kept his penlight on the motionless bag. Then the bag moved. At first Sam thought he was seeing things, but the bag moved again, accompanied with sounds of rustling and *chittering*.

The bag began to writhe as a flood of rats flipped the plastic lid open and spilled out and over the lip of the garbage bag. Sam's eyes bugged out as the rats, maybe a dozen or more, charged at him across the floor. Every fiber in Sam's body told him to run, but the best his terror-addled brain could handle was a step backward. This proved to be a bad choice as he stumbled backward over one of the kitchen chairs. He hit the floor hard and knocked the penlight from his hands.

Sam scrambled to get away, but his socked feet and sweaty hands failed to give him any traction. In his frenzy to get away, Sam kicked the penlight on the floor. It spun and illuminated the kitchen like a rotating police cherry. With each spin of the penlight, the horde of rats drew closer. Sam froze, terror in his eyes.

Several rats climbed onto Sam's feet, traversing up his legs and towards his knees. Others headed towards his crotch. Feeling their weight on his body sent him into a tailspin of panic. Sam's chest rose and fell with heavy hitches, his face painted with sweat. The spinning penlight slowed to a stop, and back-lit the advancing rats with its blinding brightness. A mound of fur rose against the light, larger than any rat he had ever seen. For a brief moment, he thought he was looking at a cat, that somehow Piper had risen from the dead. Sam shut his eyes tight in hopes he was just dreaming it all, but when he opened them again, the smaller rats had advanced and the larger rat, clearly the leader, had crawled up onto Sam's inner thigh. The smaller rats had parted to make way for the alpha rat, and Sam was the rodent's red carpet.

Oh Jesus Oh Jesus Oh Jesus… Sam screamed in his head, but the words never made it out.

BRADLEY AWOKE WITH a start, having heard commotion coming from outside his room. He swung his feet out of bed and headed for the bedroom door. He cracked it open in a slow arc. Something was happening in the kitchen, but he couldn't see anything except the glow of light and moving shadows cast on the walls.

"Sam?" he said half whispering, as he stepped out of his room and down the hallway in slow, determined steps. When he passed the TV room, he saw the couch with its makeshift bed sat empty. "Sam?"

In the kitchen, Sam heard Bradley's approach. He tried to scream for help again, but his voice betrayed him again. Nothing but dank fear escaped from his open mouth.

The alpha rat moved up onto Sam's chest. Perched there, it felt about the weight of a newborn. Sam would later estimate the alpha rat's weight as about ten pounds, more than an adult chihuahua. Its whiskers vibrated and its long, oily, white-tipped tail quivered and flipped back and forth as it slapped against Sam's legs. The other rats held back, as if they were waiting for a cue from their leader. The alpha rat extended its neck and smelled Sam's face. It opened its mouth to reveal two long, yellowed and blood-stained incisors in silhouette. Sam caught a whiff of its breath, which smelled like a mixture of shit and spoiled meat. The alpha rat ground its teeth to sharpen its incisors. The smaller rats joined in. The sound reminded Sam of chewing tin foil as a kid, sending shivers up his spine and raising the hairs on the back of his neck once again.

"Sam?" As Bradley passed the bathroom, the floor creaked under his weight.

The alpha rat cocked its head and huffed at the other rats. They turned and scrambled back under the sink, just as Bradley rounded the corner of the hallway and stepped into the kitchen. He found Sam sprawled on the floor next to an upturned chair and Sam's penlight. Bradley turned on the kitchen light. It buzzed, flickered and eventually lit up. The kitchen was cast in a cold, bluish white glow.

"What are you doing on the floor?" Bradley said.

Sam looked down his chest, over his legs and towards the garbage bag under the sink. Not a rat to be seen. He relaxed his head to the floor and panted heavily.

"Are you wasted?"

Sam looked at Bradley and sensed the anger that reflected off him. "Do I look wasted?" he said between breaths. Sam extended his arm towards Bradley. "Give me a hand."

Bradley hesitated, then walked over and grabbed Sam's hand to pull him up. "Ugh, you're all sweaty. You weren't… uh, you know… having *man time* were you?"

"What? No!"

"Then what *were* you doing on the floor?"

"Don't ask." Sam righted the chair on the floor and grabbed his penlight. He clicked it off.

Bradley wiped his hand on his shirt. "Believe me, I'm not going to."

"See you in the morning." Sam staggered past Bradley and down the hallway to the TV room.

Bradley looked around the kitchen for anything out of the ordinary. Except for the open door under the sink, with the limp garbage bag hanging off it, everything seemed normal.

Bradley walked to the garbage, raised the lid, and looked in. The bag was empty, just as he had left it after he had taken out the garbage earlier in the evening, except for a single strip of pizza crust in the bottom. Sam must have had a midnight snack.

Perplexed and still in a sleep stupor, Bradley closed the sink door, turned off the kitchen light and returned to his bedroom. As he drifted back to sleep, he tried to piece together what he had (or hadn't) seen in the kitchen. It didn't make sense. Sam was hiding something.

HOPE

Sam sat at the kitchen table and baited an old, rusty snap trap. His eyes were grainy and his skin felt like it had ants crawling all over it. He was beyond tired. What little chance Sam had had of getting some decent sleep the previous night had been shattered by his encounter in the kitchen. His senses had been heightened by adrenaline coursing through his veins, and every little noise in the apartment set off a feeling of panic.

What if they come back? What about the big one, that big fucking rat?

He tried to divert his fear by figuring out the best plan to get rid of the rats. The only solution he knew of that would work was to use snap traps. He had found an old Victor snap trap in a kitchen drawer, mixed with other odds and ends left from the last Super. According to the words stamped on the wooden base of the trap, Victor was the "world leader in rodent control since 1898" so that was good enough for Sam. As for bait, he decided upon peanut butter, because all rats are supposed to love peanuts.

Choosy rodents choose Jif.

Bradley strolled into the kitchen at eleven o'clock in the morning, still wearing his pajamas, and rummaged through the cupboards.

"About time you got up," Sam said. "The day's half over."

"Maybe for you." Bradley watched Sam engage the kill arm on the snap trap. "What's that for? We got rats?"

"What was your first clue?" Sam opened the door under the sink and placed the snap trap inside. "We got rats. And not the rubber variety."

Bradley looked at Sam sideways. "Is that what last night was about?"

Sam ignored the question, and instead chose to focus on setting the trap under the sink.

"You need to go shopping." Bradley slumped into one of the chairs at the kitchen table. He stuck his finger into the peanut putter and scooped out a mouthful.

"Do you do that at home?" Sam grabbed the jar of Jif and put the lid on it. "Grow some manners."

"But there's nothing to eat in this place."

"You need to know where to look." Sam opened the fridge and pulled out the box of last night's pizza. "Enjoy," he said as he threw it on the table.

Bradley grabbed a cold slice out of the box. "I thought rats liked pizza. Especially New York City rats."

Sam shrugged. "What are you talking about? I'm not going to waste good pizza on a rat."

"But New York City is the home of Pizza Rat!" Bradley stared at Sam with an incredulous look.

Sam stared back. He had no idea what Bradley was going on about. "Okay?"

"Seriously?" Bradley laughed. "You haven't seen Pizza Rat?"

Sam shook his head. "No. Should I?"

"Oh my God. Yes." Bradley disappeared down the

hallway, and returned ten seconds later with his phone. "I'll assume there's no wifi signal?"

Sam gave Bradley a sideways look. "You're kidding, right? In case you haven't noticed, I'm not exactly on top of technology these days."

"Gonna have to use my data, but this is worth it." He worked the touch screen with his fingers for a moment. "Watch this." Bradley handed the phone to Sam.

"What am I looking at?" Sam said.

"Press play," Bradley said. "That little white triangle."

"Right, like VCR controls," Sam said.

"VCR?"

"Never mind." Sam chuckled at Bradley's ignorance of obsolete 90s technology and pressed play. On the screen, he watched a rat carry a slice of pizza down a flight of stairs.

"Well?" Bradley watched Sam for his reaction. "What do you think?"

"Impressive," Sam said. "But I'm still not going to waste a slice of pizza on a rat."

"Over nine million views!"

"Nope." Sam shook his head. "My stomach is going to win every time. These rats are getting plain old peanut butter."

"Still, you gotta admit, it was pretty cool," Bradley said.

"Yeah, I'll give you that." Sam grabbed one of the leftover slices of pizza and nudged the box toward Bradley. "Hurry up and eat. Today you're going to learn a new skill." Sam headed down the hallway.

"What new skill?" Bradley's curiosity was piqued.

Sam walked to the TV room and laid down on the couch. "We leave in fifteen minutes."

Sam and Bradley stood in the elevator as it hoisted them to the third floor, groaning under their weight. They both wore gray coveralls that had seen better days and had work gloves jammed in their pockets. Bradley floated a bit in his coveralls, not quite big enough to fill them. On their heads were flipped-up welding visors and under Sam's arm was a rolled up rubber mat. Between them sat a large arc welding unit on a rolling platform.

"My friends have told me about these things." Bradley examined the arc welder's controls. "They're nowhere near as big as this."

"This one's special," Sam said. "It has an on-board battery pack, so I can weld in hard-to-get-to places if I need to. It also makes the thing too damn heavy to lift."

The elevators opened up on the third floor. Sam wheeled the arc welding unit out of the elevator and next to the fire escape window. He uncoiled the power cord and handed the end to Bradley.

"Plug it in over there." Sam pointed to a nearby outlet.

Bradley plugged the unit in. "What are we working on?"

"I'll show you." Sam pulled the window open. "After you," he said.

Bradley ducked his head through the window and stepped through. The platform creaked under his weight. Sam handed him the rubber mat.

"Is this fire escape strong enough to hold the both of us?" From the third floor, Bradley had a great view of the alley and dumpsters below, but the sound of scraping metal on metal rattled his nerves.

"We'll be fine." Sam pointed to the corner of the fire escape platform where several pieces of metal had broken away. "Lay the mat out over there. We're going to repair the corner."

Bradley did as he was told and laid the rubber mat down along the length of the platform, aligned with the edge. Sam stepped out onto the fire escape, pulled the electrode and return cables out and placed them down on the mat. It was cramped working quarters for both of them, but the mat was big enough to accommodate them. Sam reached back through the window and grabbed an electrode, hand clamps and a few strips of metal.

"You got to use metal clamps," Sam said as he fastened the reinforcing metal strips to the corner of the platform. "Plastic ones will melt."

"How hot does it get?"

"Hot enough to melt iron, so I'm guessing damn hot," Sam said. "Ready to do some welding?"

Bradley nodded. "Let's do it." He finally got to do something cool. Sam could see his eagerness.

"Okay. First we need to connect our return to complete the circuit," Sam said. "Clamp it to the platform, close to where we're doing the work." Sam handed the return cable to Bradley and he fastened it to the platform, close to the corner.

"This a good spot?" Bradley looked back.

"That'll work," Sam said. "Next, we insert the electrode into the stinger." Sam held up the handle of the electrode cable and an electrode to Bradley.

Bradley examined the electrode as he turned it around in his hand a few times. "It's the clean, metal end that goes in, right?" Bradley paused for Sam's approval.

"Yup."

Sam poked his head into the window and turned on the power. "Okay, we're live. Put your gloves on." Sam returned to the rubber mat and slipped his hands into his leather gloves. Bradley did the same.

"Stay on the mat or you'll get one hell of a shock," Sam said. "Believe me, it's not fun."

"Has anyone been electrocuted while welding?" Bradley's earnest concern showed through his brave front.

"Not that I know of," Sam said. "You just have to use your common sense." Sam shifted his weight to get a good position. The platform groaned beneath them. "First thing I do is lay down a few tacks. They help hold the new metal in place. Ready?"

"Yeah."

"Visors down." With both of their faces obscured, Sam began to breath with slow labored breaths. "Brad… I am your FATHER," he said in his best Darth Vader impression. When there was no response, Sam lifted up his visor to see Bradley staring at him.

"Seriously?" Inside his head, Bradley was laughing, but he kept it buried. It would take more than a Star Wars reference to get him to open up. He was nowhere near ready to accept Sam as his dad.

Sam shrugged. "I thought it was funny. Okay, visors down, for real this time."

They both flipped down their welding visors again. Sam held the stinger in his gloved hands and brought the electrode close to the metal strips clamped for repair. Several brief showers of sparks burst from the tip of the electrode.

"Your journey to the first weld is now complete," Sam said as he flipped up his visor.

"Stop with the Star Wars jokes already." Bradley tipped his visor back. "Can I try now?"

Sam could sense Bradley's impatience. "Not yet," he said as he examined the tacks to make sure they looked strong. "Just watch for now."

"Why? I've taken shop at school," Bradley said. "I know how this shit works."

Sam looked at Bradley, tired of his attitude. "They teach you welding in school?"

"No, but—"

"Then you'll watch and listen for now. That's it." Sam held Bradley's gaze until he looked away. "We have all summer."

"You're such a douche," Bradley said.

"I'll pretend I didn't hear that."

Before Sam could continue with the next weld, a female voice sounded from behind them. "Are you the Super?"

Both Sam and Bradley turned to look at the source of the voice. Their annoyance at each other melted away and made room for other questions, like who was this young woman with the pixie cut, darkly dressed and sitting on the sill of the fire escape window? Her black jeans were covered hip to foot in rivets and metal rings, with zippers on the front and back of both legs, and chain ropes criss-crossing from the back to her pockets in the front. "The Ramones" was stamped on her shirt, the long sleeves made of coarse mesh and ending mid-bicep, connected only with an arm-length strip of riveted leather. A small, silver horseshoe ring hung perfectly balanced between her nostrils.

"Uh, yeah." Sam took in all the adornments. "I try and

keep this place from falling apart. But call me Sam. And this is my s… this is Bradley."

"Hi," Bradley said with a small wave. He noticed the black Vans she wore were tied with big, sloppy bows with knots at the ends of the laces.

"I'm Hope. I'm moving in today." Hope leaned down and thrust her hand out, her various rivets and hoops jangling. Recognition of her voice flashed through Sam's mind as he shook Hope's hand. Her handshake was firm and confident. A good start.

Bradley caught himself glancing down Hope's shirt and looked away. He worried that she had caught him taking a peek. He noted that she wasn't wearing a bra.

But Hope had caught his glance. There wasn't much she didn't pick up on, and instead of taking offense, she played it cool. She thought it might be fun to have a teenage admirer.

"Right! You called about a place last week." Sam flashed his best smile. "In fact, your place is just down the hall. Could you do me a favor and turn off the power to the welder? Big red switch, you can't miss it."

Hope swung her legs back into the building and hopped down. She found the switch right away. "Got it."

"Give me a sec." Sam turned to Bradley and handed him his visor. "Let's pack it in for now. I'll get Hope sorted out and be back to help you clean up."

Bradley began to remove clamps and coiled up the cables, annoyed that his welding session had ended before it even began. Sam stood and walked to the fire escape window. With each step, and unseen by both of them, a securing nut holding the fire escape to the exterior wall loosened, rotating a quarter turn.

I_T DIDN'T TAKE_ Bradley long to pack up the arc welder. He rolled it to the elevator and pressed the call button. Bradley looked at the floor indicator and saw that the elevator was already on its way up. He unzipped his coveralls and stepped out of them. He threw them on top of the welding unit.

Ding.

The elevator doors seemed to struggle: the gap between both doors hesitated, then parted with their usual scraping. Hope and Sam stood in the elevator. They both carried boxes of books.

"Done already?" Sam walked down the hallway and talked over his shoulder.

"There wasn't much to do." Bradley found his eyes drawn to the curve of Hope's black jeans.

"Good. Get the welder back to our place and grab a box from the truck out front. We could use your help."

We could use your help, Bradley mimed in a mocking fashion as he rolled the welding unit into the elevator.

Even with the use of the elevator, lugging boxes of Hope's books left Sam winded. "How many books do you have?"

Hope grinned. "Just a few more."

"How many's a few?" Sam heard the elevator doors begin to scrape. "Hey Brad," he called out before entering Hope's apartment. "Thanks." Sam smiled as the elevator doors met and locked Bradley from view.

If Sam had been any closer, he would have seen the scowl on Bradley's face, but Sam's gratitude felt genuine and evaporated his little black cloud before it had a chance to form.

"Hey, I forgot to ask," Sam said. "How did you get in the building?"

"I can pick locks with the best of them." Hope gave Sam a sly smile. "Seriously though, luck was on my side. A lady was leaving just as I arrived."

"Scottish accent?"

"Yeah."

"That's Mrs. Baxter." Sam paused for a moment as he remembered his last interaction with her, breaking the news about Piper. "Great lady. She lives across the hall from you."

"Cool."

They both disappeared into Hope's apartment.

EVEN THOUGH HOPE'S apartment was the same size as Sam's, and the layout of the apartments from floor to floor was identical, it felt smaller due to all her stuff. The shared living room and kitchen area contained a slim-style sofa and coffee table, a television on a cheap press-board pedestal, and a kitchen table with basic wooden chairs. It was a lot of furniture for such a small space, and all of it seemed a notch below Ikea in quality. Any free surface was occupied with boxes of books.

Sam dropped his box atop another and wiped his sweaty brow. "I hope you've got shelves for these." He caught his breath and felt the warmth of soon-to-be-aching muscles. Sam didn't consider himself old, but he wasn't young either. Helping Hope lug her furniture and boxes up to the third floor had taken its toll on his body.

"Shelves? What are those?" Hope smiled. "I'm going to have to get some eventually."

Sam picked up a book from one of the boxes. "The Rodent Brain: Perception and Neuroplasticity."

"What? Oh yeah. I majored in zoology."

Sam flipped though the pages, many with full color pictures of rats in various environments. "And rodents have brains?"

"Absolutely," Hope said. "They're very intelligent creatures."

Sam felt a shudder move through his body as he recalled his kitchen episode. He placed the book back in its box. "You're going to fit right in around here."

Bradley entered with a box in his arms. "This is the last one."

"Music to my ears," Sam said.

"It's different than the rest. Super light." Bradley looked at the box's sides. "Plus it has holes in it."

Hope's ears perked up. "I'll take that one." She carried the box into what Sam called the TV room in his own apartment.

"Hey, thanks a lot." Hope returned from the other room. "I'd offer you guys a beer if I had some."

"We don't drink," Sam said.

"Aww. You're no fun." Hope flashed a friendly smile towards Bradley and Sam, one that they had both begun to admire, but for different reasons. "What about coffee?"

"Now you're talking." Sam headed towards the door.

"Oh, one more thing." Hope leaned on a stack of boxes. She looked exhausted, but happy. "It's always one more thing, isn't it? Can you hook up my cable?"

Sam and Bradley shared a look.

"I don't know about Brad here," Sam said, "but I'm the Super and I can do anything."

Bradley shook his head. "Gag."

"I'll get my toolbox."

"And I'll make some coffee," Hope said. "I saw my coffee maker somewhere around here."

Sam and Bradley headed down the hallway and stopped at the elevator doors. Bradley pressed the call button.

"What do you think of our new tenant?" Sam said.

"I think you like her." Bradley watched the floor indicator start its slow creeping arc.

"Sure, I like her." Sam rocked on his feet. In the short time since his release, he had kept to himself most of the time. He appreciated the sight of a new face around the building, even if that face was studded with metal. "Seems like a nice person."

"No, I mean you *like* her, as in… you know."

"She's a little young for me." Sam clued in on Bradley's comment. "Wait. Are you jealous?"

Bradley looked at Sam. "What? No way."

"You're blushing."

"I am not."

"Yeah, you are."

Bradley returned his gaze to the elevator's floor indicator. "Whatever."

"Don't worry. I won't say anything," Sam said. "Your secret's safe with me."

The elevator doors opened, and Sam and Bradley stepped inside. Bradley pressed the button for the first floor. The doors began to scrape closed.

Sam smiled. "Your first crush."

"It's not my first. You missed that one." Bradley's little black cloud began to form again.

Sam's smile faded as the two of them stood in silence for the rest of the elevator ride.

SAM LAY TWISTED around the stacks of boxes and the old television pedestal, his open toolbox beside him and within arm's reach. Hope moved a box of books off the sofa and made room on the coffee table for two mugs of coffee. She dug through another box and found a jar of Coffee-mate and a box of sugar cubes.

"This thing's an antique. It doesn't even have a proper coax connection." Sam crammed behind the television. "I hear flat screens are pretty cheap these days. That's what Brad says."

"If that one blows up, I'll think about it." Hope dropped two sugar cubes into her coffee. "When it's not broke…" She went to stir her coffee and realized she had no spoon. Up again, she searched for a spoon, but the best she could find was a Bic Cristal ballpoint pen. It would have to do. She returned to the sofa and stirred her coffee with the end of the pen.

"I hear you. Mine is even older than this." Sam squeezed out from behind the television and found a box to sit on. "I take it black."

"Easy to please." Hope handed the cup without the sugar in it to Sam. "I need my sugar and cream, if you can even call this stuff cream." She flipped the plastic top of the Coffee-mate open, dumped some powder into her mug, and swirled it with her pen. "Have you lived in New York long?"

"Born and bred. You?" Sam blew on his coffee and took a sip. Strong and surprisingly good.

"Indiana," Hope said, "but I've been studying at the University of California in Santa Barbara for the past six years."

"My son lives in California."

"Brad's your son?"

Sam nodded.

"Wanted to make sure." Hope warmed her hands on the mug. "So, you have joint custody, or…"

"No," Sam said. "He's just visiting for the summer. First time in over fifteen years. But he hates it here. Probably hates me, too."

Hope sipped her coffee. "Divorce sucks. Sorry, I just assumed."

"Assumed right," Sam said. "Going on thirteen years now."

"Got me beat. You never remarried?"

"Never had time for it." Sam stared at his coffee and remembered the times with Claire that were good, so many years ago. Hope studied Sam's face. "Not being there for him when he was growing up, that's one of the worst mistakes I've ever made."

Hope flashed her eyebrows in surprise. "One of?"

Sam shook his head. "Never mind. Hey, the day's disappearing. I should leave you to unpack."

"Wait." Hope's eyes lit up. "I've got something to show you." She stood and disappeared into one of the rooms off the hallway.

Sam found himself watching Hope's butt move in her

black jeans. The thick silver chains attached at the back danced and jangled with every step. He contemplated whether or not she was too young for him, then pushed the thought away.

Hope returned, carrying a cage, and set it down on top of a box. A white rat ran around inside the cage. The hairs on the back of Sam's neck stood at full attention as his mind raced. Irrational thoughts crept in from the dark recesses of his memory. His hands began to tremble. Sam set his mug down and balled his hands into fists to fight the shakes.

"This is my family." Hope's smile did nothing to relax him. "Sam, meet Harriette."

Sam's body tensed. "You live with a rat?"

"What?" Hope's smile wavered. "Pets are allowed here, right? The ad said—"

"I know what the ad said." Sam remained aware of Harriette's every move. "I just wasn't expecting a rat."

Hope opened the cage and reached in. "Harriette. Come here, girl."

Harriette made a beeline to her hand. Hope lifted the rat out of the cage and nuzzled her. Sam's eyes remained locked on Harriette.

"You should really keep that thing in the cage." Sam watched Hope stroke Harriette, from her twitching whiskers to her pink tail. Harriette's white fur bore a striking contrast to Hope's black clothes.

"Nah, she'll be fine," Hope said. "Want to hold her?"

"Keep that thing away from me," Sam said.

"She's not a thing. She's a beautiful *Rattus norvegicus*, an albino Wistar strain."

Sam hadn't heard a word Hope was saying. His world

began to close in around him and he felt an uneasy dizziness begin to float in his head.

"Don't worry," Hope said. "She won't bite, will you Harriette?" Hope extended her arms, and brought Harriette closer to Sam in her cupped hands.

"Jesus Fuck!" Sam scrambled backward, off the box he was sitting on, and landed on his large, open toolbox. An exposed screwdriver carved a bloody gash into his back.

Hope, surprised by Sam's unexpected reaction, returned Harriette to her cage and locked the latch.

"I told you to keep that *fucking* thing in the cage." Sam sat up and fresh pain shot through his back. "Fuck."

"Sorry." Hope's watchful eyes were full of remorse.

Sam reached behind his back to check his injury, and felt a warm stickiness through his shirt. Images of Piper's eviscerated body flashed through his head. Sam looked at his bloodied hand, and confirmed what he had felt moments ago.

"Shit, you're bleeding." Hope extended her hand to help Sam up. Being the only offer available, he took it. "Sit."

Sam resumed his seat on the box.

Hope handed him his coffee. "Drink," she said as she headed down the hall and into the bathroom.

The mug of coffee was still warm. Sam's hands still trembled, but holding the mug with both hands helped mask how obvious it was.

"You sure are bossy," Sam said.

"You haven't seen nothing yet." Hope's voice echoed out of the bathroom and down the hall.

Blood began to clot into the back of Sam's shirt. He stared at Harriette in the cage. Harriette and her red eyes stared back, whiskers vibrating. But it was a different red than those he had seen last night in the kitchen. Those eyes seemed to *glow*, like they could burn if touched.

Hope returned to the box-filled living room with a package of maxipads, paper towel and some scotch tape.

"Hey… You're not going to—" Sam imagined how such a scenario would have played out in prison.

"It's all I could find." Hope ripped open the package. "The scrape's too big for a band-aid."

"But a fucking tampon?"

"Relax. It's a maxipad. With wings, apparently." Hope blotted Sam's wound with a paper towel. "Besides, who's going to know? Take off your shirt."

"I'm fine." Sam sipped his coffee.

"It's going to get infected," Hope said.

"What are you, my mother?" Sam tried to twist around to look at Hope, but the pain stopped him. "I've been through worse."

"Look, I'm trying to apologize here." Hope stepped from behind to face Sam. "The least you can do is let me clean you up."

Sam could tell trying to convince Hope of anything else at that moment would be a fool's errand. Slow and reluctant, Sam removed his flannel work shirt to his t-shirt underneath. Tattoos covered his arms.

"T-shirt, too." Hope took his work shirt and held out her hand, beckoning.

Soon, you're going to know more about me than my own son, Sam thought. He didn't like the idea. Sam lifted off his plain white shirt, stained with his blood on the back, and revealed his muscular back, chiseled and weathered, and covered with hard core prison tattoos and many small scars. Across his back from shoulder to shoulder in black Gothic text were the words "Property of Franklin Correctional Facility."

Hope studied Sam's tattoos as she applied the maxipad to his wound, then affixed it to his back with tape. She admired the raw artistry.

"Wicked tats," she said. "The scrape missed most of them except the 'O' in 'Correctional'. What did you do?"

It was a detail of Sam's life he preferred not to share. He grabbed his t-shirt and redressed, fighting through the pain spread across his shoulders. His blood on the t-shirt had already dried and stiffened, and made it inflexible and itchy.

"Look, I got to go," Sam said. He grabbed his toolbox and headed towards the door. "Thanks for the coffee... and the tampon."

Hope grabbed Sam's work shirt and stopped him at the door. "Maxipad." She pressed the bunched-up work shirt to his chest. Even though the layers of crumpled fabric, she could feel his hard pectoral muscles. Hope imagined what kind of tattoos sprawled his chest. And those small scars.

"What? Oh yeah." Sam took the work shirt. "Thanks. If you need anything, apartment 102." Sam headed down the common hallway towards the elevator.

"Thanks!" Hope said. Sam shook his work shirt like a pom-pom in response. She closed her apartment door and shook her head. "That went well."

Sam stood inside the elevator and waited for the doors to close. He set his toolbox on the floor of the elevator car and examined the back of his work shirt. The rip was small and most of the blood had soaked into his t-shirt. He slipped his work shirt back on and pressed the first floor call button. The elevator car jerked to a start and scraped its way down.

Tattoo

The constant hum of outside traffic noise was no competition for Bradley's heavy breathing. He was dead to the world, sleeping soundly with a full belly. Sam had splurged on dinner, if the $14.50 Superbox from Kingsley's could be called splurging. It was enough fried chicken and mashed potatoes for three, maybe four people, but between Sam and Bradley they had eaten all of it. The food and an afternoon of lifting furniture and boxes had tired them out. Sleep came easy.

It was just past three o'clock in the morning when the rustling began. First in the corner of Bradley's room, out of the closet, the light pitter-patter of small rodent paws traveled to the clothes Bradley had left in a heap four hours earlier. They still held the essence of fried chicken where Bradley had dropped a greasy chicken leg on his pants. The rat's nose twitched, working overtime. It dug through the pile, searching for the source.

The rat poked its nose up out of the clothes and stood up on its hind legs to test the air again. Its whiskers quivered as the rodent narrowed in on the source of the smell like a guided missile. Its white-tipped tail seemed to glow in the dim city light, flicking back and forth.

The rat hopped off Bradley's clothes and ran along the

baseboard like it was on rails. It stopped once to sniff and reassess its path. The bed was the source of the irresistible smell, the rat was sure of it, but the shortest route meant traveling diagonally across the room, a dangerous proposition. Crossing open areas left the rat exposed to danger, but the smell of fried chicken was too big a draw.

The rat stood motionless and tried to determine any danger in the room. When it felt safe, the rat made a hurried beeline to the corner of the bed and crawled up and underneath the light top sheet. Bradley had stripped the other sheet off the bed after his first night. Keeping it on the bed had made it too hot to sleep.

With slow stop-start movements, the rat bump moved its way up the bed, getting ever closer to Bradley and what the rat determined to be the source of something tasty. Bradley stirred, rolled on his right side and brought his hands close to his face. The rat stopped, sniffed, whiskers vibrated, then moved ever closer.

The rat emerged from under the sheets at Bradley's hands. This was it. Saliva began to flood the rat's mouth as it opened its jaws, slow and wide. The rat waited no longer. Its jaws clamped down with twelve tons of force. The exposed yellow incisors, the same ones that had already gnawed through concrete, metal pipe, and Piper's toned muscles, sunk into the fleshy pad of Bradley's index finger like a hot knife through butter.

Sam had learned to be a light sleeper in prison. It was a necessary survival skill. Bradley's scream was plenty loud enough to wake him, and possibly Gustavo on the second floor. The fallout from that would be fun.

Sam was off the couch like a shot and burst into Bradley's room. Sam stood in the doorway, breathing heavy. "What's wrong?"

Bradley sat on the edge of his bed and held his index finger. Despite Bradley's age, Sam could tell he was fighting back tears. He wanted to look strong, but instead Bradley looked like a little boy who just wanted to be comforted. Sam imagined how many times he had looked like that with Claire over the years. Tonight was Sam's turn.

"Something bit me," Bradley said.

Sam turned on the bedside light and sat next to Bradley. "Did you see what it was?"

"What do you think?" Bradley was in no mood to answer questions. "I was asleep."

"Let's get you cleaned up."

Bradley followed Sam into the bathroom.

Sam turned on the tap and adjusted the temperature of the running water. "Wash the bite. And use soap."

"I'm not stupid, you know." Bradley wet the tip of his index finger, already red and swollen, and winced at the contact.

"Soap."

"I am!" Bradley said. The mysterious bite had left him with no opportunity to defend himself or run. His nerves shot, he held himself together by threads. "Just back off."

Sam took a step back and watched.

Bradley worked up a soapy lather in his other hand, applied it to his index finger, and grit his teeth against the sting. The longer he washed the puncture, the less it hurt. He rinsed the bloody froth down the drain in spirals.

Sam handed Bradley a towel. "Can I take a look?"

Bradley wrapped his finger with the towel and squeezed. Fresh pain flooded his hand with the increased pressure. As he removed his finger from the towel, not just one, but two puncture wounds could be seen, engorged with blood once again.

The color drained from Sam's face. The shape of the bite was unmistakable.

Bradley's anger at Sam dissolved into panic. "What?"

"Keep pressure on it," Sam said. "Did you wash up before going to bed?"

Bradley re-wrapped his finger with the towel. "I can't remember."

"You're not going to like this, but that's a rat bite," Sam said.

Bradley could tell from Sam's tone that he meant business. "How do you know?"

Sam's eyes went distant. "Believe me, I know…" He trailed off. The world closed in. He reached out to steady himself on the sink before everything went black. Sam could hear their clammy feet as they ran along cold concrete. It wouldn't be long before the bites would start.

"Sam?" Bradley tugged on Sam's sleeve. "You're sweating."

"What?" Sam's face glistened and he could smell the funky odor of his own nervous fear. He wiped his face with the sleeve of his work shirt.

"You zoned out," Bradley said.

"How long?"

Bradley thought for a moment. "Maybe a minute or two."

"Shit, I'm sorry." Sam exhaled and rubbed his face with open palms.

"You okay?" Bradley tried for once to make eye contact with Sam.

Sam shook off the dark memory. "Uh, yeah. About the bite, might have been the smell of fried chicken on your hands."

He grabbed a band-aid from under the sink and handed one to Bradley. "Keep it clean and covered. If things don't improve in a few days, we'll go see a doctor."

"Couldn't I get rabies?" Bradley unwrapped his finger and looked at the two small punctures. The bleeding had stopped. He peeled back the adhesive strips on the band-aid and applied it to his finger.

"I don't know. Maybe that funky phone of yours has some answers," Sam said. "Back to bed."

"I can't sleep now," Bradley said. "Could you?"

Sam nodded. "Good point."

SAM AND BRADLEY sat in the TV room, Sam's makeshift bed of blankets shoved to one side. The television played a rerun of *Welcome Back, Kotter*. The Sweathogs were cracking jokes and looking for any excuse to avoid school work. Bradley nursed his index finger, squeezing it every once in a while to make sure it still hurt. It did.

Bradley searched for information on rabies on his phone. "It says here that rats almost never get rabies and there's no documented cases of rats spreading rabies to humans."

"*Almost* never."

"What do you mean?"

"Almost never isn't the same as never."

"So I *could* be infected?" Bradley squeezed his throbbing finger again. It still hurt.

"Probably not." Sam grinned. "I'm just busting your balls. I wouldn't worry about it."

Bradley eyed Sam wearily as he put his phone back in his pocket. "Is there anything else on, besides this old stuff?"

"What's wrong with *Welcome Back, Kotter*?" Sam said. "It's a classic."

"It's old." Bradley stared at the ceiling. "Twenty years ago it was old."

"What can I say?" Sam shot Bradley a look. "It's four in the morning and I got three channels."

"You need a flat screen," Bradley said. "Imagine the Sweathogs in glorious HD."

Sam shook his head. "Can't swing it on my income—"

SNAP!

Bradley looked at Sam. "Was that the…" They were both thinking the same thing.

The rat trap!

Sam was up and off the sofa, headed to the kitchen, with Bradley following close behind, the bite on his finger instantly forgotten.

Sam flipped the switch to the solitary light in the kitchen. It flickered in an unpredictable cadence until it decided to stay on. He crept toward the door under the sink. Images of the last time he opened the door in the middle of the night flashed through his head.

"What are you waiting for," Bradley said. "The trap went off. The thing's dead."

Sam raised his index finger to his lips and mouthed the word "quiet." His agitation was obvious.

Sam pulled the door under the sink open and was shocked by what he saw. The snap trap sat exactly where he had placed it the day before, with a plastic straw clamped under the kill arm. There was no trace of peanut butter and no dead rat.

"What the hell?" Sam said, puzzled.

"What?"

Sam pointed to the trap under the sink. "Take a look."

Bradley stepped forward. What he saw surprised him as much as Sam.

"Did you put the straw there?"

"No," said Sam. Then he turned to look at Bradley. A sly grin crept across his face. "Your phone work in low light?"

It didn't take long for Bradley to catch on. He disappeared down the hallway, returning seconds later with his phone. Sam grabbed the snap trap and placed it on the counter. He opened the fridge and took out the peanut butter.

"We'll have to shoot in time-lapse," he said. "I don't have enough storage for full motion, but we should be okay if I play it back frame by frame."

"Whatever you say," Sam said. "It's all Greek to me."

Sam extracted the plastic straw from the snap trap. He grabbed a spoon from a drawer and scooped a glob of peanut butter onto the bait pedal. He pulled the kill arm back and engaged the trigger.

"Get a nice shot of it," Sam said as he placed the trap back under the sink.

"I'll make it fairly wide." Bradley opened the opposite door under the sink and placed his phone facing the snap trap. He framed up the shot but the phone wouldn't stay upright.

"Got anything heavy to prop my phone up with?" he said.

Sam racked his brain searching for ideas. "Just a second." He rummaged through the counter drawers, then through the cupboards. "How about cans of soup?"

"That'll work."

Sam handed Bradley a can of Campbell's Tomato soup and one of Cream of Mushroom.

"Big spender," Bradley said.

"They taste great mixed."

"Yeah, right," Bradley said as he used the two cans of soup to prop up his phone. He pressed record. The little red recording indicator blinked in the bottom corner of the phone's screen.

"Those little bastards better not gnaw my phone." He headed down the hallway. "I'm going to find something better to watch than the Sweathogs."

"Good luck," Sam said. He admired the surveillance operation set up under the sink for a moment before he closed the doors.

SAM STOOD SHIRTLESS and faced the mirror in the bathroom. There in front of him was the story of his life, a prison tableau of permanent black ink. Fifteen years of initiation, affiliation, attrition and retribution that would never let him forget his mistakes.

He turned on the faucet. Water splashed into the sink, first a gusher, then a slow trickle. He adjusted the hot and cold knobs to try to increase the flow, but the water remained no more than a rapid drip.

"Shit." Sam could hear Gustavo in his head, complaining about his water pressure. This confirmed some kind of plumbing problem, and it was probably beyond his skill set.

Annoyed, Sam shut the water trickle off. He turned his body and his head to manage a glance at the maxipad on his back. It had begun to sag from his sweat and body movement. He grabbed one corner of the maxipad and tugged it. The tape that held the pad to his back pulled free. Some of his clotted blood had dried to the cotton pad and made removal of the pad painful in spots. Slow was the order of the day. Bit by bit, Sam began to remove the maxipad off his back.

Bradley knelt in front of the television. He rotated the channel-changing knob round and round. The same three channels came up, and Bradley hoped as if by magic one of them might change to something good with just one more turn. At this hour, the choices were reruns of *Barney Miller*, an infomercial for the ShamWow with Mop and an animated cartoon called *The Mighty Hercules*. He was familiar with the ShamWow, but the other two shows were off his radar.

Bradley stood and walked out into the hallway. The bathroom door was ajar and the light inside cast a diagonal slash across the hallway.

"Sam?" He approached the door and gave it a knock, which caused it to swing open wider. "Sam, do you—"

Bradley froze in the doorway to the bathroom and stared at Sam's tattoos.

"Shit…" Sam lowered his head. "Do I what?"

Bradley was speechless. Profanity and death mixed with artistry and scars covered Sam's upper body and flowed across his shoulder blades and down his arms. Two large spider webs spread out from his elbows. A watch face without hands wrapped his left wrist. On his back, underneath the words "Property of Franklin Correctional Facility," was a skull intertwined with a snake. On his chest, the words "Motherfucker for Life" and "Murderer." On his left oblique, spilling onto his abdomen, was a headstone with his name on it and the date of his sentencing. On his right was a revolver shooting beer cans.

"I don't have all day," Sam said.

Bradley stood in the bathroom doorway, fascinated and repulsed at the same time, still processing Sam's tattoos and their possible meanings. This was something he found far more interesting than television.

Bradley cocked his head to one side. "Is that a... maxipad?"

Sam pushed the bathroom door closed. He hadn't wanted to reveal himself to Bradley this way, but what was done was done.

Perhaps it will make things easier, Sam thought.

He braced himself on the sink. Sam grabbed one end of the maxipad and ripped it off in one swift tug. He gritted his teeth through the brief sting as parts of the wound reopened and welled with blood.

Sam balled up a towel, placed it behind his back and leaned against the wall. The pressure felt good.

Bradley changed out of his pajamas and into his clothes for the day, a comfortable pair of Levi 501s and a t-shirt emblazoned with the words "Home is where the WIFI connects automatically." He attached his raccoon tail to a belt loop on his jeans.

He headed toward the kitchen, pausing outside the

bathroom door. He contemplated checking on Sam, but thought better of it.

Inside the bathroom, Sam heard Bradley's footsteps stop, then continue. Redressing his wound would be easier with two people, but Sam couldn't bring himself to ask for help. The shame that surrounded his tattoos gripped him in his own private prison.

Bradley opened the door under the kitchen sink. The phone and the trap were right where he had left them, except instead of a dead rat, the snap trap had clamped an old toothbrush under the kill arm. He grabbed the snap trap and his phone and sat down at the kitchen table. He examined the snap trap further, and couldn't find a trace of peanut butter on it.

Sam stepped away from the wall and removed the towel from his back. It was peppered with small blood stains, but the bleeding was less severe than he had initially thought.

He cracked open the bathroom door and peered out into the empty hallway. Sam walked to the bedroom, but hesitated at the door. He wanted to respect Bradley's space, but there was no other place to store his clothes.

"I need to grab a shirt out of the dresser," Sam said. "Okay to enter?"

"Sure, no prob," Bradley's voice sounded back from the kitchen.

Sam dug out a plain, black t-shirt from the bottom drawer of the dresser. If his wounds bled, they'd be less noticeable on dark fabric.

On his way to the kitchen, Sam popped into the TV room and grabbed his long-sleeved work shirt and slipped it on. Bradley sat at the kitchen table, eating dry cereal by the handful. He watched videos on his phone.

Sam made a beeline to the coffee maker.

"New rule," he said. "Whoever gets up first makes coffee."

"But we were both up already," Bradley said.

"You know what I mean."

"By the way, you're out of milk," Bradley said between crunching mouthfuls of cereal. "And you're out of your league."

Sam turned from the coffee machine, puzzled. "What do you mean?"

Bradley slid his phone and the snap trap across the table towards Sam. "Take a look."

The first thing Sam noticed was the toothbrush held under the kill arm of the snap trap. A bright pink, it wasn't any toothbrush he owned.

"I'll assume that's not your toothbrush," Sam said.

"No shit, Sherlock."

Sam pulled back the kill arm and released the toothbrush onto the table.

Bradley picked up his phone and handed it to Sam. "Press play. I think you'll find that more interesting."

Sam took the phone and touched the triangular play icon on its screen. His eyes went wide as he watched the short video play.

"You're not pulling a fast one on me, are you?" Sam said.

Bradley shook his head.

The video ended and Sam pressed play again. "Is this typical rat behavior?"

"No idea."

"I'd be amazed if I didn't hate the little fuckers so much," Sam said. When the video ended, he played it one more time.

METROPOLIS

HUNTS POINT HARDWARE was a dumpy little store on the corner of Drake Street and Randall Avenue, but in the five months that Sam had worked as superintendent of his building, it always had what he needed. Today was no exception.

Sam and Bradley roamed the cramped aisles. The store focused on tools and hardware, but the owners stocked pest removal supplies as well. Since Hunts Point was the home of many food-processing facilities for New York State, mass quantities of stored food meant pests were a certainty. It wouldn't take long for cockroaches, ants, carpet beetles, mice or rats to destroy an unsecured food supply.

"How about this?" Bradley held up a box of rat poison. "Says it stops rats dead in their tracks."

"Yeah, but the rat lives just long enough to crawl into the walls before it dies," Sam said. "Ever smelled a dead rat?"

Bradley shook his head.

"Trust me, it's sickening." Sam shuddered. "The smell lingers for months."

Bradley grabbed an electronic pest repellent. "This one's state of the art," he said. "Repels pests with ultrasonic sound." Bradley turned the box around in his hand, smiling at the illustration of the rodents, bugs and snakes fleeing for their lives.

"All those do is cause the bastards to move from one side of the building to the other, if they work at all." Sam said. "Snap traps are where it's at. They're cheap and they work."

Sam spotted a bulk box and began grabbing traps.

"How many?" Bradley joined Sam as he collected the individually wrapped bounty.

"A dozen to start would be good."

When they were done, the box had one trap left in it.

"Ah hell, make it thirteen," Sam said, "and we'll take the box."

Sam and Bradley made their way to the cashier, a crusty old guy who wore an eye-patch and still managed to chew gum with what little teeth he had left.

"Do you think this is going to be enough?" Bradley said.

"Going to have to be," Sam said. "This practically breaks my budget."

"Got rats, eh?" The cashier eyed the box of traps.

"Yeah." Sam motioned to the box. "There's thirteen in there."

"Yah look honest, but I'm gonna have to count 'em." The cashier dumped the box onto the counter and began to scan each trap individually. Bradley stared at the cashier's eye patch.

"Lost it in 'Nam, August, 1963." The cashier pointed to his eye patch. "Rats got to it. Damn near the size of dogs." He raised his left hand and revealed a shiny, metal prosthetic hook. "Got my hand, too."

"You're a regular Captain Hook," Sam said.

The cashier finished scanning the traps, unfazed by Sam's joke. He had heard them all. "Yup. Thirteen."

"What's the total?"

The cashier punched numbers into the old cash register. "Let's call it forty-five, even," he said.

Sam dug into his pocket, brought out a wad of ones and fives and began counting.

Bradley held up his index finger. "A rat bit me last night."

"Yer lucky it didn't take yer whole finger," the cashier said. "Once they taste blood, there's no stoppin' 'em. Got a fever yet?"

"Fever?" Bradley looked at Sam, alarmed.

Sam had heard enough. He handed over the cash and pushed the traps back into the box. "Thanks. Brad, let's go."

"If yah see one rat, there's ten yah can't," the cashier said. "Remember that. And those bastards are smart."

Sam and Bradley exited the store and began the walk back to the apartment.

"What did he mean about getting a fever?" Bradley said.

"Nothing. He was spouting bullshit."

"Are you sure?"

Sam stopped and faced Bradley. "If a rat bite can kill, I'd be dead." Sam paused to let his words sink in, then wondered if he had said too much.

"What do you mean?" Bradley thought he had found some common ground for a real conversation.

"Nothing," Sam said.

"No, I want to know."

"Drop it." Sam focused on the sidewalk ahead. "How's your finger doing?"

Bradley checked the band-aid. "Good. It barely hurts at all anymore."

"I think you're going to be okay," Sam said.

As Sam and Bradley turned right up Casanova Street, they passed the same prostitute they had driven by a couple of days earlier. This time she wore black heels, a denim mini-skirt, and a matching denim jacket over her body-hugging white tank top.

"Hey, honey," she said. "Haven't seen you for a while. You must be *so* lonely."

"You know, keeping busy." Sam paused, and if he had been asked, he would have said he was just being polite.

The woman ran her eyes over Bradley, head to toe and back. "Aren't you going to introduce me to this tall, cool drink of water?"

"Right," Sam said. "Carmela, this is Brad, my son."

Bradley felt heat rise up the back of his neck and curl around his ears.

"Your son?" Carmela flashed her eyes wide. "You been holding out on me, honey."

Sam shrugged a smirk.

Carmela picked up Bradley's raccoon tail and let it flow through her fingers. "That's a fine piece of tail. Maybe I should show you mine sometime." She winked at Bradley, enjoying toying with him.

Bradley's legs felt like hot jelly.

"The things I could show you." Carmela leaned forward to Bradley's ear. "I'd be gentle."

"Alright, Carmela," Sam said. "Have a good day."

Carmela, Sam and Bradley parted ways. "I have a few ideas how to make it a better day," she said.

"Bye, Carmela," Sam said.

Carmela waved back. "Bye Sam. Bye, *Brad*."

Bradley managed a weak wave, then turned to Sam. "You know her?"

"Well…" Sam searched for the appropriate words. "Let's just say we're business associates."

"Holy shit." Bradley smiled. "What's she like?"

"Nope." Sam could sense the gears working in Bradley's head.

"Come on!"

"I'm not talking about that with you." Sam glanced at Bradley. "And don't get any ideas. You couldn't afford her anyways."

"How would you know?"

"I know."

"Whatever." Bradley jammed his hands in his pockets.

"Let's go," Sam said. "We got work to do."

SAM AND BRADLEY found themselves standing in front of Gustavo's apartment. The first "2" from "202" was missing, which left behind a darkened area like a nuclear shadow.

Bradley held the box of snap traps.

"Brace yourself," Sam said. "This isn't going to be fun."

Sam knocked on Gustavo's door.

Footsteps approached from the other side of the door. A deadbolt slid and clicked within the door. Gustavo threw the door open and looked upon Sam and Bradley, scowling as usual.

"What the hell do you want?" Gustavo barked.

"Good morning to you, too," Bradley said, under his breath.

Sam shot Bradley a look. "Hey Gustavo, I'll get to the point," Sam said.

"Thank Christ for small miracles."

Sam continued. "I've discovered the building has a rat problem."

Bradley handed Gustavo two snap traps.

"I haven't seen any rats," Gustavo said.

"Trust me on this one."

"Trust you?" Gustavo laughed. Sam recoiled at the odor of Gustavo's breath. It smelled like something had crawled into his mouth and died.

Maybe it was a rat, Sam thought. He fought to hold back a smirk.

Across the hall, in apartment 201, Melvin heard the knock on Gustavo's door and the sounds of conversation. He walked to his door and looked out the peephole. Carny pricked his ears and followed. As soon as Melvin recognized Sam and Bradley, he opened his door.

"What's all the damn racket?" Melvin said.

Carny stepped out into the hallway and began to growl. Bradley responded by sneering back at Carny. The little dog's growl transformed into the ever familiar and annoying *yip-yips*.

"You mean that racket?" Bradley said.

"Carny! Quiet!" Melvin pushed Carny aside with his foot.

Gustavo pointed at Sam and held up his two snap traps. "He's playing exterminator today."

"News flash," Melvin said. "New York City has rats."

"Do me a favor and use the traps," Sam said. "Peanut butter works best."

"Do me a favor and fix the damn water pressure." Gustavo flung the snap traps back into his apartment where they landed with a clatter. "I haven't had a decent shower in weeks."

"The rats are my first priority," Sam said.

Gustavo shook his head. "You're so full of shit."

Bradley handed Melvin two snap traps. "Don't let your rat, I mean *dog*, near these."

Melvin snatched the traps from Bradley's hand. Sensing anger in Melvin, Carny began to growl at Bradley again.

"What about those plastic traps." Melvin turned the traps around in his hands, examining them. "These are too hard to set."

"Too expensive," Sam said.

"You need to hire an exterminator." Gustavo said.

"I can handle it." Sam switched his gaze between Gustavo and Melvin. "Just use the traps. Save us all some money."

Gustavo slammed his door and locked it.

"This is a problem you can't fix." Melvin threw his two traps back into the box. "Even with your god damned traps." He walked to his door. "Carny! Git!" Carny hustled into the apartment and Melvin shut his door. The deadbolt slid into place with a *thunk*.

Sam looked at Bradley. "See the shit I have to deal with? At least we're finished with Tweedledum and Tweedledee."

"Should be Tweedledumb and Tweedledumber."

Sam laughed. "I'll have to remember that one."

The two of them walked to the elevator.

"Let's use the stairs." Sam opened the door for Bradley.

The stairwell was dimly lit, with a single flickering incandescent bulb over each landing. The unpainted concrete stairs were cracked and crumbling in parts. In the corner, closest to the door, a water pipe ran the height of the building, from floor to floor, and supplied water to the sprinkler systems.

"I'm beginning to think the elevator is safer," Bradley said.

"It's all reinforced with rebar." Sam headed up the stairs, two steps at a time. "Nothing to worry about."

Bradley stopped dead in his tracks. "Did you hear that?"

Sam stopped and listened. "I don't hear anything. Your ears are playing tricks on you."

"I thought I heard rustling." Convinced by silence, Bradley followed Sam up the stairwell to the third floor.

Concealed in the corner of the second floor landing above Bradley's head, where the water supply pipe ran, a young rat sat on a securing bolt and watched Sam and Bradley's every move. When they passed the mid-floor landing, the rat scurried down the pipe and disappeared into the wall, white-tipped tail flipping as it went.

Sam and Bradley exited onto the third floor and made their way to Mrs. Baxter's apartment. The brass lion door knocker reminded Bradley of Piper.

"Want to do the honors?" Sam said.

"Can you take this for a while?" Bradley handed the box of snap traps to Sam, and was about to grab the door knocker when they heard what sounded like a muffled yell.

Sam looked at Bradley. "Did you heard that?"

Bradley nodded. "That wasn't Mrs. Baxter."

"No," Sam said. "That was from the second floor."

"Gustavo."

"Yeah."

They both paused for a moment longer and after being met with silence, Bradley grabbed the door knocker and tapped it three times.

"Who is it?" Mrs. Baxter said through the door.

"It's Brad and Sam, Mrs. Baxter," Sam said. "I know it's early, but I… we need to talk to you."

"Hold yer horses." Mrs. Baxter disappeared into her apartment for a moment, then returned and unlocked the door. "Had to get decent for me two favorite men. It's not often I get visitors at eight in the morning."

"Sorry about that," Sam said.

"What's this about?"

"There's a rat problem in the building," Bradley said. "We're handing out traps." He grabbed two traps from the box and handed them to Mrs. Baxter.

"Thank you, dear." Mrs. Baxter took the traps and set them on a table by the door.

"We don't know for sure yet," Sam said, "but they may be responsible for Piper's death."

Bradley looked at Sam, surprised.

"You don't say!" Mrs. Baxter sneered and shook her fist. "I'll molicate 'em!"

"Use peanut butter for bait," Bradley said.

"I will, Brad." Mrs. Baxter took Brad's hand and shook it firmly. "Thank yea. Does the bonnie lass across the way know?"

"We'll tell her next," Sam said. "Good luck."

"I'll skin the toaty bastards!" Mrs. Baxter shook her fists again. "You have my word."

She had almost closed her door when Sam said, "Oh, by the way, was that Gustavo we heard? A few minutes ago?"

Mrs. Baxter scowled. "Aye. The tossbag's always cussing up a storm down there," she said. "All hours of the day and night. I'm surprised you can't hear it."

"I'll have a chat with him," Sam said.

"Thank you kindly, Sam." Mrs. Baxter closed her door and engaged the deadbolt.

"You never said anything about rats killing Piper," Bradley said.

"It was just a theory. Plus it lit a fire under Mrs. Baxter. We need all the help we can get."

"Why?"

"Let's just say I had an encounter in the kitchen the other night that changed my mind." Sam knocked on Hope's door, just below the numbers "301." They were haphazardly affixed to the door. Sam made a mental note to straighten them when he had a chance.

"You mean when I found you lying on the floor?" Bradley said. "A few nights ago?"

"Yeah." Sam found Bradley's focus uncomfortable, and tried to break the tension by knocking on Hope's door again.

"What happened?" Bradley pressed Sam for an answer. "Were you attacked?"

"I'm not getting into this right now," Sam said.

"You brought it up."

Sam turned and walked back towards the elevator, fingers white from clutching the box of traps.

"Dad…" The word was out of Bradley's mouth before he could stop it.

Sam froze in his tracks. The word made his blood run cold. He had dreamed of this moment but was unprepared for the power it had over him.

Sounds of a deadbolt unlocking echoed behind them and Hope stuck her head out into the hallway.

"Oh, hi guys." She rubbed sleep out of her eyes. "What's up?"

"We need to talk to you," Sam said. "It's about rats."

Hope looked at Sam, then Bradley. "Um, sure." She swung the door wide open, inviting them in. The living room looked better but boxes still lay around.

Sam and Bradley looked for a place to sit.

"Shut the door." Hope walked down the hallway. "Give me a second to get dressed."

Bradley watched Hope walk to her bedroom. His sixteen year old eyes traced her bare legs. She wore a black t-shirt, just long enough to cover her behind. Just above the hem, in bold white letters, were the words "Stop staring at my ass." Above that was an icon of a donkey.

Sam nudged Bradley in the shoulder. "Stop staring at her ass."

"I'm not!" Bradley found a clear spot on the couch and sat down.

"Just busting your balls." Sam chuckled to himself and sat next to Bradley. "Hey, did you call me 'Dad' back there?"

"No," Bradley said. "It was a mistake."

It's the anger talking, Sam thought. Still, Bradley's response stung.

Hope walked out of her bedroom and down the hallway, now dressed in basic black jeans and a t-shirt. "So, boys…" Hope looked at Sam and Bradley. "What's so important that you had to wake me from a Tom Selleck dream?"

Bradley scrunched his brows. "Tom Selleck?"

Hope laughed. "You're so cute."

"We have a rat problem." Sam handed Hope a couple of snap traps. She took them and looked at Sam and Bradley, confused.

"Humor me," Sam said. "And take a look at this, will you?" Sam turned to Bradley. "You got the video ready?"

Bradley dug into his pocket and pulled out his phone. He worked the touch screen with his fingertips and cued up the video.

Hope took the phone from Bradley and pressed play. "What am I looking at?"

"That's under my kitchen sink," Sam said.

"You shot in time-lapse mode," Hope said. "Smart move."

"Thanks." Bradley managed a smile, although in his head, he chuffed at Hope's comment.

"Does the camera have motion sensing mode?"

"I'm not sure," Bradley said. "I'll have to check that out later."

"If it does, you should try that next." Hope paused the video. "If it doesn't, I'm sure you could find an app that does."

"Hate to break up the geek-fest, but let's get back to the video," Sam said.

"Hey." Hope pointed at Bradley. "This geek got you your video." She pointed at herself. "And you're asking this geek for her opinion. At eight fifteen in the morning. On a Saturday."

Sam held his hands up. "Backing off."

Hope looked at Bradley and winked at him. "Us geeks have to stick together, right?"

Bradley blushed and nodded. "Right."

Hope turned her full attention back to the phone's screen and pressed play.

The video image was badly degraded due to low light, but it was sufficient to see the snap trap, baited with a glob of peanut butter. Hope concentrated on the image. Behind the trap, she could make out a few rags and some cleaning supplies. The white garbage bag that hung from the back of the door glowed like a ghost.

Bradley watched Hope as she watched the screen. He tried to memorize her features, jumping from her eyes and her long black eyelashes, to her nose with the silver horseshoe ring, to her lips. He focused on her lips for what seemed like a long time to him.

Hope must have sensed Bradley's gaze, because she shot a quick glance at him and gave an awkward smile. Bradley looked away, self-conscious.

Hope refocused on the phone. The image remained unchanged for almost a minute before a rat appeared in one corner of the screen, dragging a toothbrush clamped in its mouth. It skittered up one side of the trap and dropped the toothbrush in front. The first rat was followed by a second, who ran to the opposite side of the trap.

Hope looked at Bradley. "Is there a way to reduce the playback speed?"

"Yeah." Bradley pointed to a control on the bottom corner of the screen. Hope touched it and a draggable control appeared. She reduced the playback speed and backed up the video to watch what she had missed.

The second rat moved up alongside the trap, opposite to the first rat. The second rat positioned its snout past the bristles on the end of the toothbrush and found a good spot on the handle to clamp its jaws on. The first rat re-sank its teeth into the handle of the toothbrush.

With widening eyes, Hope watched as the two rats worked together and lifted the toothbrush with their heads, up and onto the bait pedal and triggering the trap.

"They've done this before," she said, eyes glued to the phone's screen.

The kill arm swung hard onto the toothbrush and clamped it to its wooden base. The trap bounced slightly. It was difficult to tell for sure, but it appeared as if the two rats didn't flinch at all when the trap was sprung.

The two rats crawled on top of the trap and licked the peanut butter off the bait pedal, before they disappeared into the darkness.

"Wow," Hope said. "That was cool."

"Have you ever seen anything like this?" Sam said.

Hope rewound the video and paused it when the two rats sprung the trap. She studied the screen for a moment, then handed the phone back to Bradley.

"I have to show you something," she said.

Hope led Sam and Bradley down the hallway to her closed bedroom door.

"Promise me you won't evict me," she said.

"I can't do that without seeing what's behind the door," Sam looked at Hope, trying to convey both seriousness and sincerity.

"Promise me," Hope said.

Sam looked at Bradley. He nodded.

"I'd do it," Bradley said. "What's the worst that could happen?"

"I'll promise to be fair," Sam said. "Now open the door."

Hope took a deep breath and pushed open the door. The bed and dresser had been pushed to one side of the room, which left more than half of the room devoted to an expansive rat city.

A maze, tubes, little wagons, conveyor belts and other equipment populated the raised platform. In the middle of it all sat Harriette in her cage. She busied herself washing her small furry face. Harriette stopped as soon as she heard voices, and ran in the direction of Hope.

"Holy shit." Sam was overtaken by the intricacy of Hope's setup.

"Remember when I said I was studying at UCSB? Well, I'm actually doing my doctorate on rat behavior." Hope looked at Sam with expectant eyes. She was nervous and did her best to hide it. "So… am I evicted?"

"I don't know yet," Sam said.

"This is fucking cool." Bradley stepped up to the edge of the rat city.

"Brad, language," Sam said.

"Sorry." Bradley leaned in to get a close look at Harriette and how her cage connected to the city. "You built all this?"

"Yup. Every last bit." Hope smiled. It was easy to tell this project was her pride and joy. "I'm much more than just a pretty face."

Bradley blushed again, but still remained impressed.

Hope stood next to Bradley, and pointed to the white rat in the cage. "This is Harriette. Normally, I'd take her out and introduce you to her, but…" Hope looked back at Sam. "That didn't go so well last time."

"Understatement of the week," Sam said. "How'd you get all this in here? I helped you unpack."

Hope flashed her addictive smile. "Let's just say I don't have that many books."

Sam approached the platform, keeping one watchful eye on Harriette in her cage. He scanned the rat city, all its nooks and crannies. Not too far from Harriette's cage, Sam saw a small wooden log with handles on both sides. When he reached out to pick it up, Harriette must have sensed his movement and made a beeline toward his approaching hand. Sam withdrew his hand just as quickly.

"Don't worry," Hope said. "Harriette just thinks it's playtime. That's one of her favorites." Hope reached over and picked up the little wooden log and placed it in Sam's hand.

Sam felt its heft. "This is for a rat? It's pretty heavy."

"Two rats working together can lift it." Hope took the log from Sam's hand and dropped it into a hole in the raised platform. The log triggered a treat to drop from a nearby dispenser.

"Treats! That's why she wants to play." Bradley watched Harriette track the treat with her eyes and nose.

"Yup." Hope tweezed the treat with her fingers. "Positive reinforcement. It's all part of successive approximation." She held the treat to the bars of the cage. Harriette was ready and waiting to grab the treat from Hope's fingers through the bars.

"How does this explain the video on my phone?" Bradley said.

"This is so exciting." Hope's eyes sparkled. "There's so few people I get to talk to about this stuff. Brad, to answer your question, new generations of rats keep traits of their parents. A young rat that's never encountered a cat will still panic at the smell of one. It's kind of like genetic memory."

"So, the rats in my apartment learned to do that stuff from their parents?" Sam said.

"No," Hope said. "They were born with the knowledge."

"Born? Are you shitting me?" Sam found it all hard to believe. Bradley on the other hand would believe anything

Hope said, even if she told him the clouds were made of ice cream.

Hope shook her head. "There's something else. Come on."

She led Sam and Bradley back to the living room. Hope dug through a box of books and pulled one out. She flipped it open and riffled though its pages, before tossing it aside in search of another. The second book had what Hope was looking for.

AMBUSH

GUSTAVO SLAMMED HIS door and locked it. The two snap traps that he had thrown over his shoulder moments earlier sat in disarray on the floor. The corner of one of the wooden platforms had split and part of the wood had sheered off.

He knelt on one swollen knee and picked the traps up off the floor. Over the past several years, Gustavo's knees had began to give him more and more grief, and for some reason it always seemed to be worse during summer. This year was the worst it had ever been. Any unnecessary bending made his knees throb and picking up the traps had started the day off on the wrong foot.

"Fucking rat problem, my ass."

Gustavo walked to the kitchen and dropped the traps on the counter. He stared at them for a long while. His eyes traced the metal hinges and the simplicity of the coiled mechanism.

"How hard can it be?" he said.

Gustavo took the trap without the broken base and pried the kill arm back. He hooked the latch to the bait pedal but it kept slipping off. This trap had a hair trigger. He tried two more times before the latch caught.

"Hah! Take that, fucker." His triumph didn't last long.

Gustavo looked at the bait pedal and realized his mistake. In his haste, he had forgotten to bait the trap before setting it. A rookie mistake.

Gustavo held the kill arm down with one hand and unlatched the bait pedal. He was unprepared for the strength of the kill arm. It slipped out of his grasp, swung around and caught the tip of his index finger on his other hand.

"Fuck!" Gustavo's cursing was loud enough for his neighbors to hear most of the time. This was no exception.

If the kill arm had sprung unrestricted, it would have shattered Gustavo's index finger. His other hand had managed to slow it down enough to avoid broken bones, but not enough to prevent splitting the skin. The pain was immense and fresh blood rushed to his fingertip.

Gustavo gritted his teeth as he brought his hand to the kitchen sink and turned on the tap. Instead of water to wash his wounded finger, the faucet choked and sputtered. No water. Again.

"FUCK THIS!" Gustavo threw the snap trap across the counter. It smashed against the back splash. He grabbed a flashlight from a drawer and slammed his apartment door closed. The "02" that remained on the door rattled and swayed. He locked his apartment door behind him and headed down the hallway toward the elevator.

The elevator doors creaked open and Gustavo stepped inside. He pressed "B," and left a smudge of blood on the button. He wrapped his finger in his shirt tail and squeezed. It hurt like a son of a bitch but the bleeding was slowing. Or so he thought.

Gustavo had forgotten about the warfarin his doctor had prescribed for him since having a stroke last year. Warfarin is an anticoagulant, and as a result of taking the drug, bleeding from scrapes and cuts took a lot longer to clot. His shirt became saturated so he held his arm up to stem the flow. Warfarin is also a common ingredient in rat poison. The irony was lost in Gustavo's rage as he descended into the basement.

The elevator opened up to reveal old brick and water-stained, crumbling concrete lining the basement. A solitary incandescent light bulb hung overhead and accentuated the cracks. Gustavo stepped out and a wall of mustiness hit his nose.

He flicked on his flashlight. Unfinished joists and old pipes crisscrossed overhead and faded out into darkness, beyond the flashlight's reach. Just past the elevator was the door to the building's common laundry room.

A sound emanated from the blackness. Gustavo stopped and cocked his head to one side. He was lucky to still have reasonably good hearing at his age. Most of his friends needed hearing aids. Ahead he heard a dripping sound, then something else.

Scurrying? Gustavo thought as he re-aimed his flashlight in the direction of the noise. Nothing.

The elevator doors screeched closed and its mechanics clunked into action and reset the elevator car to the first floor.

Gustavo walked into the darkened basement, following the dripping sound. His feet hit a puddle of water and he stopped. A slow line of his blood flowed from his raised finger, down his arm and collected around his elbow, dripping when the blood drops got too heavy. He watched as a drop of blood fell. It splashed and mixed with the puddle.

He moved closer to the dripping sound. Above his head, and in silhouette, a rat ran across a pipe. Gustavo, alerted to the patter of paws, adjusted his flashlight aim, but just missed revealing the rat. What his light did reveal was the source of the dripping. A large pipe leaked water onto the concrete floor, regular and predictable.

"Bingo," Gustavo said as he walked closer to the leaking pipe. He reached up and touched the water. The drips mixed with blood from his finger and flowed down his arm and onto the floor, where a large puddle had already formed.

More rustling sounds caught Gustavo's attention, this time coming from behind him. He spun around and cut the darkness with the beam of his flashlight.

"Who's there?" Gustavo scanned the basement, eyes wide, his pupils large and black. He picked up almost every detail within reach of his flashlight beam. But he was met with silence.

"Is someone there?"

Something fell in the darkness ahead, but it was too far to be revealed with light.

"Show yourself!" Gustavo's raised voice echoed through the old joists, garbage, pipes and concrete walls, then fell silent. Only the sounds of dripping water and his own rapid breathing remained. His guts turned to water. Gustavo sensed twinges of panic creep up in the back of his mind and he felt a sudden urge to shit. He spotted a two-by-four propped up against an old paint can and grabbed it.

"Whoever you are, you're going to be sorry." Gustavo advanced into the basement, his whole body tensing up. More rustling. He readjusted his light again and refocused on the source of the sound to reveal what looked like an old rusty shelving unit.

The sounds continued. Gustavo moved closer and focused the beam on a black rag bunched up on the middle shelf.

Then the rag moved. It wasn't a rag at all, but the haunches of a black rat as big as a cat. It had one grizzled ear, and a white-tipped tail that whipped and flashed behind its substantial bulk. The alpha rat turned to face Gustavo. Its eyes reflected his light back in two bloody pinpoints.

"You the one been chewing on the pipes?" Panic crept closer to the surface and Gustavo fought to keep it in check. He raised the two-by-four, now slicked red with his blood.

The alpha rat stared back at him. Its whiskers twitched and its nose caught the scent of blood and fear that exuded from Gustavo despite his attempt to conceal it.

"I'm gonna beat the shit out of you." Gustavo's desire to kill the alpha rat grew with every step. The hulking black rat sat there in the center of the metal shelving unit, unflinching, watching his approach.

Gustavo's misguided blood lust took over. He focused all his intent on the alpha rat in front of him. He imagined smashing the rat's head into a pulp, grinding bits of the rat's skull into the pavement. His rage blinded him to his surroundings. If he had used his flashlight to check behind him, he would have seen one rat turn into ten, then into hundreds, all emerging from the shadows to follow his footsteps. Their glowing red eyes floated along the floor like a demented swarm of ladybugs. They hunted in coordinated packs, as they advanced on Gustavo's heels with silent stealth.

One more step brought Gustavo closer to his prize. He

sneered, his greasy mustache rising in disgust. The alpha rat maintained its position on the shelf. Its tail whipped around so fast it blurred into the darkness.

The alpha rat raised its snout and ground its teeth. To Gustavo, it sounded like a mix between fingernails on a chalkboard and a chisel on stone. A second rat, much smaller than the alpha, nosed its way onto the shelving unit and settled beside the alpha, flicking its tail as well.

Gustavo pointed the two-by-four at the alpha rat. "First dinner…" He re-aimed his weapon at the small companion. "Then dessert."

A third small rat appeared one shelf down from the other two. Then a fourth and fifth rat scurried into position. Within seconds, the shelving unit and the floor in front were covered with rats, too numerous to count. The alpha rat's backup had arrived and seemed to have emerged from thin air.

It didn't take long for Gustavo to realize that he was outnumbered. Panic overtook him, and he reversed his advance, all the while keeping his flashlight beam targeting the alpha rat.

From the horde behind, one rat bolted ahead and scrambled into and up Gustavo's left pant leg. He spun around with surprise, a scream trapped in his throat. The light beam revealed an undulating brown carpet of rats making quick work of surrounding him. Their little glowing red eyes moved around his feet and reflected his light like polished buckshot.

Gustavo swung the two-by-four towards the floor and the advancing horde. He smashed the heads of several rats with sickening pops, but his defense did little to stop the rats from moving ever closer. In fact, it seemed to enrage the rats even more as they pushed forward over their dead comrades.

Another rat bit Gustavo's right foot. His panic gave way to terror as he yelled and changed his direction of attack. He swung the two-by-four wildly, and missed more than he killed.

Rats closed in on Gustavo from all directions. As he took another evasive step backward, his foot fell on a rat's tail. It spun around and sunk its teeth through his slippers and into the fleshy ball of his foot. Gustavo pulled his foot up, but the rat's jaws remained clamped. Its furry body hung squirming from his foot, its white tipped tail flipping back and forth. He tried to kick the rat off, but lost his balance and fell to the floor. His wind was knocked out of him as he landed hard on his back.

The rats moved faster than Gustavo's attempts to get away. The horde had the advantage as they scurried around his flailing limbs. Rats leapt one over another to get on top of Gustavo's soft belly. The smell of his fear mixed with acrid sweat provoked the tiny attackers into a frenzy as they began to burrow. They were under his shirt and inside his pants in seconds, biting, digging and tasting his flesh. The fact that Gustavo's blood contained traces of warfarin didn't matter. The rats had the blood lust now.

Gustavo squirmed on the floor. He swung the two-by-four blindly, his body peppered with painful bites. The rats covered his neck and scrambled up onto his head. He opened his mouth to scream, but a rat clambered inside, bit his tongue and muffled his attempt. Eyes wide with white-hot terror, Gustavo dropped the two-by-four. He grabbed the rat's half-black half-white tail and pulled it out of his mouth as more rats attacked and bit his hand.

Every rat Gustavo managed to pull off his body was replaced by three or more. Vastly outnumbered, soon Gustavo was obscured by a blanket of brown furry bodies, slicked with watery blood. Their tails churned and painted the concrete floor a deep maroon. He lost his grip on the flashlight. It bobbed and bounced atop the horde, its beam cast in random directions. The two-by-four lay by Gustavo's side, forgotten.

With his last ounce of strength and breath, Gustavo managed to rise above the layer of writhing vermin and release a blood curdling scream. It would be his last. Blood stung his eyes and the darkness and weight of a thousand hungry rats closed in on him. He fell backward, into a sea of razor sharp incisors and sharp claws.

The alpha rat remained perched within the shelves, unmoving and vigilant, and oversaw the rapid and efficient rending of flesh and bone that was once Gustavo.

"Here." Hope opened the second book to a full page photograph of a rat with a white-tipped tail. "Look at this." She placed the open book in front of Sam.

"So what?" Sam said. "It's a rat. I don't get it."

"It's a Gambian," Hope said. "Native to Africa."

Sam flipped the page. More photos of the Gambian rat in its natural habitat surrounded some statistics and a small write-up.

"It says here that these things can reach up to eight times the size of a regular rat." Sam flashed back to his episode in the kitchen when the alpha rat had climbed onto his chest.

He tried to estimate its weight. The alpha rat could have easily been that size.

"Yup," Hope said. "Three feet long from head to tail."

Sam shuddered. "Thank god those aren't the rats we're dealing with."

"Look again." Hope flipped through another book. "Their tails are white-tipped. There's only one species of rat that has tails like that."

"She's right, Sam," said Bradley, his phone already out of his pocket. "Look."

Bradley advanced the time-lapse video forward, frame by frame. Even in the grainy, low-light video, the two rats in the video had distinctly white-tipped tails.

Sam shook his head. "They're too small."

"Yeah, you're right. But I heard about an outbreak in Florida." Hope set her book down. "They probably migrated and mated with the rats here."

Sam scoffed. "Florida's a thousand miles away."

"Never underestimate a rat's will to survive." Hope's usual sparkle was replaced with dead seriousness.

A muffled scream emanated from the heating vent on the floor.

The hair stood up on the back of Bradley's neck. "Did you hear that?"

Sam and Hope exchanged a look, concern mixed with fear. The scream, even though it was distorted by the heating ducts, was human.

Hope dropped to her knees, her ear over the vent. "Where do those vents go?"

"The basement, where the boiler room and furnace are," Sam said.

Hope looked up at Sam and Bradley. "Let's go."

As the elevator doors creaked open, Sam clicked on his pen light and led Bradley and Hope out and into the basement.

Bradley covered his nose. "Ugh, what's that smell?"

"Smells musty, like water damage." Hope grimaced.

"There's something else." Sam inhaled. "Something bad."

Hope stopped and listened, tilting her head to one side. Bradley noticed two small black bobby pins in her hair that kept her bangs out of her eyes. He imagined what she looked like with her bangs down.

"Over there." Hope pointed into the darkness. "Can you hear it?" All three stopped and listened.

"I hear dripping," Bradley said.

Hope made a beeline for the water sounds. "Follow me with the light. I don't want to trip and break my neck." Sam and Bradley followed close behind, Sam illuminating their way. For a small pen light it was surprisingly bright.

The three of them moved through the basement. The solitary hanging bulb outside the elevator now seemed very small behind them.

"Shine the light up here." Hope found a bucket nearby and flipped it over. She used it as a stepping stool to examine the source of the leak.

"You got a big problem," she said. "Look at this, in the dust. Those are paw prints. I'm sure of it."

"Let me see." Sam handed the penlight to Bradley. He placed one foot between Hope's, reached up to a securing bolt and pulled himself up onto the upturned bucket. Had they not been supporting some of their weight with their arms, the bucket would have buckled. It was close quarters for the two of them, close enough to sense each other's body heat, but it worked.

Bradley kept the penlight on the pipe, but he couldn't help notice how close Sam and Hope were. Jealousy rose in his mind.

"They're everywhere." Hope pointed out sections of damage. "Rats chewed through the pipe. You can see the teeth marks."

Sam extended his hand. "Can I have the light for a sec?"

"How about a please." Bradley said under his breath as he slapped the penlight into Sam's hand.

"What?" Sam shone the light on Bradley's face. "Did you say something?"

Hope watched the interchange with interest. *He's jealous*, she thought with a small grin. *Too bad neither of them have a chance.*

Sam ran the light beam along the top and sides of the pipe. "Damn it. This is going to cost a fortune to fix." He looked at Hope. "I'm going to have to raise everyone's rent to pay for it all."

"Wouldn't the owner of the building kick in for repairs?" Hope said.

Sam shook his head. "They don't like doling out cash. And my paycheck is directly related to how much they save."

A rat scurried past on an overhead pipe. Sam caught the movement in the fringes of his vision and pushed off the bucket. Genuine fear flashed in his eyes.

"Holy shit." Bradley tried to follow the dark, furry

silhouette with his eyes. "Did you see the size of that thing?"

"Hard not to." Sweat poured from Sam's brow as his eyes flitted erratically, scanning the pipes overhead with the penlight for any other rats.

"Yeah, it was Gambian too." Hope stepped off the bucket and scanned the overhead pipes as well, but excitement coursed through her instead of fear. "Just like your video."

A *scrittering* noise sounded from the corner. Sam took another step backward, and shone the light everywhere and nowhere. "What was that?" he said.

"Give me the light." Bradley extended his hand. "Please. You're making me sick."

Both Hope and Bradley could see the tremble in the hand Sam used to hold the penlight. Bradley felt compassion wash over him as he looked at Sam, his dad, trying to hide his terror. He reached out and steadied Sam's hand with his own, before he took the penlight.

"It's okay, Dad." Bradley pointed the light in the direction of the noise. "Stay here."

Bradley moved away from Sam and Hope, and into the darkness of the basement. Fear chipped away at his confidence, one step at a time.

Then he saw it.

"Holy fuck." Bradley froze, the penlight targeted the floor.

"What is it?" Hope said.

Bradley swallowed hard. "It's a hand."

"Is this one of your jokes?" Sam said. "Because if it is, I'm going to—"

"Dad… I'm serious."

The hand had been uncleanly severed at the wrist. A sporadic trail of blood revealed the path the dragged hand had taken across the floor.

Bradley took a few more steps forward, as he traced the blood path backward. Hope followed. Not wanting to be left behind, Sam shuffled after Hope.

"What is that?" Hope squinted, trying to decipher what she saw.

Just beyond the penlight's reach, the bloody path led to a darker mound on the floor. The air hung heavy and humid, with a metallic odor Bradley couldn't place.

"I can't tell," he said. "I'll get closer."

All it took was three more steps. The penlight's beam settled on a human head reduced to a mass of flesh and sinew, half the face ripped off to reveal bright white bone underneath. A familiar gray mustache, now stained with pink, poked out under a torn piece of cheek. Three rats sat atop the forehead and gnawed ragged strips of flesh. Their white-tipped tails were stained pink with blood. Upon being discovered, the rats scattered, sluggish from full bellies and jaws clamped around chunks of ripped meat.

Bradley turned to one side, fell to his knees and vomited.

"What the hell?" Sam said, concern in his voice. "Brad?"

Bradley spat on the concrete floor to try and clear his soured mouth. He looked back at Hope and Sam. "I think it's Gustavo."

Dumpster

It wasn't normal to have a death in the neighborhood before noon. The ambulance sat in front of the building, lights flashing and spinning. The coroner's vehicle and a police cruiser were parked further ahead, the cruiser's lights engaged as well. The scene drew a small crowd from neighboring apartments and businesses. Sam, Hope and Mrs. Baxter stood close by and off to one side of the stairs that led to the building's entrance. Sam held the iron gate open.

Melvin stood on the opposite side of the stairs. In his arms he held Carny, who barked and growled at anyone who got too close. In this case, it was the police officer who guarded the stairs. He ignored Carny's *yip-yipping*.

A spectator approached Sam. "What's going on?"

"Some kind of accident." Sam looked at Hope, then back at the spectator. "Not sure what exactly."

"Have you noticed any rat activity in your building?" Hope said to the spectator.

Sam turned to Hope and looked a question at her. *What the hell are you doing?*

The spectator shrugged. "No more than usual. Why? Is that what this is?"

Hope caught Sam's glare. "I don't know. Just curious like you, I suppose."

Bradley led a second police officer, a coroner and two paramedics out of the building. He held the door open as they wheeled a gurney out with a black body bag spread out on top. Sam noticed that one end of the body bag hung off the gurney mattress and dripped blood through the zipper seam.

One more thing for me to clean up, Sam thought.

The paramedics navigated the gurney down the stairs to the sidewalk. The officer and coroner hung back at the front entrance with Bradley.

Carny squirmed in Melvin's arms, so much so that Melvin had a hard time controlling him.

"Carny!" Melvin yanked at his collar "Shut it!"

The little dog barked and gnashed his canines at the paramedics as they rolled the gurney past. He was in another world, whipped into a frenzy by the scent of Gustavo's blood.

"We've already talked to your father and the other residents," said the second officer. "Is there anything you'd like to add?"

"Make sure your report says rats did this," Bradley said.

The coroner smirked and turned to stifle his chuckle, but Bradley saw enough of his reaction to feel an instant dislike for the man.

"Right. Rats." The second officer nodded and maintained her professionalism. She wrote and underlined the word "rats" in her notebook, perhaps a bit too emphatically. "You've made it very clear that rats are responsible."

"I saw them with my own eyes," Bradley said. "So did my dad and Hope."

The second officer nodded. "We have their statements." She turned to the coroner. "Do you have any questions for…" She looked at her notepad. "… For Brad?"

The coroner shook his head. "No. I got all I need in that body bag."

"Okay. We're done here. Thanks for escorting us into the building, Brad." The second officer removed a stack of business cards from her breast pocket and handed one to Bradley. "If you have any other information, please let me know."

The second officer and the coroner headed down the stairs and joined the first officer.

"Rats, my ass," the coroner said out of the corner of his mouth.

Bradley followed them down the stairs. As the officers and the coroner headed towards their vehicles, the crowd began to disperse.

Bradley stood next to Sam. "They don't believe us, Dad."

"Believe what?"

"That rats killed Gustavo."

"They haven't done an autopsy yet," Sam said. "Maybe they'll change their minds."

"They had to use shovels to move the body," Bradley said.

"You sure developed an iron stomach quickly," Sam said. "Not too long ago you were puking your guts out."

Bradley shrugged as he watched the paramedics load the gurney into the back of the ambulance.

"I almost feel sorry for the right bastard," Mrs. Baxter said.

Bradley shook his head. "Not me."

"Come on." Sam tapped Bradley's shoulder. "Show some respect. Gustavo was an asshole, but no one deserves to die like that."

The paramedics hopped into the cab and drove away, followed by the police cruiser and the coroner's vehicle.

"Well, that was exciting." Hope looked at the time on her phone. "Anyone hungry?"

Sam grimaced. "You're joking, right?"

Hope stuck her tongue out at him in response.

Melvin hooked Carny's leash into his collar and placed him on the ground. Carny sniffed, searched, and paused to lick the drops of Gustavo's blood off the concrete. Melvin looked across the entryway to Sam, Bradley, Hope and Mrs. Baxter. As hardened as Melvin was, Sam could see sorrow in his face. Gustavo, his comrade and drinking buddy, was gone.

"What the *fuck* are you looking at?" Melvin turned and walked away down Casanova Street, Carny *yip-yipping* at his heels.

"He's a rude wanker." Mrs. Baxter headed up the steps and into the building. "He'll get his, and I hope his sad excuse for a dog gets it, too."

"Amen to that," Bradley said, too low for anyone to hear.

"So, Hope…" Sam said. "Some would say that a certified rat expert moving into an apartment infested with rats is an incredible coincidence."

"Some would say that." Hope looked at Sam and flashed him a sly smile.

The three headed up the stairs to the building entrance.

"Well?" Sam said. "Do *you* say that?"

"Busted." Hope sat down at the top of the stairs. Bradley and Sam followed suit.

"What can I say?" she said. "I wanted to study rats in a real-world setting. I researched the areas of New York City with the most rat complaints, and here I am. The Gambian angle is just icing on the cake."

"Great," Sam said. "And here I thought you liked the building."

Bradley tried to look Hope in the eyes, and managed to do it for a second or two before his shyness kicked in. "Why New York City? There's rats all across the country."

"Why not?" Hope raised her hands in front of her like she was addressing a crowd. "I mean it's New York City! The greatest city in the world! I'm a little disappointed that I'm not living in Manhattan, but all in the name of science, right?"

Bradley ran his raccoon tail through his fingers. "It's a long way to come for science."

"I'm in it for the long haul," Hope said.

"Have you ever seen anything like this before?" Sam said.

"Not first hand, until now." Images of Gustavo's partially consumed corpse flashed through Hope's mind and sent a shiver up her back. "The rats I studied were omnivores but never ate meat. Gambian rats do. They've killed and eaten kids before. That's a documented fact. It's not much of a stretch to graduate to adults."

"They should just demolish the building," Bradley said.

"Fuck that," Sam shot back. "I haven't been here long but this place is my home, *and* my livelihood, damn it. I'm going to fight for it. Everyone here depends on me."

"Less one asshole," Bradley said.

"It wouldn't matter anyway," Hope said. "The rats would just find another way in. They're very intelligent."

"Dad, do you still think Piper was killed by rats?" Bradley asked.

Sam nodded. "After what I saw today, it's more than likely."

"Wait." Hope faced Bradley and Sam, her interest piqued. "Who's Piper?"

"It's Baxter's cat," Sam said.

"Was her cat," Bradley said.

"Right. Was." Sam clenched his fists. "Discovered the body a few nights ago."

Hope's eyes lit up. "I need to see the remains."

MRS. BAXTER STOOD outside the door to her apartment, keys in hand. Gustavo's death and all the hoopla that surrounded it had reminded her of Piper again. Most things reminded her of Piper. His death was still fresh in her mind and the time between flashbacks was still mercilessly short. It would get better with time but that was no blessing for the present.

Piper had always known when she was back from the grocery store, scratching his greeting on the door from the inside. Mrs. Baxter always had a treat for him, usually a few morsels of fresh fish, and he always repaid her with loud, friendly purring and a nuzzle or two.

Mrs. Baxter unlocked and opened her door. Piper wouldn't be there to greet her, even though she half expected him to run down the hallway, meowing.

Crestfallen, she entered her apartment and locked the door behind her.

She kept the lights off. The noonday sun cast a square of light and warmth on the floor next to the dinner table. Yet another favorite sleeping spot for Piper. Its reflected ambiance was enough to see everything in the shared living room and kitchen.

She walked to the table where she had set up a small shrine comprised of a framed picture of Piper, with his collar and vanity tag hanging off one corner, and a votive candle beside it. Mrs. Baxter sat facing the shrine and picked up the picture.

"Aye, you were one bonnie cat." Mrs. Baxter kissed the picture lightly and placed it back on the table. She lit the candle with a match and placed it in front of Piper's picture.

In the nearby glow of the candle sat a baited snap trap. The glob of peanut butter glistened atop the bait pedal. Mrs. Baxter eyed it with contempt.

"Damn you, Piper," she said. "Why'd you go and mess with those bastards?"

She grabbed the snap trap and placed it on her kitchen counter.

"As for you *vermin*…" Mrs. Baxter glared at the trap. "Your days are numbered."

She walked to her bedroom and laid down. *Just a wee nap*, she thought.

Sleep came fast and heavy, a rarity since Piper's death, and with it dreams filled with the antics of Mrs. Baxter's best friend.

"THIS IS IT," Sam said. "Chez Dumpster. Moist and rancid as the day is long." He presented the dumpster like a maitre-d'. "Any volunteers?"

Hope and Bradley stood and forced clenched toothy smiles at Sam. Their looks said "no fucking way." Sam wasn't surprised. He grabbed the lip of the dumpster and hoisted himself up and in.

"Digging through the dumpster twice in one week." Sam popped his head out. "That's a record."

"Did you make sure there weren't any rats in there first?" Bradley said.

Sam's face went white. "Shit, never thought."

"I think you'll be fine," Hope said. She caught a whiff of the contents of the dumpster and felt her stomach do a back flip.

"If I'm not back in an hour, call the police." Sam disappeared into the garbage and filth. As he waded through the refuse and rotting food, he could feel the moisture seep into his shoes. His clothes he could wash, but his shoes, they might have to be replaced.

"It had a blue tie—" Bradley said.

"Found it."

Sam lugged a green garbage bag secured with a blue twist tie out and over the side of the dumpster, and dropped it in front of Hope. It landed on the pavement with a sticky *plop*, like a lump of overripe dough.

"Fill your boots." He swung his legs over the lip of the dumpster and landed on the asphalt of the alley with a *squelch*. He left wet, sour footprints.

"Do you always get this excited about road kill?" Sam said.

"Just when it involves rats." Hope dug into her pocket

and pulled out a tube of Vick's VapoRub. She squeezed a glob onto her finger and applied it just below her nostrils. "I saw this on TV once. It works really well. Want some?"

Sam took the tube and applied some to his nose. "Brad?"

"Nah, I'm good."

Sam returned the tube to Hope. She slipped on a pair of rubber gloves and untwisted the tie on the garbage bag. The smell that emanated from the bag had a solidity to it, as if it could plug her nostrils permanently if given enough time. After the dumpster, Sam wasn't sure washing his clothes would work. Even with the VapoRub Sam and Hope struggled to maintain their composure.

"Holy shit." Bradley covered his nose and mouth and twisted away from the bag in retching fits. "Sorry."

"No apology needed," Hope said. "The smell of death is unpleasant for a reason."

Hope opened the bag up wider and folded down the edges so she had easy access to its contents. She dug through the remains and picked up Piper's skull. Hope examined its surface, rubbing away clotted blood and fur as she rotated the skull in her hands.

"It was rats, alright," she said. "Look at these teeth marks."

Bradley tried again to get a closer look, but succumbed to gags. He ran around the corner of the dumpster and vomited. Sam and Hope heard the tell-tale splash on the asphalt.

"What happened to that iron stomach of yours?" Sam said.

"It's the smell, Dad." Bradley gagged and heaved from behind the dumpster. "I can't get past it."

"Want to try the VapoRub?" Hope said. "It's in my front

pocket. My hands are all goopy so you'd have to dig it out yourself."

Bradley ran the scenario through his head. His hand in Hope's front pocket searching for the tube of VapoRub, maybe feeling the hem of her underwear if he was lucky, his hand closer than he'd ever get in other circumstances. Bradley felt stirrings deep within his body. He wanted to say yes, but the fetid odor of Piper's decomposing body was too much.

"Thanks, but I'm done," he said. "I can't get any closer. I'll wait for you at the stairs." Bradley walked out of the alley and toward the front of the building. He gave the dumpster a wide berth. Once he got to the entrance, he realized that he didn't have the key to the wrought iron fence. He propped himself against the bars. His mouth was still awash with the sour taste of vomit. Maybe he'd see Mrs. Baxter return home from a trip to the grocery store and require assistance. Anything to help settle his stomach would be a welcome change.

Sam held his breath and leaned in for a closer view. He could see the bite marks Hope had talked about on the skull. Blood had collected in the grooves and made them stand out against the white bone. They encompassed the skull and it reminded him of the scars that peppered his body.

"Those are the same kind of marks we saw on the pipes in the basement," Sam said.

"And this…" Hope tweezed something long and brownish-yellow out from the bone of the skull. She wiggled it until it slipped out. She placed the skull back into the bag and dropped her prize into her palm. She rolled it back and forth, where it left short red streaks. "This is one of their incisors."

"Holy shit." Sam's eyes went wide with astonishment. "That's an inch long."

"Inch and a quarter, I'd say." Hope dropped the tooth into the garbage bag and gathered the edges, twisting the bag closed again. "As much as I love rats, you need to get an exterminator out here. You can't do this yourself."

She tied a knot in the bag and tossed it back into the dumpster. "The longer you wait, the more they multiply."

Hope peeled off her rubber gloves inside out, trapping maroon sludge inside. She threw them into the dumpster over her shoulder where they landed in a heap next to the garbage bag.

"I hope garbage pickup is soon." Hope wafted at her nose with her hand.

"Amen to that," Sam said.

The two walked out of the alley to join Bradley.

Professionals

From the outside, Detest-A-Pest looked like it was closed for business. The brick facade was weathered and dirty from years of neglect. Graffiti that depicted pests of all kinds, including wasps, ants, termites, cockroaches, and rats, covered the exterior. All the windows were barred and beside the equally nondescript main entrance were two loading bays, both with motorized corrugated garage doors.

In one of the two parking spaces out front sat the company vehicle, a white windowless panel van decorated with a hand-painted Detest-A-Pest logo. Rust spots encroached from all corners. From a distance the van looked like it was being swarmed by cockroaches. Without the van out front, there was no indication of what kind of business was located there.

Beside the van sat a white 1956 Buick Century, which looked brand new compared to the van. The chassis had been lowered, which gave the sedan a "don't fuck with me" attitude. The impeccable interior was classic red with silver and black accents, and the vinyl seats were worn smooth and slick from years of use.

The inside of the building looked no better than its exterior. A narrow counter stretched the width of the reception area, and separated customers from the back office. Its Formica surface was scratched and chipped. On the left side, the counter top swung up and over to allow the staff of two easy access to the stockroom.

The back office was in a shambles and had a rear door and blinded windows that looked out into the stockroom and work area. There were papers, invoices, coffee cups, traps and magazines everywhere. In the center of it all, sixty-something Bertha O'Connor, short and stout, reclined in her chair, feet propped up on her paper-smothered desk. A pellet gun sat in her lap and her jaws clamped down on a smoldering cigar stub. Like a badge of honor, a blood-stained snap trap stuck out of the breast pocket of her coveralls. This office was her filing system and she knew where everything was located.

"Don't fuck with my space," she had told Washington when she hired him ten years ago. "I know more ways to kill a man than you'd care to count."

Washington, an African American in his fifties, was over the hill and gaining speed. Pest control was a hard business, with all the killing, even if it was killing pests. The job had taken its toll on him. Gray had begun to pepper his tightly cropped hair.

He sat in the back of the stockroom and took inventory of the company's instruments of death. The shelves that contained rat poison, bait, and traps towered above. They were low in stock. He reached up to grab a box of Contrac Cake from the top shelf, but upended it by mistake and spilled the last remaining brick on the floor.

O'Connor cradled a rotary phone receiver in the crook of her neck. Muzak floated out of the telephone's speaker. She raised her wrist to look at her watch. "How long do I have to wait? Jesus."

To pass the time, she flipped through an exterminator supply catalog as she blew smoke rings across the office.

"Fuck, I'm in the wrong business." O'Connor spoke loud enough to be heard through the rear door that led to the stockroom. "I should be selling this crap." She began to inventory supplies in her head. "Washington!"

Washington picked up the Contrac Cake brick and placed it back in its box. Contrac Cake was nasty stuff. Its one and only selling feature was to cause a rat to spontaneously bleed to death.

Got to remember to wash my hands, Washington thought as he looked towards the office. From his vantage point, all he saw was the glow of the office fluorescent lights through the rear door and the blinded windows. O'Connor loved to yell at him from her office.

She took the cigar out of her mouth and leaned toward the rear office door. "Washington!"

"What?"

"How are we fixed for gas?"

Washington looked at the shelf that contained rows of one-pound cannisters of propane. They looked like little plump green soldiers. "We're good."

"And batteries?"

Washington focused on another shelf. "Month's worth, maybe."

"Okay. How are we—" O'Connor's phone clicked in her ear, the muzak cut out and was replaced by a sales rep. "You sons of bitches better not put me on hold again if you know what's good for you."

The phone rang, the second line button flashing.

O'Connor pressed the button and took the call, placing line one on hold.

"Take that, ya bastard," O'Connor said. "Yeah?" She paused and blew another smoke ring. "Sorry, I only serve the Bronx." She switched back to line one.

"Look. I need—you still there?" O'Connor paused. "Good. I need five hundred snap traps. And by five hundred, I mean five hundred. You people shorted me last time."

O'Connor tossed the catalog across the office, and watched it land close, but not in, the lone waste basket. She didn't care.

"Shit," she said. "What? No… Just don't screw up again or heads are going to roll." O'Connor leaned back and yelled towards the back door. "How are we on pellets?"

"Low," Washington said.

"How low?"

Washington began to count the cans, then stopped. "Low enough."

"Three boxes of pest pellets, flat-head, twenty-two caliber," O'Connor said. "That's it. Got it?"

O'Connor listened to the sales rep as she blew smoke rings across the office. She raised her pellet gun, and aimed at the floating rings.

"I'd say we're done here," she said. "Don't fuck it up this time."

O'Connor slammed the phone back onto its cradle and blew more smoke rings. She raised her gun again, aimed, and fired. A pellet blasted through the center of the smoke rings and into the well-punctured head of a rubber rat nailed to the wall on the opposite side of the office.

"Bull's eye." A wide grin spread across O'Connor's face.

But her glory was shattered by the phone's ring. She picked up the receiver. "Yeah?"

It was Sam on the other end of the line. "Do you kill giant rats?"

O'Connor took her cigar out of her mouth and let her feet drop to the floor. "What do you mean by *giant*?"

"I mean bigger than a cat," Sam said.

"You better not be shitting me." O'Connor leaned forward in her chair.

"I'm not. A cat and a man are dead already."

"A cat... *and a man*?"

"That's right."

"And you're in the Bronx?"

"Yeah."

O'Connor grabbed a pen and paper. "What's your name?"

O'CONNOR POKED HER head out the back of the office. "Is the van stocked?"

Washington looked up. "Should be. That's what you pay me for."

"Alright, get your ass in gear. I'll move Bruce." O'Connor grabbed two sets of keys from a hook on the wall. "This job could put us on the map." She waited as the automatic garage door raised up into its housing, then stepped out into the afternoon sunshine.

O'Connor opened the heavy door to the Century and slipped into the driver's seat. She pulled her key-chain out of her pocket and engaged the ignition. The V8 roared to life like a lion claiming its territory, then eased into a low growling rumble.

"Bruce, baby, I never get tired of hearing you purr." O'Connor shifted into drive and navigated the Century into the open garage door. The car disappeared into the darkness of the building.

Washington was clad in heavy work boots, his white hazmat suit printed with his name on the front and the Detest-A-Pest logo on the back. He loaded some last minute items into the back of the panel van. Taser rods were a new addition this year. Similar to an electric cattle prod, the taser rod produced a high voltage electric shock at its dual pronged business end, but the main difference was the lethal amperage delivered. When triggered, the rod stopped a rat dead in its tracks, and sometimes caused them to explode. That was a side effect Washington didn't care for and was the main reason he avoided using them.

But O'Connor had no problems with exploding rats. The bloodier the better. She ducked out of the garage before the door closed and hobbled toward the back of the van. She favored her left leg with an almost imperceptible limp. No one, except for Washington, ever noticed.

"Suit up." Washington tossed O'Connor a set of coveralls in the company colors. She stepped into the hazmat suit without a single complaint, which surprised Washington. It was normal for O'Connor to bitch and complain about the suit, how it was too small, too white, too hot. Not today.

O'Connor spotted several taser rods secured onto the back shelf and smiled. "We're going to make ourselves some rat kebabs today," she said. "Ready to rock and roll?"

"Are we ever truly ready?" Washington loaded a few green propane tanks into the van.

"Stop it with your zen bullshit, will yah?" O'Connor jingled her keys. "Get in. I'm driving."

By the time Washington had secured their equipment and closed the rear doors, O'Connor was already revving the engine. He made his way around to the passenger side and hopped in.

"Haven't seen you this excited about a job since, oh, never," Washington said. "Where we going?"

"Hunts Point. 616 Casanova at Spoffard." O'Connor backed out onto the street without looking, then floored the gas, leaving a trail of gravel, dirt and burned rubber behind.

"What's so special about Hunts Point?" Washington watched O'Connor's eyes sparkle with excitement.

"You'll see." O'Connor clamped down on her cigar stub with her teeth.

"Watch where you're going," Washington said. "I don't got a death wish like you."

The Detest-A-Pest van flew down Colgate Avenue as O'Connor rocked the steering wheel. She shot a dismissive look at Washington. "Bitch, please. You know I drive better than you."

"That's some bullshit. Look at your speed." Washington shook his head. "Take Bruckner—"

"Bruckner, yeah I know," O'Connor said. "We'll be there in ten. Then you can lose your shit."

O'Connor turned right onto Bruckner Boulevard and floored it again. Washington grasped the door handle with his right hand, and pulled a pendant of a rat's skull encased in amber from under his shirt with his left.

"No no no. Uh-uh." O'Connor spotted the pendant in

Washington's hand and shook her head. "That thing stays hidden."

Washington didn't have the will to argue. He had had the "pendant talk" before with O'Connor and knew it would go nowhere. He slid the pendant back under his shirt, but kept his hand on it. Its round, smooth shape calmed him, even through the fabric of his shirt.

"So why is this job so special?" Washington said. "We've had jobs in Hunts Point before."

"Not like this one."

"Fuck, O'Connor. Throw me a bone, here."

"How about a human femur?" A sly grin crept onto O'Connor's face as she weaved in and out of traffic. "That a big enough bone for yah?"

The gears in Washington's head ground to a halt. "A human—"

"Femur."

Washington stared back at O'Connor in silence, dismissing her unsafe driving for a moment. Washington's world began to close in around him.

"That's right." O'Connor nodded. "These rats have killed a man."

"Fuck me." Washington faced forward. The color drained from his face.

"Oh, and a cat, too," O'Connor said. "Isn't that great?"

Over the past few years, Washington had struggled with the idea of quitting, but never seriously. He could never commit. That all changed in an instant. He still had at least thirty years left in him, and he'd be damned if he was going to let a bunch of rats take those years away, especially rats that made a habit of dining on human flesh.

"What's the matter, Washington? *Rat* got your tongue?"

O'Connor bellowed with laughter, and reached over to punch Washington's shoulder. "Get ready. We'll be there in five."

Get ready? Washington thought. All he wanted to do was run the other way. He crossed himself. O'Connor caught the gesture but let it go. She could tell Washington was spooked.

O'CONNOR TOOK A hard left off Randall Avenue and shot north up Casanova Street to where it met Spoffard Avenue. She slammed on the brakes and the van's front right tire bounced up onto the curb. Equipment flew off the shelves in the back and clattered onto the floor. From the sound, Washington suspected taser rods, but it could have also been pellet guns or even snap traps. Any closer or faster, the van's front bumper would have taken out the wrought iron bars that surrounded the stairs to the entrance.

"This is it." O'Connor pulled a Zippo from her breast pocket within her hazmat coverall and relighted what was left of her cigar. "616 Casanova."

"616…" Washington trailed off.

"What are you going on about?"

Washington looked out the passenger window of the van to the numbers over the crumbling arched vestibule. "616. True number of the beast."

"Don't start with your religion shit," O'Connor said.

"Just a strange coincidence, don't you think?"

"Fuck coincidence. Let's move."

O'Connor and Washington hopped out of the van, and

slammed the rust-pocked doors closed with a scraping metallic *clrunk*.

Washington opened the back of the van to reveal the results of O'Connor's erratic driving. Equipment lay scattered across the floor of the van. Washington picked up a taser rod.

"These are custom-made." Washington shot a look at O'Connor. "We can't do our jobs if our equipment is smashed."

"It's your job to tie our shit down," O'Connor said.

"All that could be tied down, was tied down." Washington glared at O'Connor. "There's some expensive shit in here."

"Okay. Just stop nagging me," O'Connor said. "We're not married, for fuck's sake."

"Just protecting the company's assets."

"Alright." O'Connor looked Washington in the eye. "I'll try to drive safer."

"I almost believe you." Washington began to assemble their gear and placed it in duffel bags: video camera, flashlights, taser rods, propane torches, pellet and tranquilizer guns.

O'Connor scanned a clipboard and checked off the equipment.

"We good?" Washington said.

"Yep."

Washington closed the rear doors to the van. The two sole employees of Detest-A-Pest walked to the wrought iron bars in front of the building and dropped their duffel bags full of equipment on the sidewalk.

O'Connor looked up at the bars and the way they curved

down at the top, like upside down fish hooks. *I wonder if they've ever tasted blood*, she thought.

Washington tried the gate and found it locked.

"No prob." O'Connor puffed out a smoke ring, and pulled out an old cell phone. She referenced her clipboard and found Sam's name. Before she could dial, Washington pulled out his pendant and kissed it.

"What did I say about that?" O'Connor said. "Leave the hocus pocus shit at the door, alright? This could lead to more work so don't screw it up."

"I got rituals," Washington said. "Besides, I've never worked a job with human fatalities. Have you?"

O'Connor ignored the question, but Washington was right. She had never encountered a human death due to a rat attack either, but would never admit that. O'Connor gnawed on her cigar and puffed out a plume of acrid smoke in Washington's face. She found Sam's name on her clipboard and dialed the number.

"I should have stayed in bed this morning," Washington said.

"And I'd have fired your ass." O'Connor lowered the cell phone from her ear slightly. She could hear Sam's phone ringing through one of the open exterior windows. "He lives on the first floor."

An audible click sounded through the cell phone. O'Connor returned it to her ear.

"Yeah?" Sam's voice crackled through the receiver.

"Detest-A-Pest for Sam Shaw," O'Connor said.

"Hold up." Sam's voice was distorted by old electronics. "I'll let you in."

O'Connor hung up and threw the cell phone in one of the duffel bags. Washington crossed himself again.

"Do that one more time. I dare yah." O'Connor said.

Washington ignored her. He knew O'Connor well enough to know that she was usually full of hot air.

Sam appeared at the front entrance, followed by Bradley.

"I'll hold the door." Bradley stood in the vestibule and propped the door open with his body.

"Thanks." Sam ran down the stairs. "Sorry about the gate."

"You get a lot of crime here?" O'Connor said. "Or are the bars to keep out the *giant* rats?"

"No more crime here than anywhere else." Sam pulled out his keys. "And the rats I've seen are too smart for these bars."

He unlocked the wrought iron gate and pushed it open. "Can I take one of your—"

"We got it under control." O'Connor picked up her duffel bag of equipment. "I'm O'Connor. This is Washington." Washington grabbed his bag.

Sam followed Washington and O'Connor up the steps. "You know, you guys were my last chance," he said. "Every other exterminator I called laughed in my face."

O'Connor stopped half way up the stairs. "That's what sets us apart." She faced Sam. "Our competition is really no competition at all. They're all a bunch of idiots that don't know when opportunity is slapping them across the face. We're lean, we're mean… and we have a *secret weapon*."

"What would that be?" Sam's curiosity was piqued.

"All in due time." O'Connor blew a smoke ring towards the building.

Washington continued up the stairs. He stopped and offered his free hand to Bradley. "The name's Jimmy Washington, but everyone just calls me Washington."

"Like the character from *Welcome Back, Kotter*," Bradley said. "My dad's into that show."

"Close." Washington smiled. "That was a Freddie, not a Jimmy. What's your name?"

"Bradley, but you can call me Brad."

"Good to meet you, Brad," Washington said. They shared a firm handshake. "Hey, I like your raccoon tail." He pointed at the furry appendage attached to Bradley's belt.

Bradley formed an instant fondness for Washington. No one ever noticed his raccoon tail straight off.

O'Connor pushed her way through the front entrance. A plume of acrid, blue smoke followed her head. "What's with all the lollygagging? We got rats to kill."

Sam met Bradley and Washington at the front entrance. "Well, you heard the woman."

All four disappeared into the building to face what had become Sam's new nightmare.

Basement

Melvin stood in his kitchen and rummaged through his cupboards. There was plenty of human food, like crackers, cereal, rice, and cans of condensed soup, but no dog food. Not even a box of kibble. Carny paced back and forth and whined.

"I know you're hungry, damn it!" Melvin had a short fuse most days, but after Gustavo's death every little thing set him off. "I'm looking. Shut your trap."

Melvin pulled out one of the boxes of crackers and the contents spilled onto the counter and floor. He examined the box and found a hole in the back corner just big enough to allow a cascade of crackers to flow through it. Carny's hunger took over and he scrambled to hoover the bounty on the floor. It didn't matter that the crackers were seasoned with rosemary, olive oil, and salt, and didn't have an ounce of meat in them.

"Great," Melvin said. "Now you're going to shit the bed. Well, I ain't cleaning it up." He grabbed his keys and unlocked his apartment door. Carny tilted his head and looked at him.

"We got to get you some food," Melvin said. "Now git, you good for nothin' varmint." Carny bolted past Melvin and into the hallway.

Melvin emerged from the elevator with Carny clutched in his arm, just as Sam, Bradley, O'Connor and Washington spilled into the front entrance way. Upon seeing new faces, Carny went nuts barking his loud *yip-yip* and leaped from Melvin's arms. The dog tore a path toward Sam and the group.

"Is this the rat you were telling me about?" O'Connor pointed at the approaching ball of fur.

Sam laughed. "I wish."

"Couldn't we just, like, take him out by accident?" Bradley grinned.

Sam gave Bradley a gentle elbow. "Keep your voice down."

Washington stepped forward and knelt down to Carny's level. "Why so angry, puppy?"

Carny dug in and raised the intensity of his barking. He lunged at Washington and bared his fangs.

"What are you doing?" Melvin said. "Get away from him or I'll knock your block off." He picked Carny up, but that did nothing to stop the onslaught of *yip-yips*.

Washington stood up and looked down at the bald patch on Melvin's head. He was a good foot taller than Melvin.

"You're going to knock *my* block off?"

Melvin looked up at Washington. He knew he was out of his league but refused to back down. Sam, Bradley and O'Connor watched with amusement.

"I think you better re-evaluate your options." Washington nodded towards Carny. "For the dog's sake."

"Out of my way, *nigger*." Melvin pushed through the group and out the front entrance.

Bradley's jaw dropped. He looked at Washington and expected a reaction.

"A ray of sunshine *and* a bigot," Washington said. "Got to love human diversity."

"He's not worth another second of your time." Sam opened his apartment door and directed O'Connor and Washington inside.

Washington leaned toward Bradley as he entered the apartment. "You've never heard the n-word for real, huh, Brad?"

"No."

"I hope it's the last time." Washington thumbed back toward the front entrance. "Believe me, I've heard worse."

Bradley nodded and followed Washington into the apartment and closed the door.

O'Connor dropped her duffel bag on the floor and raised her clipboard. She scanned it slowly.

"Sam Shaw… 616 Casanova." O'Connor sucked her cigar. The end glowed like a dying sun. Tendrils of smoke rose from the corners of her mouth. "You said you got Gambians, eh bub?"

"Yeah."

O'Connor pushed past Sam and examined the baseboards around the kitchen. "You need a lesson in home decor."

"And that'd be from you?" Sam chuckled. "No offense, but if it ain't broke…"

Washington pulled his pendant out from beneath his shirt and held it firm in his hand. He dropped his duffel bag and walked down the hallway to investigate the bathroom, TV room and bedroom. Bradley watched Washington and his pendant with great interest.

"How do you know about Gambians?" O'Connor said.

"One of my tenants is an expert on rats," Sam said.

"Oh, really?" O'Connor thought she had heard everything, but that was a new one. "So… what did this so-called *expert* have to say?" She continued to follow the baseboards and noted evidence of dirt streaks on her clipboard.

"They're originally from Africa, three feet long, eight to ten pounds, and known for killing and eating kids."

O'Connor stood and faced Sam. "Who the fuck are you, Encyclopedia Britannica?"

"Oh, and white-tipped tails." A grin spread across Sam's face. "At least that's what my so-called *expert* told me."

"Okay," O'Connor said. "You pass the test."

Washington re-emerged from the bedroom and drifted back towards the kitchen.

"Did you find anything?" Bradley said.

Washington tucked his pendant back into his shirt. "Nothing but bad energy."

"Hey!" O'Connor glared at Washington. "Stow it!"

"Why can't you see it as an asset?"

"What, the mysticism?" O'Connor blew a smoke ring towards Washington. "It's all bullshit. A rock hanging around your neck ain't gonna save you if your number's up."

"Are the suits really necessary?" Sam said.

"I don't wear 'em to be stylish." O'Connor poked Sam in the chest with a unwashed finger, her nail clogged with oil and dirt. "Ever heard of the bubonic plague? Rats carry disease. Better safe than dead."

O'Connor strung a belt with a walkie-talkie, duct tape and a holstered tranquilizer gun around her waist. She grabbed a second belt from one of the supply bags and tossed it to Washington. He fastened it around his waist.

"So… do we need suits, too?" Bradley looked at O'Connor, then to Sam. "I mean we live here."

O'Connor shrugged. "Sorry, fresh out." She hobbled to the refrigerator with a more noticeable limp, and directed her flashlight into the gap between the side of the fridge and the wall. "Where did you see that…" O'Connor consulted her clipboard. "… *horde* you were telling me about on the phone?"

"Under the kitchen sink," Sam said.

O'Connor opened both cabinet doors and revealed the underbelly of the sink. The garbage bag attached to the right-hand door swayed from its hooks like a toddler's full diaper. O'Connor took a final drag from her cigar stub, rubbed it out in the sink, and threw it into the garbage bag.

She pulled a new cigar from a pocket under her hazmat suit and floated it under her nose, inhaling its aroma.

"You can't beat a Cuban Cohiba." O'Connor pulled off the tail with her teeth and spat it into the garbage. From the same inside pocket, she took out a lighter and began to roast the end of the cigar, rotating it until the end bloomed in orange flame.

Washington leaned toward Bradley. "She always needs to be the center of attention," he said in a hushed voice.

O'Connor drew smoke into her mouth and released it, repeating until the cigar smoldered on its own, the flame replaced with an orange glow. She jettisoned the remaining smoke out of her mouth in a rolling smoke ring and clamped the cigar between her teeth.

O'Connor favored her left leg as she knelt down to get a better view. She moved her flashlight beam into the shadowy corners under the sink, and behind the rags, a bucket, and cleaning supplies. She switched between regular and ultraviolet light modes. Areas on the walls fluoresced as the flashlight's beam passed over them.

"Yup. We got an access hole here. Droppings, urine, the whole nine yards." O'Connor backed out of the cabinet and stood up. She braced herself on the counter top and turned to Sam. "We're going to need full access to the building."

THE ELEVATOR GROANED and creaked under its load as it descended towards the basement. Sam and Bradley stood in back, O'Connor and Washington in front, shoulder to shoulder. A little too close for comfort. Any more than a few floors and this arrangement would get awkward.

Washington's wandering gaze stopped on the capacity sign posted above the call numbers.

"It says this elevator can carry a maximum of eight people," he said. "Can you imagine four more of us in here?"

"One more of you would be a nightmare," O'Connor said. "I don't even get this close on a first date."

Sam leaned in close to Bradley's ear. "These two are like an old married couple."

"Enough from the peanut gallery," O'Connor said. "I may be old but I got ears like a cat."

Washington raised his eyebrows. "Wait. Since when do you go on dates?"

"Not that it's any of your business, but there's this guy in my car club that's a primo hunk of meat, let me tell yah." O'Connor pulled the memory to the top of her mind. "His name is Jack, or Joe, or somethin'. Recently widowed and one-hundred percent beefcake. I got plans to ride his engine, if you know what I mean." O'Connor pumped her fist back and forth.

"Gross." The thought of O'Connor being sexual in any way gave Bradley a shiver up his spine.

"Bah." O'Connor sucked on her stogie and released a Cohiban miasma. "Youth is wasted on the young."

The elevator hit bottom, jerked and bounced before the doors creaked open.

"Finally," O'Connor said. "I thought we were in hell for a second."

The smell from O'Connor's cigar overpowered the mustiness of the basement, an unexpected but pleasant surprise for everyone. Sam clicked on his penlight and led Bradley, Washington and O'Connor into the darkness.

"The foundation of this building is in serious need of repair." Washington held a GoPro modified for night vision in his hand. He moved the camera in sweeping arcs. The video image appeared on a phone in his other hand.

"Cool," Bradley said in awe. "You can see so much more."

"Gotta love technology, eh Brad?" Washington winked at him.

O'Connor scanned her surroundings with her UV flashlight combo, and uncovered fluorescing areas in the darkened corners of the basement.

"Smell that?" O'Connor sniffed.

"What?" Sam inhaled.

"Rat shit. It's everywhere."

"I don't smell anything except that cigar."

O'Connor put her arm around Sam's shoulder and grinned. "That's why you're paying us the big bucks."

"Look." Washington raised the phone's video screen and

followed a rat's path with his camera. "There goes one now. No, scratch that. There goes three."

"Make that five." O'Connor focused her flashlight in the same direction as Washington's camera and tracked the five rats as they scurried along a wall.

Sam looked away, grabbed a overhead pipe and tensed up, shutting his eyes tight. In his head, he imagined hundreds of starved rats as they emerged from the darkness and made a beeline for his legs. He struggled against his urge to run.

O'Connor sensed Sam's apprehension and dropped her arm from his shoulder. "What's up with you, bub?"

"He's afraid of rats," Bradley said.

Sam continued to clutch the pipe and tried to calm himself with deep breaths. It wasn't working. He fought back the visions.

"That's okay," Washington exchanged glances with Bradley. "Today, I am too, but don't tell anyone."

The rats disappeared into the shadows and escaped the reach of both O'Connor's and Washington's surveillance.

Bradley placed his hand on Sam's shoulder and gave it a gentle squeeze. "They're gone, Dad."

Sam relaxed and loosened his grip. His hand left a sweaty palm print behind on the dusty overhead pipe. He opened his eyes and sent Bradley a nod of gratitude.

O'Connor found the leaking pipe and tapped it with her flashlight. "You better fix this leak."

"I'm dealing with the rats first," Sam said between breaths.

"Where'd that guy bite it?" O'Connor swept the area with her flashlight.

"Brad knows," said Sam, his world almost back to normal.

"Over here." Brad walked to the scene of Gustavo's evisceration. A large patch of the concrete was still stained with blood and would remain a marker of the danger all four were walking into. "It was crazy. I've never seen anything like it."

"You got one up on me, kid." O'Connor directed her flashlight on the overhead pipes and followed their paths. "We're going to have to shut off the water to the building. Where's the master shut off?"

"Damned if I know," Sam said. "I'll have to dig out the plans to the building."

Washington caught movement on his video screen. Two, four, then eight rats ran along the back wall. "Bogies, dead ahead!"

Bradley stood next to Sam. "It's okay. Just don't look."

Sam nodded and grabbed Bradley's wrist to steady himself.

Washington moved forward. He watched his video screen and followed the exodus. More rats emerged and scurried along the back wall. They all disappeared into a hole in the back corner of the basement, a hole big enough for a person to crawl into.

O'Connor aimed her flashlight on the hole as Washington approached it with slow and careful steps. Sam hung back and held his ground, watching, with Bradley by his side. He released his grip on Bradley's wrist.

Sam saw Bradley rub his forearm. "Sorry."

"No worries." The finger-lines that remained from Sam's grip changed from white back to flesh color as the blood flow returned to Bradley's hand.

"Where does this hole go?" Washington crouched to his knees to try and frame up a better shot. The infrared camera's range illuminated the small tunnel for a couple of feet. Fear rattled the doors of Washington's mind as he looked at the dark, jagged portal that led to a place only God and rats knew about.

"No idea," Sam said.

O'Connor and Washington exchanged a look.

"Aw shit," Washington said. "I'm not crawling in there."

"That's what I pay you for." O'Connor puffed on her cigar.

"Fuck me." Washington handed the phone to O'Connor. He knelt and crawled into the small tunnel, his outreached arm swallowed up by a maw of darkness. Almost immediately, he retracted it again and dropped the camera. A fresh scratch on his forearm welled up. Pinpricks of blood rose to the surface of his skin.

"Damn! What in the hell was that?" Washington looked at the fresh scratch on his arm.

"Looks like some exposed wire." O'Connor handed him the phone. "Take a look."

Washington studied the image on the screen. "It looks like it's only on the right side." He handed the phone back to O'Connor and knelt at the opening to the tunnel. "I hate this job more and more every day."

"No, tell me how you really feel." O'Connor blew a smoke ring toward the tunnel entrance.

"Be careful," Bradley said.

"Thanks, Brad." Fear flooded Washington's senses. "I'm glad someone cares."

O'Connor nudged Washington with her boot. "Get your fat ass in there."

Darkness swallowed Washington up as he moved forward into the tunnel. He pressed his body to the left to avoid the exposed wires and moved his hands over the rubbled surface of the tunnel. Reaching blind, his fingertips found the GoPro and he grabbed it in his right hand.

"You got visuals?" The tunnel dampened all sound.

O'Connor crouched to the entrance of the tunnel. "Visuals five by five."

Washington wriggled forward. There was not much space to move. Washington thought he detected motion, but the vast blackness ahead deceived his senses. The blinking red LED light on the GoPro was his only anchor to reality.

O'Connor watched the video feed on the phone. Washington's camera moved past the exposed wire and rough concrete edges, and opened to a bare, tiled floor that led to blackness. It was as if the room was filled with black smoke.

"We've got some kind of room back here." Washington's fingers felt the square tiles and the grout in between.

Back at the entrance to the tunnel, O'Connor could barely hear Washington's voice. He panned the camera back and forth and scanned the hidden room. The phone showed nothing but white institutional tile and black grout.

A pair of white dots appeared. Then four. Then eight. O'Connor recognized them instantly. They were eyes. Dozens of pairs of eyes emerged from the black beyond.

"Washington!" O'Connor watched as the pairs of white dots drew closer on the phone's screen, the forms of rat heads more clearly defined. "Get the fuck out now!"

"What?" Washington couldn't make out her words over

the echo of his voice. Silence closed in on him again, except for… except for…

What is that?

It was the soft pitter-patter of rat feet. And teeth gnashing and grinding.

When he saw the red eyes, fear broke through and flooded Washington with terror. He reversed himself and worked back though the tunnel. He snagged his right arm again on the exposed wire and dropped the GoPro.

Washington squirmed out of the tunnel and pulled his right arm out. What used to be just a scratch was a deep, bleeding gash.

"Move your black ass!" O'Connor said as she pulled Washington to safety.

On the phone's screen, a horde of rats scurried past the GoPro left in the tunnel, hot on the scent of Washington's blood trail. They emerged at the opening of the tunnel and held their ground, whiskers twitching, teeth grinding, red eyes blinking randomly.

Sam remained frozen in his tracks as more rats appeared, gnawing and chittering. Bradley saw sweat pour down Sam's face and could sense the fear that emanated from his body. He stepped in front of Sam to try and shield him from the rising tide of vermin.

O'Connor pulled Washington back to a safe distance while keeping her flashlight focused on the tunnel entrance. The horde filled the bottom half of the opening. Rats jostled for position and their greasy heads and red eyes poked in and out of the mass of fur.

O'Connor monitored the entrance with her flashlight. With the phone's screen within visual range and held loosely at O'Connor's side, Sam was the first to see the alpha rat appear. He recognized it in an instant. The grizzled ear and white-tipped tail were unmistakable.

Sam couldn't talk, but broke through his fear enough to point at the phone's screen. Bradley followed Sam's finger line and saw the alpha rat. He nudged Washington. "You getting this?"

Washington cocked his head to listen, but kept his eyes on the tunnel entrance. "What?"

"The phone," Bradley said. "Look."

Washington grabbed the phone from O'Connor. His eyes went wide as he shared a look with Bradley. "Holy shit." He tapped O'Connor's arm and held the screen up. "You're gonna want to look at this."

The alpha rat stared into the camera, like it was grandstanding, like it knew what a video camera was. The grainy black and white video image was clear enough to see streaked, stained teeth and the flicking white-tipped tail.

O'Connor watched the massive rodent knock the GoPro on its side as it shuffled past. "It's definitely a Gambian."

"What'd I tell you?" Washington said. "Bad news, hocus pocus or not."

O'Connor shook her head. "God damned foreigners don't belong in America." She noticed Bradley shoot her a look of disapproval. "What? I'm talking about the rats." O'Connor pointed at Sam. "If I were you, I'd be more concerned with Mister Catatonic here than my views on immigration."

Bradley looked back at Sam, drenched with sweat. "Can you put the phone away?" Bradley said. "Please?"

O'Connor grunted, blew a cloud of Cohiba smoke at Bradley, and slipped the phone back into her pocket. Sam's shoulders relaxed enough to be noticeable.

"Shit." Washington held his arm above his head. "The camera. I'm not going back in there to get it."

"We'll come back for it," O'Connor said.

"We better. It's got a custom built lens. Cost a fortune."

"It's recording?"

"As long as the battery holds."

O'Connor directed her flashlight back at the tunnel opening. Some of the smaller rats had moved aside and left a gap in the center that recessed back into the tunnel. O'Connor could see the alpha rat's nose and its vibrating, blood-stained whiskers that poked out beyond the shadows. Its eyes remained shrouded in darkness, but reflected back bright pink circles of light the size of glass marbles.

O'Connor stepped up to Sam and pulled him aside. "Snap out of it. I want to talk to your *expert*."

SEARCH

SAM, BRADLEY, WASHINGTON AND O'CONNOR emerged from the elevator and headed down the hallway towards Sam's apartment.

"You need to grease that elevator or something." Washington cradled his arm. His white hazmat suit was smeared with swaths of maroon red. "It feels like a death trap."

"Sounds like one too," Bradley said. "Is the signal from the camera dead?"

O'Connor puffed away at her cigar, now noticeably shorter in length. "The signal's not dead, we're just out of range."

"Anyone want a coffee?" Sam said.

"Maybe later." Washington held his arm up. "Right now, I'd rather have bandages instead." The blood flow from his gash had slowed, but his soaked shirt sleeve still dripped a trail all the way from the basement.

"Brad, can you get Washington set up?" Sam said.

"Sure." Bradley led Washington to the bathroom. Washington closed the lid to the toilet and sat down while Bradley rummaged under the sink for bandages. He didn't find much of use except some cloth tape. First aid supplies were not a priority for Sam.

Washington rolled up his sleeve. "I'll start cleaning it." He approached the sink.

"Let the water run a bit," Bradley said. "Trust me on that."

"You better hope those bastards don't follow your blood back here," O'Connor said from the kitchen. "At least not yet."

"Bring it," Washington called back. "We're ready for them."

"I'll go get our resident rat expert," Sam said.

O'Connor sat down at the kitchen table, inclined her chair and propped her feet on the table. "I'm looking forward to it." She blew a smoke ring across the kitchen.

"Dad!" Bradley ran out of the bathroom. "Ask Hope for another maxipad."

"Another… *maxipad?*" A smile broke across O'Connor's face.

Sam groaned. "Jesus, Brad. Could you say that a little louder?"

O'Connor watched the father-son dynamic playing out and began to laugh.

"You have no first aid kit," Bradley said. "It'll be better than nothing."

"Is asking for feminine hygiene products from your female neighbors a habit of yours?" O'Connor broke into a full belly laugh.

"It's a long story," Sam said.

"Sure it is." O'Connor laughed so hard she almost fell off her chair.

"I just asked because you had one on your back earlier," Bradley said.

"Oh, *you* use them too!" O'Connor roared.

"It's okay, Brad." Sam tried to ignore O'Connor's hysterics, which proved to be difficult due to her volume. "I'll ask."

Washington poked his head out of the bathroom, the right sleeve of his hazmat suit rolled up and arm exposed. "What in the hell is so damn funny out here?"

"Nothing." Sam shot a look at O'Connor. "Not a word."

O'Connor went deadpan. "Sure thing… *Mr. Maxipad*." But she couldn't maintain it and fell back into a laughing fit, slapping her knee.

"For fuck's sake." Sam disappeared down the hallway.

Bradley returned to the bathroom. Washington had somehow managed a clean trickle of water from the faucet and had already begun to rinse the gash in his forearm.

"Shit, that doesn't look good," Bradley said. "Do you think it'll need stitches?"

Washington brought his arm close to get a good look. Cleaning the wound had awakened the bleeding. "I hope not. I don't got time for that. But I'm lucky, though."

Bradley looked at the ragged and irregular punctures and tears in Washington's right arm as they oozed blood into the sink. At one point blood dripped faster than the water from the faucet. "This is what you call lucky?"

"If it was a blade that had cut me, I'd be useless," Washington said. "I probably would have bled out."

"Not today." Bradley grabbed a towel and handed it to Washington. "Put this on it."

SAM STOOD IN front of Hope's apartment door, his eyes closed. He still felt jittery from his encounter in the basement. He tried to picture Hope's face instead of the alpha rat with its red pinpoint eyes that pierced the shadows, but the damn rat kept winning out.

Those eyes. Those fucking red eyes.

He took a few deep breaths and calmed himself. Sam opened his eyes to the "301" on Hope's door, still misaligned. He gave the door a knock. The numbers rattled against the wood. His mental note to fix the numbers wasn't sticking.

Sam stood and listened to footsteps pad their way to the front door. He tried to picture Hope in black socks, but even that image didn't stick.

Hope opened her door. "Hey Sam. What's up?"

Sam looked at her feet. He had gotten the color right, but instead of black socks, she wore her black Vans with the laces loosely tied. Over bare feet. *Toenails probably painted black.*

"Hey, Sam," Hope bent down to break his stare. "I'm up here."

"Oh, sorry," Sam said. "Can I borrow you for a sec?"

"Uh, yeah. Okay." Hope grabbed her keys.

"Oh, and can you spare another… maxipad?"

Hope did a double-take. "For your back?"

"No, no. It's not for me."

"Brad?"

Sam shook his head. "My exterminators had a little accident."

Hope tried to imagine a scenario in her head that would fit, but nothing came to mind.

"Look, I'll buy you a new box later," Sam said.

"One second." Hope disappeared into her bathroom and

returned with two maxipads. "At this rate, you'll need to buy me a box today."

She held the pads out to Sam, which he took. "These are the best. Super absorbent." Hope could see the red flush of embarrassment spread across his cheeks, neck and ears.

"Do you get embarrassed buying condoms too?" Hope locked her door.

"I can't remember," Sam said. "I haven't bought condoms in over fifteen years."

"Might want to get on that." Hope's words were out before she could stop them. "I mean, just in case. Uh, you know…"

The two made their way back to Sam's apartment, both feeling the warmth of their own embarrassment on their faces.

SAM AND HOPE returned to the apartment.

"The intrepid Mr. Maxipad returns!" O'Connor said. "Everyone rejoice!"

Sam pointed his finger at O'Connor. "If you want this job, you better shut your damn trap."

"Take it easy," O'Connor said. "Just bustin' your balls."

"Brad!" Sam said. Brad poked his head from the doorway to the bathroom. Sam held out the maxipads. "You wanted these."

"Thanks." Brad took the pads and returned to the bathroom. "These will help."

"Maxipads, huh?" Washington nodded and took the pads. "Good thinking."

"O'Connor," Sam said. "This is Hope."

O'Connor gave Hope a once-over. "The rat expert."

"Expert?" Hope looked at Sam and sent home a look of thanks. "Maybe on rat intelligence, yeah, you could say that," Hope said. "You must be the exterminator."

"What was your first guess?" O'Connor blew a smoke ring across the kitchen.

Hope's eyes lit up. "Sick! You got to show me how to do that."

"Maybe later."

Hope looked at Sam. "Has she seen the video?"

Sam shook his head. "It's on Brad's phone."

Hope stuck her head into the bathroom. "Brad, can I borrow your phone? For the video."

"Yeah, sure." Bradley dug his phone out of his front pocket and handed it to Hope. She disappeared for a second, then reappeared at the door.

"Mind if I take a look?" Hope said.

"Sure," Bradley said. "Washington, this is Hope."

Washington looked up, unfazed by Hope's appearance. "Are you the source of our medical supplies?"

"The men in this apartment apparently can't seem to get enough of my maxipads." Hope flashed a friendly smile that made Bradley's knees turn to jelly and his stomach buzz like it was full of bees. He didn't seem to notice that she was talking about feminine hygiene products.

Washington waved with his left hand. "Good to meet you, Hope. You have my gratitude."

"No prob." Hope stepped closer to look at Washington's arm. "That's nasty. Worse than the one Sam got in my apartment."

Hope noticed the wheels turning in Washington's head. They both shared a glance. "It's not like that. God no."

Hope laughed. "He was fixing my TV, plus he's old enough to be my father." Hope paused. "Eww."

Bradley smiled to himself upon hearing of Hope's lack of romantic interest in Sam. *Maybe she's into younger guys*, Bradley thought.

"Hey, I'm not one to judge," Washington said. "Brad, could you tear me some strips of tape?"

"Sure." Brad tore off six inch pieces of cloth tape and placed them hanging down off the sink. Washington placed one of the maxipads over the gash on his arm and secured it in place with the tape.

"There." Washington pulled down the sleeve of his shirt and hazmat suit and flexed his forearm. "Good as new. Thanks Hope, Brad." He nodded to them both.

"No prob," Hope said.

"Now if you'll excuse us, Brad and I have a job to finish."

"We do?" Bradley said.

"Damn straight." Washington stood up and went to the door of the bathroom. "Let's move."

Hope glanced at Bradley. "Better listen to the man," she said.

All three filed out of the bathroom.

"We'll be back." Washington headed for the door with Bradley close behind.

WASHINGTON AND BRADLEY stood at the rear of the Detest-A-Pest van. He pulled out his keys and unlocked the back. Most of the equipment had been loaded into Sam's apartment already, but one item remained. A large rectangular box, hinged handles at both ends and sided with textured aluminum, sat by the doors.

"What the hell is this?" Bradley ran his hand across the box's raised diamond plate surface.

Washington placed his hand on the box. "You remember O'Connor talking about our *secret weapon?*"

"I heard her say something to my dad," Bradley said. "But I wasn't paying much attention. This is it?"

"Yeah. This is it."

Bradley detected a mournful note in Washington's voice. "What does it do?"

"I'm not going to get into too much detail," Washington said. "Let's just say it's the ultimate rat trap. A Detest-A-Pest exclusive."

Washington grabbed a handle and pulled one end of the metal box out of the van. "Give me a hand. It's heavy."

Heavy was an understatement. Bradley grabbed the handle on the opposite side of the box and felt the muscles in both his arms pulled to their maximum extension. They lugged the box out of the van and dropped it to the curb.

"What do you have in this thing?" Bradley massaged his arms. "It weighs a ton."

"All will be revealed." Washington closed the back of the van and locked the door. "I got to get you to sign a non-disclosure agreement first."

"What, really?"

Washington grinned. "No, not really. Now let's get it up to your apartment. I have a feeling we're going to need it."

Bradley had had the forethought to prop the wrought iron gate open, and together they lugged the box up the stairs and into the building.

O'CONNOR REPLAYED THE video on the phone, fascinated by what Bradley's time-lapse video had captured. Her cigar sat between her fingers instead of clamped in her teeth, an irregular occurrence.

"See? Right there," O'Connor said. "You can see one of them buggers check out the trap and disappear. The next time, there's two of them, and they're carrying that toothbrush."

"Yup," said Hope. "That's successive approximation at work."

"We ain't all Harvard graduates, honey," O'Connor said. "English, please."

"Through trial and error, these rats have learned to work together."

O'Connor rolled her eyes. "Any rat can do that. I thought you were smart."

Hope ignored the jab. "When you combine cooperation with the knowledge of how to disarm a snap trap, you've got something amazing."

"I'll give you that," O'Connor said. "I've seen a lot of strange shit in my day, but nothing like this."

Hope nodded. "I've seen behavior like that in crows, but never in rats other than in the lab. And they've got the characteristics of both a Gambian and a brown rat."

"Or a giant white-tailed rat from Kuranda." O'Connor grinned and placed her cigar back between her teeth.

Hope stared at her, and raised an eyebrow.

"That's in Queensland. Australia," O'Connor said. "I'm

not just a pretty face, honey. I know shit, too. And what we've got is a bigger, smarter, more aggressive hybrid."

"Not to mention an increased breeding cycle."

"From what I saw in the basement today, we could be dealing with thousands of those bastards." O'Connor and Hope shared a knowing glance. "You wouldn't be looking for a job, by any chance, would ya?"

"Thanks," Hope said, "but I'm more into the science and not the killing."

A knock sounded at the door. Hope opened it and let Bradley and Washington into the apartment. Their arms strained against the weight of the metal box.

"What's that?" Hope said.

"The question of the day," Bradley said between heavy breaths. He and Washington navigated the box to the side of the kitchen and dropped it with a thud. Bradley nodded toward Washington and O'Connor. "Their *secret weapon*."

Sam entered the kitchen holding an old, water-stained roll of paper. "I found this buried in the bedroom closet."

"That better be plans to the building," O'Connor said, "or we're fucked."

Sam unfurled the roll of paper on the kitchen table and revealed faded blue drafting lines describing the building's layout. The plans were water damaged in parts and pests had eaten holes in a few areas, but they were largely intact.

"I guess we're not fucked," Sam said. "Looks like the master shut off valve is either in the boiler room or the laundry room."

O'Connor unzipped one of the duffel bags and took out a box of steel wool and an aerosol can of insulating foam. She placed them in the center of the plans.

"We need to block perimeter access holes," O'Connor

said. "Where there's rat piss, there's a way in and out. The process is simple. Fill the holes with steel wool, then seal it in with the expanding foam. Should hold them for a while."

O'Connor began to divide up supplies. Bradley stepped up to get his share.

"Who are you, again?" O'Connor held back Bradley's supplies, as if he had to pass a test first to get them.

"Brad."

"Right. Sam's kid." O'Connor relinquished the aerosol can and steel wool to Bradley. "You and Washington seal any access holes here, except under the kitchen sink."

Bradley looked at Sam. "I want to go to the basement with you." He glared at O'Connor. "And I'm not a kid."

"Look," Sam said. "Your mom would kill me if anything happened to you."

O'Connor grabbed Bradley's arm, firm enough for him to know she meant business. "Washington knows how to kill these bastards. And he doesn't jump ten feet in the air when he sees them, either." O'Connor motioned at Sam. "Understand?"

Bradley nodded and felt both disappointed and embarrassed.

Sam felt the heat of their stares on him and there was nothing he could say. It was the truth. His fear was a serious shortcoming.

"Me and Brad got it covered," Washington nudged Bradley, to try to bolster his mood. "Don't we, Brad?"

"Guess so," Bradley said.

O'Connor grabbed a UV flashlight from a duffel bag and handed it to Bradley. "These have a UV mode. The switch is on the side. Anything with rat piss on it will—"

"Will glow," Bradley said. "I know."

"Smile, kid. You'll live longer." O'Connor looked at Sam and Hope. "You two come with me."

O'CONNOR, SAM AND HOPE stood in the basement as the elevator doors scraped closed behind them.

"Does the elevator always sound like that?" Hope listened to the elevator car grind its way back to the first floor.

"Afraid so," Sam said. "It's old, but does the job."

Hope looked around the basement. She aimed her flashlight along the dingy bricks and water-stained concrete. "Remind me to take the stairs back."

O'Connor pulled out a crude, quickly drawn sketch of the basement plans. "Hope, you check out the laundry room."

"Alone?" With one word, Hope's fear came through loud and clear.

"You're used to rats." O'Connor consulted her sketch. "What's the problem?"

"It's this basement that creeps me out more than anything."

O'Connor handed Hope a walkie-talkie. "You're a big girl. We'll be a hundred feet away, if that. Yell if you get stuck. Besides, Sam needs his hand held."

"Fuck you," Sam said.

O'Connor laughed and puffed a cloud of cigar smoke into the shadows. "That's the spirit."

Hope moved around the exterior of the concrete elevator shaft and followed the sloppy, hand-painted signs to the laundry. Ahead, a flickering light bulb hung from the exposed joists and pipes. Most of the time it didn't light at all. When the light bulb was within reach, she reached up and gave it a couple of taps, then a twist. The bulb flashed twice, then settled back into its flickering. Hope tried to ignore the shadows that seemed to close in around her with every step. Instead, she focused on the flashlight beam that traced a path in front of her.

Sam and O'Connor headed out in the opposite direction, toward where the boiler room was supposed to be. O'Connor led the way. In less than a minute, the only tether between Hope and O'Connor was the walkie-talkies clipped to their belts.

"You okay?" Sam noticed O'Connor's limp, which grew more noticeable with each step.

"What?" O'Connor alternated between scanning the floor and the overhead pipes with her flashlight.

"Your leg."

"Oh. Yeah." O'Connor patted her leg with her hand. "It acts up once in a while."

"Hey." Sam had been so focused on O'Connor's limp that he had failed to notice where he was: back at the tunnel where he had last seen the alpha rat. Fear began to overtake him but he fought it back as best he could. "This isn't the boiler room."

"No shit, Captain Obvious." O'Connor dug the phone out of her interior pocket and activated the GoPro app. The display glowed in the darkness as it relinked with the video feed from the camera.

"These things totally changed how I do business." O'Connor pointed at the tunnel's opening and handed Sam her phone. "Keep light on the entrance. I need to get that camera."

"O'Connor," Sam said. "Aren't you're forgetting something?"

"What?"

"Your cigar."

"Hell no," O'Connor said. "They go where I go." She knelt down on the concrete and slipped her flashlight into her hazmat suit. Then O'Connor butted out her cigar on the rough edge of the tunnel and slipped it next to her flashlight.

"You're on lookout duty," she said.

"Great." Sam could feel sweat build up on his brow. *As long as I don't see them, I'll be fine*, he thought.

O'Connor dropped to her stomach and began to squeeze herself into the tunnel. She grabbed a loose chunk of concrete and flattened the protruding wire that had gored Washington. His blood was still fresh on the wire's sharpened barbs.

Sam checked the phone's screen. No rats to be seen.

O'Connor wriggled halfway into the tunnel. It was harder work due to her short, stout frame. Her hands flashed in front of the phone's display as she grabbed the camera. O'Connor's face and the tiled floor appeared as she scanned the mystery room. Her face looked like a gray ghost.

"I can't see a fucking thing." O'Connor tucked her chin in to yell back through the tunnel. "The camera's shooting infrared. Anything on the phone?"

"Nothing," Sam said.

"Hold on." O'Connor twisted her body in jerky stages to position herself on her back. GoPro camera in hand, she moved the camera around in a wide, deliberate arc, and captured video images of the floor and walls.

She brought the camera back to her face, with the lens pointed up. Above O'Connor's head was what she thought was empty darkness. The phone's screen told another story. Sam saw the alpha rat perched on an overhead pipe. It looked down into the GoPro's lens with eyes that glowed, turned bright white by the infrared light.

"Holy shit." Sam felt fear stab at his brain.

"What?"

Sam's silence filled O'Connor with dread. She pulled out her flashlight and clicked it on. Just as the beam of light revealed the overhead pipe, the alpha rat jumped and landed on O'Connor's chest.

"Jesus Christ!" O'Connor dropped the camera. It rolled onto the tiled floor, lens up. Her flashlight rolled into the center of the hidden room. "Pull me out!"

Sam held the phone in his trembling hands and stared at the screen. Images of O'Connor's head and shoulders as she struggled with the alpha rat flashed across its display.

"Get your thumb out of your ass!"

O'Connor's yelling broke through Sam's fear just enough for a moment of clarity to take hold. He dropped his flashlight and the phone, grabbed O'Connor's legs and pulled. Sam's feet slid on the gritty concrete floor as they searched for purchase. O'Connor began to slide.

"Hurry the fuck up!" O'Connor's yelling could be heard clear as day beyond the tunnel's opening. "Pull harder!"

Sam increased his grasp and pulled with all his strength. O'Connor burst forth out of the tunnel, still in an intense battle with the alpha rat. She had one hand wrapped around the rat's neck while she tried to punch it with her other hand. But the alpha rat fought for its life as it tried to lunge at O'Connor's neck.

Sam continued to pull O'Connor by her legs. It was the only thing he could do to keep his mind from going numb with fear. She slid across the floor until her right boot hit an exposed bolt, stopping her.

Sam pulled O'Connor's left leg clean from its socket beneath her knee. He fell backward, holding the leg, as O'Connor managed to throw the alpha rat off her chest. The rat shook off the impact and charged O'Connor again.

"What the…" Sam scrambled backward and dropped the leg.

"Use it!" O'Connor twisted her head away from the alpha rat's incisors. "Use the leg!"

"What?" Sam sat dazed on the floor.

"Hit the rat with it, you stupid fuck!" O'Connor threw the rat off her again, and again it resumed its attack. "Quick!"

Something in Sam's brain clicked and thought returned. He grabbed the prosthetic leg by the calf and swung it at the rat with all his might, like he was teeing off at some demented golf course. O'Connor's boot at the end of the leg connected with the alpha rat, and sent it flying into the darkness where it smashed into a pile of obscured refuse. This time, the rat didn't return for more. It was gone, for now.

"Nice shot," O'Connor said. Her face and neck was scratched and bloodied. "I thought my number was up for a second there."

"What the fuck." Sam dropped the prosthetic leg on the floor.

"Secret's out." O'Connor said. "I got a fake leg." She unzipped the seam on her left pant leg and rolled the cuff up past her knee. She grabbed the prosthetic leg, peeled down the suspension sleeve and positioned the socket under her stump. Using the exposed bolt in the floor for leverage, she slid the leg back on.

O'Connor stood and leaned her weight onto her prosthetic leg. The socket slid up her stump a little more. She pulled the suspension sleeve back up over the socket and her knee, securing the leg in place.

"Jesus." Sam panted. "You could have told me."

"And spoil the fun?" O'Connor smiled, the congealing blood on her face stretching with her cheeks. "Fuck no."

"You okay? You look like shit."

O'Connor touched her chest and checked her inside pocket. "No, I'm not okay." She crouched at the opening of the tunnel. She could see the flashlight a few feet away. It lay on the white tile, with her cigar right next to it.

"It must've fallen out." O'Connor crawled back into the tunnel.

Sam's eyes went wide with disbelief. "What the hell are you doing?"

O'Connor scooted forward and grabbed the camera first, then the flashlight and her cigar. She reversed direction and was back out in less than thirty seconds. It felt more like minutes to Sam. O'Connor popped out of the tunnel for the second time, the camera and flashlight in one hand and her cigar in the other.

"It's a sin to abandon a Cohiba." O'Connor clamped the cigar between her teeth. She reached into her hazmat suit, took out her lighter, and re-lit her cigar. Plumes of thick, white smoke rose from her mouth. "That's the stuff. Help me up, will ya?"

Sam grabbed O'Connor's outstretched hand and pulled her to her feet.

IT DIDN'T TAKE long for Hope to reach the laundry room. And she wasn't surprised to see it had a hand-painted sign on the door, just like the signs that led to it. Even though she had a flashlight, the dancing shadows beyond the flashlight's beam still ate away at her psyche. *I don't like this place*, Hope thought. *I hope there's a laundromat nearby.*

The door frame was roughly cut and unfinished, as was the interior of the cramped room. A solitary light bulb hung from the cracked and peeling ceiling, and illuminated one old Maytag washer and dryer set and a large wash basin on spindly legs. Hope remembered her parents singing the praises of Maytag appliances and how "they didn't make them like they used to." Here was proof, staring Hope in the face.

She leaned over to get a better look behind the appliances, and ran her flashlight in the gap between the appliances and the wall. There was no master shut off valve back there, only two small water supply hoses, one split to go to the basin and washer's water intake. Hope knew it had been a long shot.

Beside the washer and dryer was a glass-fronted vending machine with rows of metal corkscrews that pushed snacks forward to drop into the collection tray at the bottom. A single bag of chips sat inside. Either this vending machine had been forgotten or restocking it wasn't high on anyone's priority list. Probably both.

Even with the single bulb hanging from the ceiling, Hope was glad to have her flashlight. As she moved further into the laundry room, she spotted three rats scurry along an overhead pipe. She traced their path above and behind her, and followed the pipe towards the door. The shadows cast from Hope's flashlight made the rats look twice their usual size.

One rat branched off and scaled down the wall, wedging itself in the corner next to an electrical conduit. It darted out and ran behind the vending machine.

Hope lost track of the rat as she scanned the other side of the vending machine, until it emerged from a hole in the back. She followed the rat with her light as it crawled through the metal corkscrews and into the back of the bag of chips.

The bag twitched as the rat looked for leftover morsels. Hope moved closer to get a better look. The rat could see Hope's approach through the clear cellophane portions of the chip bag and continued about its business.

The bag, with the rat still inside, flipped and dropped into the hidden cavern of the collection tray. Hope stepped back and listened. She could still hear the bag's cellophane crinkle and crunch inside the vending machine.

Hope made a slow approach towards the spring-loaded door to the collection tray. She used her flashlight like a stick and pushed open the door, as slow as she could manage. The rat ran back and forth inside the collection tray, then stopped and stood up. It looked at Hope with its red eyes, whiskers twitching. The rat opened its jaws and began to grind its incisors, *chi-chi-chi-chich*. Fear rose in the back of Hope's mind. The rat could sense it. Its snout quivered and caught the scent of Hope's increased alarm.

At first it sounded like running water. Hope looked back at the wash basin. The tap was dry. She returned her gaze to the collection tray of the vending machine. The rat had disappeared but the sound of running water remained. But the sound wasn't like running water anymore. It sounded more like fingers on a keypad. Hope moved the flashlight along the length of the collection tray's opening.

Fingers on a key pad… or paws on concrete.

To Hope's horror, a dozen rats spilled out from underneath the vending machine. She panicked and stepped backward, dropping her flashlight into the collection tray door. Dozens more rats emerged from under the vending machine and through the collection tray door, propped open by the flashlight.

Hope backed away towards the door as the rats continued to advance. She grabbed her walkie-talkie.

"O'Connor, I need—" The knot in Hope's right shoelace snagged between her foot and the jagged right-hand edge of the door frame and she lost her balance. Both she and the walkie-talkie hit the concrete floor hard. The walkie-talkie cracked and shorted out. Hope pulled at her shoe, but the more she pulled, the more the knotted lace aglet dug deeper into the cracked door frame.

Hope faced the darkness beyond the laundry room door. "Sam!"

She scrambled to untie her shoe, but the laces were knotted tight, like pebbles that had been woven into the fabric. The rats continued to advance. Their pace across the floor increased. Hope tried to rip her shoe off, but yanking on the laces had fastened the shoe on her foot so tightly, she was beginning to lose feeling in it. She grabbed the door and swung it closed, sliding her caught laces under the gap between the door and the floor and barricading the rats within.

Hope tried to pull herself away again, but the laces held

tight. Fine sand and concrete dust caused her left shoe to slide. She was tied to the door frame, unable to get away.

She focused her gaze at the gap between the door and the floor. The light behind it dimmed as the influx of rats jammed their bodies into it.

Hope stared at the gap and tried to estimate its height. "Please, please, please be less than an inch." To her horror, no estimation was necessary. Already, the rats began to force their bodies under the door. If she did nothing, she'd be overcome and attacked by rats in seconds. The choice was clear. Kill or be killed.

"SAM! O'CONNOR!" Hope stood as best she could with her right foot tied to the door frame and screamed.

Rat snouts and frenzied whiskers emerged first, then heads and squirming rat bodies followed. She stomped the rats first to emerge with her left shoe as their heads poked through.

She began to kill the creatures she loved. The sound of their heads as they popped and crunched under her foot made Hope's stomach churn with repulsion and remorse.

The first one was the hardest to kill, but it got easier. Soon the concrete in front of the laundry door was greased with blood, bones, brains and fur. And the rats kept coming.

O'Connor and Sam emerged from the darkness, O'Connor holding the GoPro.

"It's about time, you bastards," Hope said.

"I thought you said you weren't into the killing side of things." O'Connor surveyed the carnage collecting on the floor.

"Just get me out of here!" Hope was in no mood for games.

O'Connor shot a look at Sam. "There's too many."

Sam ripped off his long sleeved work shirt, revealing his muscular, tattooed arms. He twisted his shirt into a thick rope, jammed it into the gap between the laundry room door and the floor, and kicked it into place.

"That'll buy us some time," Sam said.

"Shit." O'Connor took in Sam's expansive tattoos, one arm at a time. "Dig the crazy sleeves. You know my secret. What's yours?"

"Give me your lighter," Sam said.

"What?"

"Your lighter."

O'Connor dug into her pocket, grabbed her lighter, and passed it to Sam. He knelt next to Hope's right foot and struck a flame. The stuck laces burned through and freed her shoe within seconds.

Sam tossed the lighter back to O'Connor. "You okay?" he said to Hope.

"They just kept coming." Hope's eyes stared vacantly and Sam noticed a subtle tremble in her hands. "Like lemmings to a cliff." She spotted O'Connor's bloodied face, which looked like a Jackson Pollock painting if he painted in blood and used people instead as canvas. "What the hell happened to you?"

"Face to face with a pissed-off alpha rat." O'Connor tapped the GoPro. "Should have caught it all on camera in glorious HD."

Sam extended his prison-branded arm and helped Hope to her feet. "Glorious would be the last word I'd use."

"It's glorious because I'm in the shot, 'fraidy-bitch.'" O'Connor looked around the door that led to the laundry room, then at Hope. "Where's your flashlight?"

Hope thumbed backward. "In the laundry room. I can get it if you like."

"Real funny," O'Connor said. "And your walkie talkie?"

Hope shrugged a sheepish grin.

"Damn. That shit is expensive."

"Yeah, well it slipped out of my hand," Hope said. "I barely escaped with my life."

"Spare me the details." O'Connor pulled out her sketch of the basement and clicked on her flashlight. She moved back and forth between illuminating the sketch and the surrounding area. "Where *is* that fuckin' shut off valve?"

Sam glanced at Hope, then back at O'Connor. "Are you expecting an answer?"

"For fuck's sake, gimme your walkie talkie."

Sam unclipped his walkie-talkie from his belt and handed it to O'Connor.

"Washington, what's your status?"

The three were met with staticky silence.

"Washington!" O'Connor repeated.

Again, no answer.

Main

Washington moved through the kitchen. He followed the baseboards and enclosed areas, and made note of access points. Bradley followed with steel wool and expanding foam. Once he knew what to look for, the holes seemed to jump out at him.

"They're everywhere." Bradley crammed a ball of steel wool into an access point and filled it with expanding foam. "I've counted six so far."

"Yeah." Washington looked grave. "Not a good sign." Washington moved into the hallway. "How old are you, Brad?"

"Sixteen."

"Ah, sixteen." Washington cast his mind back to better days and smiled. "Handsome guy like you must have to fight off the girls, huh?"

"Not really."

"Oh." Washington caught himself. "Are you into guys instead?"

"No, I like girls," Bradley said, "but I have a few friends who are gay."

"My bad. I just assumed." Washington looked at Bradley, surprised. "You don't have a girlfriend?"

"Well, there is this one girl I like." Images of Hope

floated through Bradley's head and filled his stomach with bees again. "She doesn't know I like her, though."

Washington grinned. "I think she knows, Brad."

"What do you mean?"

"I've seen the way you look at Hope."

"It's that obvious?"

"Well, to me it is." Washington considered his next words carefully. "I'd guess she's ten years older than you."

"That's okay. I like older women." Bradley tried to recall how he had behaved around Hope. All he could remember was how nervous and jittery she made him feel.

"Well, Brad, don't overthink it." Washington smiled to himself. "People like to be liked."

That was an impossible proposition. Bradley was going to overthink it and Washington could see it on his face. To keep Bradley on task, he changed the subject. "Say, you like killing rats?"

"I don't know." Bradley looked at the bandage on his finger. "But I sure don't like them biting me."

"Let's see if you got what it takes, shall we?" Washington stepped into the bedroom. "Let's find us some more access holes."

Washington scanned the baseboards underneath the head of the bed. He spotted a chewed gap in the wood.

"Help me move the bed," Washington said. The two of them slid the box spring to one side, which gave Bradley easy access to the gap.

The job was easy and became second nature to Bradley in no time flat. He crammed a wad of steel wool into the hole in the baseboard and capped it with a shot of expanding foam. Bradley wouldn't have been so cavalier if he had known about the horde of rats within the wall. They recognized the smell of his blood on the bandage on his finger, and watched his every move through the access hole with their red, pinprick eyes, until they were once again sealed in darkness. The rats didn't need to attack now. Under the cover of night was always best. And Washington and Bradley would never find all the access holes. There would always be a way out.

Bradley moved the bed back and Washington continued along the baseboards. His walkie-talkie squawked into life.

"Washington, what's your status?" O'Connor's voice cracked with static.

Bradley moved to the closet. He watched Washington go to answer O'Connor's page, but stop his hand positioned over the walkie-talkie clipped to his belt.

"Aren't you going to get that?"

"I like to bust her balls every once in a while," Washington said. "Reminds her of my importance in all this."

"Washington!" O'Connor's filtered voice floated from the walkie-talkie's speakers.

"Oh, she's pissed off." Washington laughed. "Sometimes this is the only way to get joy out of this job."

The walkie-talkie came to life again. "Washington, you better not be fuckin' with me."

The joke had gone on long enough. "Yeah, we got access holes everywhere," Washington said into the walkie-talkie.

"There's one in here." Bradley filled an access hole in the closet with steel wool and foam in quick succession.

"Kitchen. Bedroom. It's like this place was a central colony at one point." Washington shared a look with Bradley. "Bad fucking energy."

"Use your hocus pocus to shine a light into the access hole under the kitchen sink, will yah," O'Connor crackled.

"See the kind of disrespectful shit I got to deal with?" Washington headed for the kitchen.

"Maybe that's all she can do," Bradley said, following.

"You're very wise for your age, you know that?" Washington opened the double doors under the sink. For a split second, Washington thought he saw movement in the shadows, but all his flashlight revealed was an access hole. "Too bad O'Connor is, and forever will be, a heartless bitch."

"I think you're wrong," Bradley said.

"Everyone's entitled to their opinion." Washington's eyes looked tired. "Mine's been stomped on for the past ten years."

"Why do you stay?"

"I don't know." Washington raised the walkie-talkie to his mouth. "What's next?"

"Jesus Christ, Washington. Did you crawl?" O'Connor screeched.

Washington turned down the volume. He smiled at Bradley. "That's better."

"Make the hole bigger."

"Bigger," Washington said.

"What are you, deaf?" O'Connor cackled like a witch on AM radio. "Don't care how you do it."

Washington sat on the floor and positioned his right foot above the small hole. He cast a look at Bradley. "Sorry about this."

"Hey, I don't live here… at least not permanently."

It didn't take much to break through the drywall. Washington's foot sailed through it like it was made of soft cheese. The result was a large hole big enough for his head and shoulders to fit through.

"Why is it that I'm always the one sticking his neck into dark places." Washington directed his light into the black gullet and down towards the basement.

"THERE!" O'CONNOR SPOTTED Washington's flashlight beam from above. Sam and Hope followed O'Connor to the area illuminated by the light's beam. "Got it!" O'Connor yelled up to Washington.

"This is the boiler room?" Hope said. "It's not even a room."

"Maybe at one point it was." Sam targeted the floor with his flashlight. "This looks like an old elevator shaft."

"And everyone knows the boiler room is always found in the elevator shaft," Hope said.

"Nothing about this building makes any sense, at least according to those plans." O'Connor scanned the walls with her flashlight, switching in and out of UV mode. The walls fluoresced yellow and magenta in the darkness. The master water shut off valve for the building jutted out of the wall, half way up, two feet from an access ladder.

"Look at all the rat piss." O'Connor followed the glowing trails along the walls up the ladder. She looked at Sam. "Leads right into your place."

Sam followed O'Connor's flashlight beam with his own. Together, they traced the fluorescent markers along the cracked concrete. His stomach sank. It felt hot and heavy, as if it was stuffed with greasy, spoiled seafood. Sweat beaded up on his brow.

Hope cast Sam a wary glance. "Lucky you."

"You've been living in a rat's nest and you didn't even know it," O'Connor said.

The access ladder embedded in the concrete began halfway up the wall, beyond O'Connor's grasp.

"Give me a boost."

Sam clasped his hands together to form a stirrup around O'Connor's boot and lifted her up. He grunted under the strain.

"Hope… ," Sam said between heavy breaths. "Could use a hand."

Hope added her clasped hands to Sam's. They both exerted all their strength to keep O'Connor raised off the floor.

"You should lay off the pound cake," Sam said.

"How about you eat my shit-kicking boots?" O'Connor grabbed the rungs of the embedded ladder and hooked her elbow into it. Under the sudden weight, the old concrete crumbled around the metal ends of the rungs. O'Connor reached out and tried to work the water shut-off valve closed.

"The damn thing's stuck." O'Connor pulled down hard on the rusted rungs of the valve.

"It's probably never been touched since it was installed." Hope gritted her teeth under O'Connor's weight. "Just hurry it up. We're dying here."

"As you wish, your highness." O'Connor made slow progress, twisting the valve a bit at a time.

"Are you turning it the right direction?" Sam said.

"You think I'm stupid? Is that it—"

A rat ran past Sam's feet. He panicked, let go of O'Connor and scrambled backward to get away. Hope tried to take on all of O'Connor's weight, but the soles of her boots dug into Hope's hands. The pain and weight was too great and she let go.

O'Connor slipped down. The ladder rung and her elbow bore all her weight. "Help me up, you fools!" The concrete around the rung's ends crumbled under O'Connor's bulk.

Sam sat several feet away, sweating and unable to move. Hope jammed her shoulder under O'Connor's backside and tried to lift her up, without success. Hope's thin frame was no match for O'Connor's weight.

The rung reached its load limit and ripped out of the disintegrating concrete wall. O'Connor dropped to the floor and landed hard on top of Hope.

The two women fell in a heap in front of Sam and distracted him enough to break through his fear. "Shit. You okay?"

O'Connor propped herself up and glared at Sam. "You got to cure yourself of that fucking phobia."

"I second that." Hope brushed herself off. "You're starting to piss me off."

WASHINGTON SLIPPED OFF the hood of his hazmat suit as he finished looking for access points in the TV room. Bradley stood beside him at the ready with his steel wool and foam.

"These goddamn suits don't breath." Washington unzipped his suit halfway down his chest. "I'm sweating like a whore in church."

"Do you really need one?" Bradley said. "I'm not wearing one and I'm fine."

"Part of the get-up. You know, branding and shit."

"You could do that with a t-shirt."

"O'Connor likes the suits. Makes our visits seem more official. More official makes more money." Washington shrugged. "Or so I'm told. Bottom line, O'Connor gets what O'Connor wants."

Both left the TV room and rounded the corner to the bathroom.

"How long have you lived here?" Washington said.

"I'm just visiting. I live in L.A."

Washington raised an eyebrow. "I've never met a person from Hollywood before."

"I don't live in Hollywood." Bradley said. "L.A.'s a big place."

"Yeah. So's New York." Washington began his scan of the bathroom. "Broken home?"

Bradley looked embarrassed by the question. "Yeah. My parents split up when I was one. I don't remember my dad at all, and my mom doesn't talk about him, even when I ask."

"Must be tough." Washington nodded. "I don't got no kids. Wish I did, though. Wish I'd done a lot of things." He sighed and looked around the bathroom, this time really seeing it instead of just looking at it as part of a task. "Now I'm married to this goddamn job, crawling around shitholes like this. No offense."

Bradley shrugged. "Could be worse, I guess."

"You got that right."

"What's something you wish you'd done?"

Washington gave the question some thought. "I'd have made a good priest… if it weren't for the booze and the women." He shrugged and chuckled at the same time. "Maybe paint pictures, be an artist. What about you?"

"I don't know." Bradley looked around the bathroom as if he'd find an answer there. "I'm only sixteen." He grinned.

"That you are," Washington said. "Get the lights."

Bradley flipped the light switch. The bathroom fell into relative darkness. The only other light came from the small frosted window adjacent to the shower. Washington turned his flashlight to UV mode and scanned the walls and baseboards. Yellow and magenta patches glowed everywhere.

"Unless you and your dad like pissing on the baseboards and rubbing your noses in it," Washington said, "you've got rats in here too."

"Weird." Bradley turned the light back on. "I've only been here a couple days. I've been bitten but I haven't seen anything."

"A rat bite is as good as seeing one in my book." Washington ran his flashlight beam under the sink, in the tub and behind the toilet. "If you see one, there's ten more you can't."

"Yeah," Bradley said. "I've heard that before."

Washington lifted the toilet seat lid and took a slow, careful look inside.

Clear water.

"Did you know rats can hold their breath for three minutes, sometimes more?" Washington closed the toilet seat lid and sat down. "Your toilet's like an open door."

"They'd give David Blaine a run for his money," Bradley said.

Washington laughed as he dug into his shirt for a pack of Marlboros and a lighter. "You got that right." He shook the package and captured a cigarette with his lips, drawing it out. He offered the pack to Bradley.

"No thanks."

Washington lit the cigarette and inhaled deeply. "Can't stand those cigars, but this… this is worth the time."

"I'll take your word for it." Bradley turned away to get a breath.

"What's up with the coon tail?"

"It's nothing."

"Nothing? I smell bullshit." Washington took a drag from his Marlboro. The tip glowed orange. "Is it your spirit animal or something?"

Bradley was surprised at Washington's knowledge and how he could strip away the layers and go right for the heart. He had liked him from the start, but this sealed the deal. "Actually, yeah."

"How'd it choose you?"

"I was jumped by a bunch of kids coming home from school one night. They beat me up and took my money and my phone," Bradley said.

"Sorry." Washington took a drag from his cigarette.

Bradley shrugged. "I wasn't hurt that bad. I was lying in a ditch, and out of nowhere, there was this raccoon. I had never seen one for real before. I didn't even think raccoons existed in L.A. We just stared at each other. I don't even know for how long. It was cool." Bradley picked up the raccoon tail and let it run through his fingers. "The next day, I saw this hanging in a shop near my house."

"It was a sign."

"Yeah, I guess so. I bought it and I haven't been bothered since."

"You discovered masks. Just like a raccoon," Washington said. "Now you can summon whatever you need… confidence, secrecy, a *don't fuck with me* attitude, anything."

Bradley nodded, secure with the knowledge that Washington understood. "What's your spirit animal?"

Washington pulled his pendant out from under his shirt and turned the rat skull encased in amber around in his fingers. "I'll give you one guess."

"A rat?"

"A rat. A god-damned rat." The ember of Washington's cigarette inched toward the filter. "That's probably why I'm so good at my job. It takes a rat to know a rat."

Bradley took a closer look. "Is that a skull?"

"Yup," Washington said. "A common New York City roof rat. Juvenile, I think. I picked it up at a pawn shop a couple of years ago."

"Cool."

Washington took one last drag from his Marlboro. "Now let's show these little shits who's boss." He stood up and raised the toilet seat lid to dispose of his cigarette butt.

A rat jumped out of the toilet, its fur slicked wet.

"Motherfuck!" Washington grabbed the towel rack to steady himself on the wet floor. "Get the door!"

Bradley slammed the bathroom door just in time. The rat saw its escape route vanish and reversed direction. It scrambled back into the bathroom along the baseboards.

Washington unholstered his tranquilizer gun and tracked the rat along the floor. He steadied his aim and pulled the trigger. The dart hit the rat just below its neck. It squirmed for a few seconds before the drug in the dart began to take effect. But the rat continued to struggle and made a pathetic but equally valiant effort to drag its body across the floor.

"Holy shit." Washington watched the rat's struggle to move. "There was enough juice in that dart to take down a dog. Look at it."

The momentum of the dart had flipped the rat on its side upon impact. Its legs moved in time with each other, like it was swimming. The image reminded Bradley of videos he had seen of sleeping dogs running at full speed, but the rat moved a lot slower.

"I'll be right back." Washington opened the bathroom door to leave. "Don't let it get away."

"What do you mean?" Bradley said. "Are you serious?" Bradley relaxed when he heard Washington's laugh from the kitchen.

When he returned moments later, he held what looked to Bradley like a stack of the cooling racks Claire used when she baked cookies.

"What's that?"

Washington closed the bathroom door and answered Bradley's question by placing the layers of welded stainless steel wires on the floor. He pulled up on the steel ring in the center. The grid of welded wires unfolded and reassembled themselves into a small cage. Washington locked the walls into place.

"That's totally awesome!" Bradley's eyes twinkled with interest.

"Thanks," Washington said. "My own design."

"Really? You should be selling these. You'd bank huge coin."

"You know, I just might do that, Brad." Washington grabbed the semi-conscious rat by its white-tipped tail, dropped it into the cage and locked it in. He grabbed his walkie-talkie. "O'Connor, I got a live one."

A moment passed, then O'Connor's staticky voice replied. "White-tipped tail?"

Washington held the cage in front of his face for a closer look. "Yeah, and it's —"

"Look out!" Bradley pointed to the toilet.

A second rat perched on the seat of the toilet and launched itself onto Washington's back. He dropped his walkie-talkie and it skittered across the floor.

"Washington?" O'Connor said through the walkie-talkie.

Washington dropped the cage and twisted to try to get the rat off his back. "The lid!"

A third rat surfaced in the toilet and jumped across the bathroom. It landed in the hood of Washington's hazmat suit.

"Close the MOTHERFUCKING LID!" Washington yelled, crouching and casting his arms behind himself.

Bradley scrambled across the bathroom to the toilet. To his horror, more rats began to surface in the toilet bowl. He slammed the lid closed with both hands, but felt the lid bounce up and down as rats inside the toilet bowl jumped against it. Bradley grabbed the toilet handle and flushed.

"No, goddamn it!" Washington glimpsed the toilet bowl begin to overflow. Water covered the tile.

"Sorry!" Bradley felt the heat of embarrassment spread across his cheeks. "What do I do?"

"There's too many." Washington unzipped his hazmat suit. "They're clogging the pipes. Stand on it."

The rat in Washington's hood bit his neck. "Fuck!" He ripped the rest of his hazmat suit off and threw it in a heap in the corner of the bathroom. It squirmed on the wet floor.

Washington touched the back of his neck and returned with his hand covered in his own blood. "Fucker bit me." He slammed his heel onto the squirming rat lumps under his hazmat suit. Crimson bloody patches soaked into the fabric.

Washington grabbed the duct tape off his tool belt and began to wrap the toilet shut. "One hundred and one uses for duct tape? That's one hundred and two."

The toilet seat lid bumped. Quivering noses, whiskers, and yellow incisors poked out between the seat and the toilet bowl. The duct tape would hold for now.

Washington slumped down to the bathroom floor, exhausted. Beside him lay the rat in the cage, now fully awake. The tranquilizer had already worn off.

"Look at that thing," Washington said. "So much for our tranq guns." He shared a concerned glance with Bradley.

Sam burst into the bathroom, sweating and out of breath.

"Don't you fucking knock?" Washington looked up. "What if I was taking a shit?"

"Your walkie-talkie went dead," Sam said.

"You don't ever want to be in the bathroom when I'm talking a motherfucking shit." Washington glared at Sam, before he broke into a wide smile and began to laugh. He looked at Bradley and motioned him to climb down. "That lid's locked down for now."

"You okay?" Bradley said to Sam as he climbed down off the toilet. The toilet lid continued to bump up and down.

"Never better," Sam said between breaths. He looked at the cage and the frenzied rat inside. "I thought your mom said no pets."

Bradley grinned.

Sam offered his hand to Washington. "We got work to do." He took it and Sam helped him to his feet.

Bradley was the last out of the bathroom and he flipped the bathroom light switch off as he passed.

If there had been a UV light in the bathroom, it would have revealed the snouts and incisors in a magenta glow, as they poked through between the toilet seat and the toilet bowl, just as before. But this time the rats had discovered the duct tape. They had also discovered how easily they could chew through it.

Onslaught

THE LOSS OF Piper had thrown Mrs. Baxter into a deep depression. Her regular sleep patterns were destroyed. She couldn't sleep when she wanted to and would drift off in the most inopportune moments. She missed her little rascal something fierce.

Mrs. Baxter wasn't afraid of growing old. She had called herself an *old bag* on more than a few occasions. But she never called herself a *deaf* old bag. Mrs. Baxter's hearing was as clear as the day she was born.

The noise that had woken her from her nap had come from the kitchen. Mrs. Baxter was still dressed in her housecoat from breakfast.

Don't need to go out today so there's no point getting dressed, she had thought when she woke this morning. And yesterday morning. And the morning before that.

Mrs. Baxter sat up on the edge of her bed and cocked an ear, more to try and identify the sound than to locate it.

Like metal chains on wood.

She slipped her feet into her slippers. They felt cool on her feet as she padded down the dark hallway towards the kitchen. Mrs. Baxter had kept the apartment lights off since learning of Piper's death. On sunny days, the apartment windows next to the kitchen table cast enough light to live by, but she had drawn the blinds the day before.

She approached the kitchen in almost total darkness. The light that spilled in from around the blinds was enough to identify the kitchen table and chairs, Piper's shrine and the counter with all its fixtures and amenities, but nothing in detail.

Except that the trap was no longer on the counter. The rattling continued. From Mrs. Baxter's vantage point, she could tell the sound came from the floor, behind the table and beyond her current view.

She turned on the light to the kitchen and approached the table wide. Her slippers *shuff-shuffled* on the vinyl flooring. There it was. The snap trap she had baited and left on the counter the previous evening was inverted, with a rat half stuck under the kill arm. The rat was far from dead, and it squirmed with renewed urgency once it realized a human was nearby.

"There yah be, yah rat bastard." If anyone had seen Mrs. Baxter at that moment, they would have said she was baring her fangs. She walked back to the kitchen counter and slid a large chef's knife out of a knife block shaped like a loaf of bread (a Christmas gift from the kids in 2013).

Mrs. Baxter shuffled back to where the rat struggled on the floor and moved closer to the sprung trap. She gripped the handle of the knife with white knuckles. The blade glinted in the kitchen light.

The rat paused, caught Mrs. Baxter's scent, then continued to writhe on the floor. Its white-tipped tail flipped like an out-of-control garden hose. Through its struggles, it had worked itself part-way out of the trap. Mrs. Baxter needed to act fast.

The trap flipped over and for the first time, the rat could see the danger it smelled. Mrs. Baxter and the rat locked eyes. The rat drew in rapid breaths, its small chest heaving up and down.

The rat smelled Mrs. Baxter as she moved closer, and resumed its frenzied struggle. It began to shit on the floor, leaving a trail of small, moist pellets.

"Now I've got you." Mrs. Baxter knelt on her hands and knees and crawled toward the rat held tight in the snap trap. She didn't encounter much need to kneel most days, but this was worth the effort.

Poised and ready, Mrs. Baxter sneered and bared her fangs again. She raised her knife, and in one swift, powerful arc, she brought the blade down through the rat and severed its spine. The tip of the blade embedded in the trap's wooden base.

The rat squealed and squirmed in pain as Mrs. Baxter raised the trap in the air like a trophy. Thick, ruby-red blood trickled down the blade's honed edge. She struggled to stand, her knees protesting. With her free hand, Mrs. Baxter pulled herself up with the aid of the kitchen table.

She hobbled to the kitchen sink, flung the rat and trap into it, and placed the knife beside the sink.

"Take that, yah rat fuck."

The rat landed with a *thud* and succumbed to its injuries without much additional struggle.

As Mrs. Baxter flipped off the kitchen light and turned to leave the kitchen, a rustling sound caught her ears.

The bugger's not dead yet.

She turned the light back on, approached the sink again, and grabbed the knife once it was within reach. Mrs. Baxter focused on the sink for any movement, but there was none.

Her eyes wandered, scanning around the sink and across the counter top. Past the coffee maker, the knife block, the toaster oven and her beloved kettle that had kept her steeped in tea for countless years.

But then she saw them. A second pair of red rodent eyes watched her from behind the knife block.

A standoff. Mrs. Baxter raised her knife again, slowly. Whiskers vibrated and the rat's white-tipped tail flipped like a metronome on speed. It advanced toward her with small, deliberate steps.

"You've met your match, you little *shit*." Mrs. Baxter brought her knife blade down hard, and caught the rat's tail just as it lunged towards her.

Lightning fast, the rat twisted around and sunk its incisors into Mrs. Baxter's hand. She let go of the knife like her body was on automatic. Blood welled up on the side of her hand, her blood this time. She was surprised by the intense pain.

The rat, pinned to the counter top, squirmed to get free and began to chew off its own tail.

Mrs. Baxter clutched her bleeding hand and watched the rat free itself. She made a slow move towards the knife block to rearm herself. A third rat emerged from behind the coffee maker. Then a fourth and fifth rat appeared from behind the kettle and toaster oven. In seconds, over a dozen rats revealed themselves on the counter top.

Mrs. Baxter took a step back and felt a searing pain in the back of her right heel. She looked down to see a rat biting at her foot. She kicked it away. Both the rat and her slipper sailed out into the middle of the kitchen floor and into the center of an advancing horde of rats. They closed in on her with the soft *pitter-patter* of rat paws and the *chi-chi-chi-chich* of grinding incisors.

Panicked, Mrs. Baxter looked back at the counter top, now completely covered with rats. Their oily, matted fur shimmered under the dim kitchen light. She had nowhere to run.

The first rat, now tail-less and free, leaped onto Mrs. Baxter's chest. She grabbed for the knife but missed and knocked it to the floor. She brushed the rat off her chest with her bloodied hand. The rat landed next to the knife on the floor, shook off the impact, and followed the blood trail from the previous bite on her right foot. The rat spun around to attack again, this time higher. Its long incisors ripped into Mrs. Baxter's Achilles tendon.

She collapsed to the floor in excruciating pain as rats approached from all sides. Frantic, she tried to fight them off as her hand grabbed blindly for the knife on the floor.

"Piper!" Mrs. Baxter flailed on the floor as the rats overtook her. Her efforts were futile. "Where are you, Piper?"

Rats burrowed into her housecoat and ripped into her flesh. She felt the warm stickiness of her blood soak into her nightgown and flow across the floor. It might have been a comfort had the attack stopped, but rats crawled over her face, latched onto her eyelids, and pulled them back like they were peeling mandarin oranges.

Mrs. Baxter screamed into the emptiness of her apartment as she clawed at her own face.

Hope and O'Connor rejoined Washington, Sam and

Bradley in Sam's kitchen. Hope squatted in front of the sink and examined the gaping hole Washington had kicked in the drywall. She leaned in to get a better look, but stopped short of putting her head through the hole.

"Any brilliant insights, princess?" O'Connor said.

Hope let the jab slide. Again. "I'm going take a look around."

O'Connor watched Hope wander out of the kitchen and down the hallway, disappointed that she couldn't get under her skin.

"Rats in the toilet?" Sam found it hard to believe what he was hearing. "Is nothing off limits to these bastards?"

O'Connor sat reclined in a chair and blew cigar smoke across the kitchen. Her legs were propped up on Sam's kitchen table. "You could always shit in the sink."

"Your sink ain't big enough for my shits," Washington said.

Bradley laughed.

"Not funny." The only thing going through Sam's mind was the image of rats in his toilet. The situation was personal now. He felt violated. Switching to a porta-potty until this invasion was over was becoming a very real alternative, and Sam didn't like it one bit.

"Sometimes you just gotta laugh." O'Connor unholstered her pellet gun and aimed it at the overhead light, at the faucet, the light switch. "At least your kid has a sense of humor."

Bradley watched O'Connor's hand cradle the gun. "Is that thing loaded?"

"Twenty-four, seven."

"Can I hold it?" Bradley was serious.

"What do you say, daddy-oh?" O'Connor looked at Sam. "Shall I let the kid have a go?"

Sam looked at Bradley. His eyes gleamed and he practically vibrated with anticipation. "Okay."

"Sick!" Bradley faced O'Connor.

O'Connor flicked the safety with her thumb and slid the pellet gun across the table. "Keep your finger off the trigger, or I'll kick your ass."

Bradley picked up the gun and felt its cool weight in his hands. He raised the weapon to eye level and squinted to aim it.

"Don't aim it at me, jack-hole." O'Connor ducked out of the way.

Bradley adjusted his aim to the back of the kitchen and imagined all the rats he could shoot with it. "This is awesome."

O'Connor held out her hand and beckoned for return of the gun. "Maybe your daddy-oh can take you to the firing range sometime."

"That'd be cool, eh Dad?"

Sam shrugged.

Bradley placed the gun in O'Connor's hand. "Thanks."

O'Connor gave Bradley a nod and a wink. A little piece of the shield O'Connor hid behind fell away. "Well, Washington?"

"Well, what?"

O'Connor stood, holstered her pellet gun, and walked to the metal box that sat near the apartment entrance. She slapped her hand down on the diamond-plate. "I think it's time to break out this bad boy."

"It's about damn time," Washington said.

Mrs. Baxter's screams filtered into Sam's apartment, low

but loud enough to hear if someone stopped to listen. That someone was Hope.

She returned from the hallway and tilted her head to one side. "Does anyone hear that?"

"What?" O'Connor said. "What are you talking about?"

"I don't hear anything," Bradley said.

Hope held up her hand, palm out. "Shut up for a second."

"It's getting serious, folks." O'Connor chuckled.

Hope shot O'Connor a look instead of a reply.

With everyone quiet, the screams were hard to miss. Even muted through the vents, the screams turned Sam's blood cold.

O'Connor took the cigar from her mouth. "Who is that?"

Bradley looked at Sam, concern in his eyes. "Mrs. Baxter?"

Sam echoed Bradley's concern. "Shit…"

"What?" O'Connor said. "Who's Mrs. Baxter?"

"Remember when I told you that these rats had killed a man?" Sam said.

"Yeah?"

Sam locked gaze with O'Connor. "I think it's happening again."

O'Connor didn't waste any time. "Washington, suit up. Full gear." She began to pull extra equipment from the duffel bags: torches with a propane backpack, and taser rods. Washington pulled out his own set of similar equipment.

"Is that a flame thrower?" Bradley said.

"Damn straight." Washington maintained a serious tone. "If you can't beat 'em, burn 'em."

Bradley's eyes bugged out. "Cool."

"What's not cool is being eaten alive." Washington cut Bradley's excitement short.

"Got enough ammo?" O'Connor tapped her holstered pellet gun.

Washington nodded. "Let's move. Maybe we can save this… Mrs. Baxter."

Sam already knew what he'd find in apartment 302. "We're too late already," he said low, under his breath.

Hope squeezed Sam's shoulder. "Maybe you're wrong."

Sam looked at Hope, but couldn't manage a smile.

THE ELEVATOR STRAINED with each new occupant. Sam, Bradley, and Hope were already inside. When O'Connor stepped in, the elevator car sank an inch below the hallway floor. The cables that held up the car gave sounds of metal fatigue. O'Connor turned and bashed Hope and Sam with her propane back pack.

"Sorry, brother." O'Connor held up her hand like she was directing traffic. "Your fat ass ain't gonna fit."

"*My* ass is fat?" Washington looked at O'Connor, his eyebrow raised. "Have you looked in the mirror lately?"

O'Connor pressed the third floor call button. As the elevator doors scraped shut, she grinned and waved at Washington left in the first floor hallway. "Buh-bye, now, sucker."

Washington stared back at O'Connor until the elevator doors had fully closed.

"Bitch." At that instant, Washington had no affection for

O'Connor at all. He didn't care if she lived or died. *I should pack my shit up and walk*, he thought.

"I heard that," O'Connor said from within the elevator. The elevator's electric motors kicked in and began the slow ascent to the third floor.

WASHINGTON PULLED OPEN the door to the stairwell and stepped in. The entire stairwell was poorly lit. The single bulb above his head on the first floor landing looked as if it was one hundred years old. The bulb's glass was thick and warped with age, with a fine patina of dust permanently burned onto it. The sturdy filament burned a fiery orange-yellow, and reminded Washington of a day-glow pipe cleaner. From his position on the first floor landing, he could see light flicker over the landing above, and what he couldn't see was shrouded in either shadow or cracked and disintegrating concrete.

"What a shit hole." Washington looked down the stairs to the basement, then up to the second floor.

He started up the stairs and unclipped his UV flashlight from his belt to help light the way. The sand and grit made each step slippery and he lost his footing more than once. Washington steadied himself on the hand railings and continued his ascent to the second floor landing. An echoing *skittering* sound stopped him in his tracks.

"What the hell was that?" he said to himself in a low whisper. "Hello?" He scanned forward and back with his flashlight. There was no one else there, no one else that he could see.

Washington slowed his pace and continued up the

stairwell. His eyes leveled on the landing between the second and third floor. There, on the center of the top step, sat a single rat. It looked down at him, its red eyes glowing in the darkened stairwell. There was no light bulb hanging under the mid-floor landings, and that made the rat's eyes even more prominent.

"Won't you look cute under my boot," Washington said.

He continued to move up the stairs toward the mid-floor landing. The rat didn't budge. It just sat there, and watched.

The little shit's got balls. It's like he's got…

Washington unholstered his pellet gun and ascended the steps. His slow, deliberate steps raised his vantage point high enough to see past the rat and onto the mid-floor landing.

It's like he's got backup.

There were rats everywhere. They advanced to the edge of the mid-floor landing to join their comrade. They ran down from the third floor landing and peeked over the edge of the steps.

Washington took a step backward, only to find rats crawling up the stairwell from the first floor. He had been ambushed, surrounded, and outnumbered by rats.

"Well, shit." Washington grumbled.

The rats began to advance and close in on Washington. It didn't take long to realize his pellet gun was useless. He holstered it and pulled out his propane torch. He opened the valve to start the flow of gas and lit the pilot flame at the end of the wand.

"Okay, motherfuckers," Washington said through gritted teeth. "Who's first to the barbecue?"

He pulled the trigger and the torch's flame sputtered.

Washington hit the valve and tried again. The torch's nozzle emitted a small puff of flame.

"Come on! Goddamn it!"

Washington waved the end of the torch's wand at the rising tide of rats, but the waning flames did little to repel them.

"Shit." Washington tried to climb the railing to get away, but the rats were on him in seconds. They bit his hands and blocked his every move. He tossed his propane torch aside and grabbed his last option, the taser rod.

Please be fully charged…

"Who's first?" Washington jabbed the taser rod forward and pinned a rat against the stairs. "Take that, you rat fuck!" He pulled the trigger and the rat shot back from the end of the taser rod, smoking and very dead.

"That's what I'm talking about." Washington pinned and fried one rat after another as quickly as he could manage. However, his feeling of victory was short-lived. There were just too many rats. He had to…

… run, damn it, RUN!

Washington made a break for the third floor landing. He bounded up the steps, stomping on rats as he went and zapping any that got too close with the taser rod. But they were all too close. Rats began to rip through his boots and into his heels.

He hobbled towards the door to the third floor and reached for the doorknob. Washington's hand, slicked with blood, spun around it like it was a greased ball bearing.

He looked behind him, down the stairwell at what looked like a never-ending wave of rats. He tased as many as he could.

This is it, Washington thought. He pounded his fist on the door and left panicked, red hand prints.

"Fuck!"

THE ELEVATOR DOORS opened onto the third floor. O'Connor, Hope, Sam and Bradley piled out and started down the hallway.

"Did you notice anything strange today," Sam said to Hope. "Any weird noises?"

"No, but I've spent most of the day so far with you guys," Hope said. "She seems to keep to herself, at least since I've been here."

"She wasn't always like that."

"What do you mean?"

"Remember that cat we showed you?" Sam could see the door to apartment 302 looming ahead. "That cat... Piper... was Mrs. Baxter's whole world."

Hope nodded.

The group stopped in front of the door. There was a light on inside. Sam looked at Bradley and tried to shake off the memory of the last time he had knocked on Mrs. Baxter's door. Bradley returned a knowing glance. The significance of the moment was not lost on him either.

O'Connor took out her UV flashlight and scanned the hallway and the baseboards. Bright yellow and magenta streaks fluoresced all the way back to the elevator.

"That doesn't look good," Sam said.

"No shit, Sherlock." O'Connor puffed on her cigar.

"A rat superhighway," Hope said.

"I like that." O'Connor grinned. "You come up with that yourself?"

Hope shrugged.

"I'm gonna steal it," O'Connor said.

Hope avoided O'Connor's gaze. "Whatever."

Bradley approached the door and raised his fist to knock, but paused. "Mrs. Baxter?"

O'Connor spotted something at the base of the door. She dropped to her right knee to get a better look and touched the substance.

"It's blood," O'Connor said.

"But is it human or rat?"

O'Connor stood and raised her blood-smeared fingers to her mouth.

"Shit," Bradley said, disgusted. "You're not going to taste it are you?"

"Gotcha." O'Connor pointed at Bradley and laughed.

"Jesus. Can you be serious for once?" Bradley said. "Show some respect." The words were out of his mouth before he could stop them. He looked at Sam, who gave him a wink and a subtle nod of approval.

O'Connor closed her mouth, and instead gave the blood a couple of quick sniffs. "It's not rat blood."

Something passed fast behind the door and cast a shadow between the bottom of the door and the floor. Then it was gone.

"Did you see that?" Hope pointed at the bottom of the door.

"What?" Sam looked and saw nothing.

Hope shook her head. "It's not there now."

Sam stepped close to the door. "Mrs. Baxter? It's Sam." He turned his head to place his ear on the door to listen.

Silence.

"I'm gonna break it down," O'Connor said.

"The fuck you will." Sam dug into his pockets for his keys. "We don't need any more of your damn bravado."

Sam isolated the key to apartment 302 and unlocked the door. He turned the handle and pushed the door open, but it struck something on the floor inside. The door had opened enough for Sam to see the pool of blood extend into the apartment. He took a step back.

"Allow me," O'Connor said.

Sam stepped aside as O'Connor squeezed in through the partially opened door. She expected fat jokes, but everyone was silent. "Aw, shit." O'Connor had seen dead bodies before, but nothing like this.

MRS. BAXTER LAY dead on her side in the hallway, just behind of the apartment door. Her housecoat trailed at her feet, soaked with blood, and her nightgown was shredded along one side. Strips of flesh had been pulled off her face and one of her breasts appeared to have been half eaten. Blood pooled around her body, and her final struggle to live had left a smeary crimson trail back to the kitchen.

O'Connor took out her UV flashlight and began to scan the kitchen for access points.

Sam popped his head through the partially open door. "Oh, Jesus." Horrified, he turned and stumbled away. He propped himself up against the wall and fought the urge to vomit. He looked at Hope and Bradley. "You don't want to see this."

Hope peered around the door. It took only a moment for

her to absorb the horror of the scene. She raised her hand to her mouth. "Oh my god."

Hope ran partway down the hallway. Sam began to follow her but stopped and faced Bradley.

"Mrs. Baxter was decent folk. She didn't deserve… that." Sam looked back at the pool of blood under the door. "Trust me, Brad. You don't need to see this."

Sam followed after Hope. Bradley looked into the apartment through the door's small opening. He could see one of Mrs. Baxter's bloodied feet and her saturated housecoat, and decided that he didn't want to change his final memory of Mrs. Baxter, as sad as it was.

There was an audible *thump*. At first Bradley thought it was O'Connor rattling around inside Mrs. Baxter's apartment. But it had come from the hallway. He headed after Sam.

"Sorry," Sam said.

"Hey, I'm the idiot who looked." Hope wiped her mouth. "I will never forget that as long as I live."

Bradley joined Sam and Hope. "Did you hear that?"

"What?" Sam cocked his head to one side.

All three fell silent. Barely audible sounds of struggle emanated from the end of the hallway.

"The stairwell." Sam felt the hairs stand up on the back of his neck.

Hope's eyes went wide. "Washington!"

They ran toward the end of the hallway.

Bradley cast all of his thoughts away in favor of one: *Don't be dead. Please don't be dead.*

More distressed noises sounded through the stairwell door next to the elevator. They heard a fist pound on the other side.

Sam and Hope slid to a stop. Sam skidded, lost his footing and landed on his ass.

"Get O'Connor!" Sam said.

Hope turned around and headed back toward Mrs. Baxter's apartment.

Bradley was already on the doorknob, twisting it open. Even with the door open a crack, he saw a wave of rats block the door from opening.

"Dad! Help!"

Sam stood and laid his weight into the door and forced it open further. He tried to ignore the rats that began to spill out from the stairwell and into the hallway.

Washington's arm snaked around the edge of the door and he navigated his way through the opening. His hand still grasped his taser rod. He left bloody hand-prints as he forced himself through. "Brad! What a welcome surprise."

Washington threw himself from the door and into the hallway. "I was ambushed!"

"No shit." Bradley looked at the third floor landing in the stairwell, undulating with rats.

Washington fell out of the stairwell. Rats followed and jumped on his legs and chest. He kicked the rats he could reach, and zapped the rest, but the battery in his taser rod was depleted.

A rat charged past Bradley and over Sam's foot. Fear overtook him. He stepped backward and tripped over his own feet. Sam landed on the floor next to the elevator, paralyzed with terror.

Washington glared at Sam as he brushed off rodents left and right. "Get off your damn ass!"

Bradley held the doorknob tight. He placed his foot on the door frame and pulled with all the strength his sixteen-year-old frame could muster. A mass of rats prevented the door from closing completely.

Sam remained on the floor, frozen in fear. His eyes tracked another rat making a beeline for his crotch.

Washington managed to get on his knees to help Bradley pull the stairwell door closed, but his hands were still slicked with blood. "For fuck's sake get up, or we are going to DIE!" Inside the stairwell, a rising tide of rats pressed against the door, but an equal amount clambered between the door and door frame and kept their progress in limbo.

"Dad! Move your *ASS!*" Bradley's command broke through Sam's veil of terror.

The rat hopped onto Sam's boot. He flung his leg to the side, crushing the rat against the wall in a red furry smear. Sam got to his feet and ran to join Washington and Bradley at the door.

"HOPE!" Sam hooked his hand through the gap in the doorway and pulled on the edge of the door. Even with the three of them, the door wouldn't close. "O'CONNOR!"

Hope and O'Connor burst out of Mrs. Baxter's apartment and ran down the hallway.

"Ramming speed!" O'Connor said as she ran towards the door.

"Wait! You gotta pull—" Washington tried to warn O'Connor but he was too late. He lost his grip when she slammed all her weight into the stairwell door. The sudden burst of force flung the wall of rats back into the stairwell just enough to give them the advantage. The door flew backward, then all five pulled on the doorknob.

O'Connor kicked the rats that regrouped on the landing and between the closing gap of the door. The rats reversed and charged at the gap again, now smaller. The weight of the tsunami of rats behind the door now helped close it. The stairwell door inched toward the door frame like a slow guillotine. The door's blunt blade sliced off heads and popped rat bodies as it was pulled closed.

"Come on, bitches!" O'Connor held the doorknob.

Washington placed one foot against the wall for more leverage. "What if the doorknob falls off?"

"That kind of thinking will get you killed." O'Connor dug her Vibram soles into the hallway carpet. "One more pull… NOW!"

The door popped into the door frame and latched closed. The rats that made it into the hallway tried to scatter. O'Connor and Bradley stomped on as many of them as they could.

"In case you're wondering, the stairwell isn't an option." Washington stood up and winced in pain. Blood began to collect around his feet. "Those bastards are hungry, too."

BRADLEY WASN'T THINKING clearly when he pressed the elevator call button. It may have been the adrenaline in his blood that clouded his thoughts, or the exhilaration of helping to save Washington's life. He could hear the old electrical motors kick in as the elevator began a slow creep to the third floor. And it couldn't be stopped.

"Why the fuck did you do that?" O'Connor's face turned red with anger. "God dammit, kid, you got shit for brains?"

"Hey!" Sam pushed O'Connor backward. "Watch it."

O'Connor took the hint and raised her hands. "Don't get your knickers in a twist." She took the cigar out of her mouth and ejected a plume of acrid smoke. "Didn't mean nothing by it."

"Bullshit," Sam said.

A small smile crept over Bradley's lips as he watched Sam defend him, but the feeling was short lived. The elevator's floor indicator was half-way between the first and second floor.

"Where's your torch?" O'Connor said.

Washington thumbed at the door to the stairs, stained around the side and bottom edges with blood and fur. "Stairwell. And my taser's outta juice."

"Ah, shit." O'Connor clamped the cigar between her teeth and looked at the blood pooling around Washington's feet. "You okay to walk?"

"Think so," Washington said.

"Better know so." O'Connor lit the pilot flame of her propane torch. She cast a wary glance at the elevator's floor indicator as its analog pointer moved past the second floor. "Ready people."

Everyone shuffled to one side of the elevator entrance. They stood in silence, except for the noise of the elevator's century-old electrical motor whirring within the concrete walls, and the hiss of the torch's pilot flame.

The floor indicator hit three.

Ding.

The elevator doors slid open, grinding with resistance.

Nothing.

"Kid, you're up," O'Connor said with a hushed voice. "Check it out."

"My name's Brad, and I'm *not* a kid." Bradley moved past O'Connor and glared at her.

"Well, Brad…" O'Connor said. "You got us into this shit storm, so…"

"Lay off, will yah," Washington said. "I've made worse mistakes."

Bradley moved parallel to the open elevator door. Each slow, deliberate step revealed more of the interior of the car. The more he saw, the more his nerves cooled. The car was empty.

"I don't see any—" Bradley watched one rat run out of the elevator and away from the group. He turned to Sam, Hope, O'Connor and Washington and shrugged. "It's just one rat."

Bradley walked back to join everyone, satisfied with his report. The rat stopped farther down the hallway and reversed its direction back towards the group.

"Why is it coming back?" Hope said.

"What?" Bradley turned to look back. The rat stopped at the open elevator door and stood up on its haunches, whiskers vibrating, eyes like red LEDs.

"Why aren't the doors closing?" No sooner were the words out of Washington's mouth than the elevator alarm bell began to ring. "What the…"

Hope saw the color drain from Sam's face. "Sam, what is it?"

"The elevator only does that if it's overloaded," Sam took a step backward. "We need to get out of here."

"Overloaded?" Bradley said. "With what?"

An avalanche of rats flowed out from a corner of the elevator and spilled into the hallway.

"The fire escape!" Sam led the way. "RUN!"

Bradley looked back at the mass of brown, oily fur filling the hallway. "Oh shit!"

Hope and Bradley helped Washington hobble towards the fire escape. His boots left bloody footprints on the floor as they went. O'Connor trailed the group and blasted a jet of flame at the rats when they got too close.

Sam arrived at the fire escape first. He unlocked the latch and tried to open the window leading out. It wouldn't budge. The rest of the group arrived moments later.

"What's the holdup?" Washington looked back at the rats closing in on them.

"The window." Sam pulled with all his strength. "It's stuck."

Washington joined Sam at the window, and pulled. The window broke free and slammed up into the top of the window frame. Sam swung his legs through, then turned to help Bradley out.

The loose nut that held the fire escape's third level to the building rattled and rotated with Sam and Bradley's every panicked step.

O'Connor sent a short blast of fire down the hallway, but it only slowed the rats at the front. "Hurry up, people. Today, we're on the menu."

Hope climbed through the window, then turned to help Sam pull Washington through. He collapsed in a corner of the fire escape platform. The nut rotated a quarter turn, then a half turn more. The fire escape platform strained under the weight of four people.

O'Connor swung her right leg over the window sill. Rats swarmed and scaled her left leg. She fired a burst of flame at the rats on her leg. The closest ones scrambled to get away and exposed the floor again. But a flame ignited the cuff of her pants.

"That's an interesting technique," Sam said.

"You ain't seen nothing yet." O'Connor grinned around her cigar.

As soon as the flame stopped, the rats resumed their attack and leapt onto her boot. She swung her leg up toward the window sill and knocked her boot against the frame. She sent the rats to the floor again and extinguished the flames on her cuff, all at the same time.

"It pays to have a fake leg sometimes." O'Connor hopped onto the fire escape. The securing nut continued to loosen, half a turn at a time now. She reached up and tried to close the window, but it was stuck. Again.

Rats advanced up the wall towards the window sill.

"Come on, you son of a whore!" O'Connor pulled on the bottom of the sliding window.

Sam backed away from the sill. "Just let them fall."

"The whole point is to kill the bastards." O'Connor yanked on the window again. It moved a quarter of an inch. "Falling three stories would only piss them off."

A rat appeared on the window sill. Then another.

"They're climbing out!" Hope said.

"Thanks for the update, egghead." O'Connor lifted her legs off the fire escape platform so the window bore all her weight. The window remained open. Two more rats scrittered onto the window sill. "Close, you piece of... SHIT!"

Hope joined O'Connor at the window and pulled with both of their weight. It was just enough to tip the scales. The window slammed down and crushed the four rats on the sill with a wet *pop*.

Blood and guts sprayed onto everyone, but most of it landed on Hope. She wiped her face in a mad frenzy, but some of the detritus dripped into her mouth before she could wipe it away.

"Ugh! Get it off—"

The nut that secured the top right side of the fire escape spun off the threads of its anchoring bolt and flew off into the summer sky. The strain of five people on the platform sheared off the three remaining bolts that supported the right side. In an instant, the bloody entrails on Hope's face didn't matter anymore.

THE RIGHT SIDE of the fire escape peeled away from the building and twisted the platform against the left side, still anchored to the exterior of the building. The stairs that led down to the second level detached from the platform and fell like a hinged trap door. Everyone dropped to their knees and scrambled for something to hang on to.

O'Connor stepped off the right side and grabbed the downspout. "Over here! Quick!"

The weight of the rest of the group was too much for the platform to bear. With the left side of the platform almost twisted into a helix, the stress ripped the four remaining bolts on the left side out of the exterior, one after another, leaving cracked and crumbling holes in the old brick.

Loaded like the kill arm of a snap trap, the third floor fire escape platform flipped down, hinged to the wall by rusty bolts at the base that were never meant to bend.

Washington joined O'Connor at the downspout. "Where's Brad?"

Sam crawled along the bars of the vertical railing, which

was now the floor. Through the rungs, he spotted Bradley hanging from the right side.

"How the hell did you get down there?" Sam said.

"I don't know." Bradley's knuckles gripped a rung from the railing. "It flipped me over."

"Hold on!" The railing bent under Sam's weight as he moved toward Bradley. He noticed the spot where he had started welding repairs.

Brad looked down. "I could jump down to the next level. It's not that far."

Sam shook his head. "If this goes, it'll take the lower platforms with it."

"Missy!" O'Connor held out her arm towards Hope, who clung to the side of the building. Their hands locked around each other's forearms and O'Connor swung Hope to the downspout. "Don't get any ideas."

Hope latched onto the downspout and dug the toes of her Vans into the mortar grooves between bricks. "No chance of that."

"Can you grab him?" Washington said.

Sam arrived at the end of the railing and climbed around the right end. He crouched and reached toward Bradley.

"Brad!" Sam locked eyes with Bradley. In the prospect of possible death, they saw who they were and who they would become. "Grab my hand!"

Bradley stretched his arm out and reached as far as he could with one hand. "Dad! I'm going to fall!"

"No, you're not."

The remaining bolts, corroded and probably a hundred years old or more, pulled free from their brick anchor spots. One by one, like unsnapping a denim shirt, the bolts released the weight of the third floor fire escape and jolted everything downward.

Bradley lost grip in his remaining hand and started to fall, but Sam grabbed his hand just in time.

"Sam!" Hope reached out from the downspout.

With Bradley in one hand and the shuddering railing in the other, Sam took a breath to shore himself up. He let go of the railing and pushed off toward Hope. He grabbed her hand and formed a human chain. The weight of Sam and Bradley combined almost pulled Hope's arm out of its socket, but she held out long enough to swing them to the downspout.

A split-second later the third floor fire escape ripped out of the building's exterior and took the second and first escape landings with it. The old, rusted iron structure landed three stories below in a crush of tangled metal next to the dumpster.

"Holy shit." Sam stared at the wreckage below in amazement. *I could have been down there, impaled on the wreckage. Everyone could have.*

"Everybody okay?" O'Connor said.

Bradley gripped the downspout tight. "I think so."

"Now what, genius?" Washington's blood-soaked boots slicked his footing.

"We climb down." O'Connor blew a puff of cigar smoke into the warm breeze. "Slowly."

"You sure about that, Missy?" Hope pointed up the downspout to the roof. "Look."

Rats poked their heads over the edge along the roof line and scurried back and forth. White-tipped tails curled and snapped. Some tested their footing on the building's brick exterior, but retreated to the safety of the ledge.

"How the fuck did they get up there so fast?" Washington said.

"They've got runs everywhere," Hope said. "Now they're choosing the best route to get to us."

"Yeah…" O'Connor looked up. "Okay, people. Let's pick up the pace."

One step at a time, the group began to lower themselves toward the ground. Sam had started his descent as soon as he saw the rats on the roof. It didn't take much to convince Bradley to move as well. It wasn't long before everyone heard the scratching sounds within the downspout. It acted as an amplifier. The rats continued their pursuit within the confines of the downspout, inch by dirty inch.

A piece of downspout, eroded from years of rain and neglect, tore open in front of Washington. Rats spilled out onto his chest. In his panic, Washington lost his grip and fell backward.

O'Connor reached out for his sleeve, but missed. "Grab his foot!"

With one hand, Hope locked onto Washington's boot as he fell backward. She slowed his descent but couldn't stop him as his blood-slicked boot slipped away.

Sam was next in the chain. He reached out with his free arm, snagged Washington's boot in the crook between his forearm and bicep, and pulled him in. O'Connor kicked the downspout breach, crimped its opening and stopped the flow of rats.

Washington hung upside down, facing Bradley. His pendant dangled down off his neck. "This is some fucked up shit, eh Brad?"

"Yeah." Bradley managed a half smile.

"Quit the chit chat," O'Connor said. "Get your asses moving."

"Wait." Washington followed the downspout to where it ended at the second floor, just below Bradley's feet. Rats that remained in the lower part of the downspout escaped onto the brick wall and clambered to the ground, where they scattered into the corners of the alley. "There's no more downspout."

"What do you mean, *there's no more?*" O'Connor said.

"It just ends," Washington said. "Back me up, Brad."

Bradley looked past his feet. "He's right."

O'Connor shot a glance at Sam.

"What?" Sam said. "It's on my list."

Washington looked past Bradley and toward the fire escape window below. "I think I can reach the second floor."

"You *think?*" O'Connor said.

Washington tried to reach the window, but he was less than a foot short. "Sam, lower me down a bit and swing me over," he said. "And hurry. My head feels like it's gonna explode."

"Gee you don't ask for much." Sam kept Washington's boot locked in the crook of his arm and navigated down to a lower ledge in the brick exterior.

Bradley shimmied down to make room, but had no more downspout to secure himself to.

"Dad, I can't go any farther."

"Okay," Sam said. "Washington, you're going to have to swing yourself."

Washington began to rock himself back and forth at his hips. His body swayed toward the second floor window and each time, his fingers came within inches.

The boot in Sam's grasp slipped. "Try harder. I can't hold you forever."

"What do you think I'm doing?" Washington reached out and missed the window again. The pressure of blood in his head from hanging upside down began to cloud his thoughts and coordination.

"Push him," Hope said.

"Hope's right." O'Connor looked down at Hope, then past to Bradley. "Give him a shove in the right direction, kid."

"That's the first time you've used my name." A subtle grin traveled across Hope's lips.

"Don't get used to it." O'Connor averted her eyes.

Hope nodded. "I get it. You're just a big teddy bear in disguise."

"Shut up," O'Connor hissed at Hope. She tried to blow cigar smoke at Hope, but it was carried away in the summer breeze.

Hope released one of her hand's grip on the downspout, and raised her middle finger at O'Connor.

Bradley timed his pushes to coincide with the apex of Washington's swings. The first push almost worked. The second got Washington even closer.

"One more time, Brad," Washington said.

Bradley pushed with all his strength. Washington swung closer but missed the window by an inch.

"Again, Brad. Fourth time's a charm."

Brad summoned what little energy he had left and focused it into one large push. Washington sailed in an arc towards the window now within reach. This was his only chance.

Washington clawed his fingers into the wood of the window frame. "Got it!"

"Great. Now open it, you fat fuck." O'Connor was back to her usual self.

Washington pulled, but the second floor window didn't move. "Uh, Sam. Are these windows locked?"

Sam closed his eyes in frustration. "Shit."

"What? Are you serious?" O'Connor said.

"It's a bad neighborhood," Sam said. "Security's important."

Sounds of smashed glass distracted Sam and O'Connor before they could go at each other's throats. Washington had taken his flashlight and smashed the window pane. He unlocked the latch and pulled the window open.

Washington pulled his body towards the open window and secured his grasp on the sill. "Sam, let me go."

"What? No way," Sam said.

"Just do it before I pass out."

"You're sure—"

Washington's patience ran out. "For fuck's sake, man, let me go!"

Sam released Washington's boot. Gravity took hold and his legs swung down. He fell hard against the bottom of the sill. The impact knocked the wind out of him, but Washington maintained his grip on the inside of the window. He pulled himself into the building.

A minute passed. Then two minutes.

"Washington?" Bradley said. "You okay?"

Washington popped his head out of the window, a shit-eating grin on his face. "Which one of you motherfuckers is next?"

Kill-O-Matic

Sam worked up his courage to get closer to the collapsible cage on the kitchen counter. The sounds of claws and teeth on metal sent a shiver down his spine. The rat inside was determined to escape. Sam moved close enough to get a good look.

The rat stopped its attempts to escape temporarily and stared at Sam with its red glowing eyes and twitching whiskers. Sam stared back.

"What makes their eyes red like that?"

O'Connor reclined in a kitchen chair, propped feet on the table and blew smoke rings. She looked at Hope "You want to field that one?"

Hope stood beside Sam and crouched to the level of the cage. "It's just a lack of pigment. Just like your eyes are brown and mine are blue."

Sam looked at Hope's eyes, which were indeed blue. A deep, almost azure blue. There it was again. A spark of something. Both Sam and Hope felt it. A light flush rose on Hope's cheeks before she looked back at the rat.

"But it's more than just the red." Sam cast his eyes back on the rat in the cage. "The eyes seem to glow, and I'm not talking reflected light and all that."

"I don't know." Hope stood up. "Maybe it's a genetic mutation."

The rat returned to its gnawing with incisors stronger than the steel cage that imprisoned it. Sam could have sworn that the metal bars had become thinner during the time he had been watching.

"Anyone getting the feeling that these little bastards have got it in for us…" Sam said, "just as much as we do for them?"

"Yeah, well not for long." O'Connor stood up. "Washington, gimme a hand."

O'Connor and Washington moved the kitchen table and the chairs to one side of the room. Each grabbed an end of the diamond-plated metal box and positioned it in the center of the room.

"The secret weapon. Finally." Bradley watched with interest and took out his phone to take a photo.

O'Connor held out her hand. "No photos, kid."

"What?" Bradley's face mixed surprise and disappointment.

"Just like you said." O'Connor gnawed at her cigar. "Our secret weapon."

"I thought you were joking," Bradley said.

"I never joke about our secret weapon." O'Connor remained stone-faced. "Put the camera away."

Washington leaned next to Bradley's ear. "She's busting your balls, Brad."

Bradley looked a question at O'Connor.

"He's right." O'Connor laughed. "Just fucking with yah, kid. Take all the pictures you want."

"Bitch," Bradley said under his breath.

"What was that, kid?" O'Connor continued to laugh. "You say something?"

"Take your photos, Brad." Washington said. "What we got here ain't no secret." He unfastened the latches and raised the lid. Spray-painted inside, in crude hand-lettering, were the words "Kill-O-Matic."

"That inspires confidence," Hope said.

Bradley shot Hope a smile and took a photo with his phone.

O'Connor and Washington unfolded the contents of the box in a very precise and specific sequence. It was poetry in motion. The cage assembled itself like a choreographed ballet, one with blood, dirt and cigar smoke.

Sam, Hope and Bradley preoccupied themselves with the Detest-A-Pest construction project in the kitchen. The toilet secured with duct tape was a distant memory. But the rats hadn't forgotten. Moist and slimy snouts and whiskers twitched and poked out from between the toilet seat and the bowl's rim. Teeth gnawed the duct tape, tearing strips away one strand at a time. As rats worked from both sides of the tape, their progress doubled. Soon, the rodents would be unencumbered again.

O'Connor and Washington lifted the unfolded contents of the box from its center. A large cage, six feet on all sides, snapped into place. Its walls were made of quarter-inch steel mesh, with smaller insulated windows inset at the top on all four sides. Under one window was a narrow door that opened outward.

Bradley stared at the cage as Washington locked the final sides in place. "That's the secret weapon? A cage?" As he walked around the cage, taking it all in, he could see traces of fur stuck to the mesh and detected a faint acrid odor of burned metal… and something else. "It's just a larger version of that other cage."

"Yeah, but this baby lights up." O'Connor smiled as she held up a power cord. "Twenty thousand volts at four amps. Enough juice to kill us all in less than a second."

"So it's just a big electrocution chamber?" Hope said.

"Give Missy a cigar." O'Connor blew smoke across the kitchen, towards Hope.

"Great. Can't wait," Hope said, unimpressed. "Speaking of cigars, you said you'd show me how to blow smoke rings."

"Yeah, and my answer was *maybe later*."

Hope held out her hand. "Okay, I'll take my cigar now, then." She grinned, sly and satisfied. "For safe keeping."

"Nobody's getting my last Cohiba," O'Connor said.

Hope's tone flipped from playful to serious. "Missy's won a cigar, and Missy wants her cigar NOW."

Bradley heard something beyond Hope and O'Connor's bickering. *A tapping?* He looked at the small cage on the counter, but the rat inside wasn't matching the sound. He looked to everyone's feet, but other than the occasional step, everyone was standing still.

In the bathroom, the rats had broken through the duct tape on one side of the toilet. The toilet seat flipped up and down. Its rubber supports made soft *clacking* sounds on the toilet bowl, as slick, waterlogged rats forced their way out, two, three, five at a time. Other rats continued to gnaw on the remaining duct tape that held the toilet closed.

"You think you're so smart," Hope said. "You don't know shit."

A hush fell over the kitchen as Sam, Bradley and

Washington watched the stand-off between Hope and O'Connor.

Clack. Clack… Clack.

"I know you're a white-bread, privileged bitch with a silver spoon stuck up her ass." O'Connor spit on the floor, the gob landing close to Hope's boots. "You've never worked an honest day in your life."

Washington began to laugh, shattering the tension in the kitchen. "You two are entertaining as shit, but we got a job to do."

"Shut up," O'Connor said.

"No, *you* shut up!" Bradley drew his fingers into tight fists, but his fists were trembling. "And listen."

"Kid, you need to—"

"LISTEN!" Bradley's face went pale as he looked at Washington. "The toilet."

Washington nodded and thumbed at Bradley. "You ought to be giving Brad the cigar."

The *clacking* sounds were more prominent, more rapid.

"O'Connor." Washington motioned for her to join him as he limped into the hallway towards the bathroom. Sam, Bradley and Hope followed. Washington pushed open the bathroom door. It swung open in a slow arc. Rats were everywhere, leaping from the toilet to the floor of the bathroom. The remaining duct tape had been chewed through, allowing easy escape.

Hundreds of red rodent eyes spotted Washington and O'Connor at the door to the bathroom. In one coordinated charge, the rats surged for the door.

"I'm getting tired of this bullshit." Washington unhooked his taser rod. O'Connor closed the bathroom door, but the rats began to squeeze underneath. As they passed under, the rats took bites out of the wood and enlarged the gap under the door. The floodgates had opened.

Washington tased as many rats as he could but there were just too many, too fast. He backed down the hallway towards the bedroom.

Hope stepped back. "It's the laundry room all over again."

"Yeah, but we got better toys this time," O'Connor said. "Push the cage door toward me."

Sam and Bradley slid the cage around and positioned the door facing the hallway. The hundreds of rats ignored everyone, except Washington. They followed the scent of his blood on the floor left by his boots.

"They seem to have issues with you," O'Connor said.

"Karma's a bitch." Washington zapped rats left, right and center, but he couldn't keep up. The horde swarmed his feet. Dozens began to claw their way up his pants. Every time Washington zapped a rat, the horde became more enraged.

"We're not going to be able to kill them all before they get to us," he said. "There's too many."

"What do you suggest, genius?" O'Connor glared at Washington at the end of the hallway.

"Fuck it." Washington dropped the taser rod and ran toward the cage. Rats that fell off his clothes joined the wet, furry mass at his feet and continued their pursuit. Washington entered the cage. The horde followed right behind to join him, already overtaking him and biting into his legs. He yanked his pendant from his neck.

"Brad! Catch!" Washington threw the pendant out of the

cage, where it bounced down the hallway. He grabbed the cage door and pulled it shut, locking it.

"What are you doing?" O'Connor said.

"Punching out. I've had enough of this bullshit." Washington's gaze locked with O'Connor. "Been nice knowing you."

"What? No! Don't do it!" Bradley grabbed the cage and rattled it.

"Let go of the cage, Brad." A hundred rats climbed up Washington's body and bit and ripped into the flesh on his hands and arms. He winced and tried to hold back the pain. "Let go and step back."

Tears spilled down Bradley's cheeks as he stepped back. His foot struck the pendant on the floor of the hallway. He knelt down, picked it up and held it tight in his right hand.

Washington looked at O'Connor. "For fuck's sake, turn it on."

O'Connor stared in disbelief, struck by how quickly her world could implode. Detest-A-Pest wasn't just herself. It was Washington too.

"You don't get to make this choice." Washington watched O'Connor's emotional armor begin to fall apart.

"That's suicide!" Hope turned to Sam. "Do something!"

Sam tried to approach the cage, but even with it locked, the rats inside with their red eyes, oily fur and white-tipped tails placed shackles of fear on him.

Washington turned to Sam and Hope. "It's okay. Y'know, the needs of the many, and all that shit." He returned his stare to O'Connor. "Now turn in on!"

"No. It's not okay," O'Connor said. "It's weak."

Frenzied rats consumed with blood lust burrowed into Washington's shoulders and back. He collapsed to his knees, gritting his teeth. "Either you turn it on, or you watch me get eaten alive. If we swapped places, I know what you'd want."

O'Connor stared at Washington as he continued to be ravaged by rats. She plugged the power cord to the cage with one hand, and held the remote switch in the other. Her hand trembled over the power switch.

"You're a real bastard, you know that?" O'Connor said. Sam could see her fighting back tears, but it was hard to tell if it was because of anger or sorrow. Either way, it chipped away at O'Connor's tough exterior and made her seem a little more human.

"Washington!" Bradley stepped forward, hands reaching for the cage. "You—"

"Don't touch it!" Sam pulled Bradley away from the cage. "It's live!"

Washington knelt, then leaned to one side in the cage. He could no longer maneuver himself on his own. Rats continued to bore into his flesh. Now on the back of his head, they ripped his scalp in strips with ruthless efficiency. "Brad… Come here, Brad."

Bradley walked around the cage so Washington could see him. His blood flowed around his nose and stung his eyes.

"Closer." Washington's voice rasped, a whisper of what it used to be.

Bradley stepped closer to the cage, but still within a safe distance. Sam stood behind, hands on Bradley's shoulders. He didn't know if he was providing Bradley comfort, but he couldn't think of anything else to do.

"Brad." Washington's voice wheezed. "Been a pleasure meeting you as brief as it was. You're a good kid… I mean man. A good man. Put on your *brave* mask." Washington rolled towards the inside of the cage. "C'mon you bastards! I'll see you in HELL!"

Rats crested the top of Washington's head and dug into his face. They pulled, bit, tore away at his flesh in a blood-fueled frenzy. He raised his shredded hands in weak protest, then fell backwards into the cage, swallowed up in the slickened crimson horde.

Hope ran to O'Connor. "For fuck's sake DO SOMETHING!"

"You want to turn it on?" O'Connor thrust the cage's remote to Hope, her hand shaking. "Be my guest."

Washington struggled and screamed, unseen under the mass of squirming fur. It was a scream of a dying man with no options left.

"I'll be damned if I'm going to let him get eaten alive." Sam looked at O'Connor. "Do it!"

O'Connor couldn't find the courage to commit. Sam placed his hand over hers, on the remote's switch. "This is the only way, now."

O'Connor nodded, tears overflowing.

"Brad, look away." Sam pressed the 'ON' switch on the remote, and held O'Connor's gaze. There was no going back.

Hope took Bradley aside and crouched, facing away from the cage, both in tears.

The light in the kitchen dimmed. Rats squealed, smoked and popped. The soles of Washington's boots melted into the cage floor and burst into flames. No escape for man or beast.

All told, the cage was live for less than fifteen seconds, but to everyone outside the cage, it felt like an eternity. Sam helped O'Connor turn the cage off. Just to be safe, Sam unplugged the cage as well.

What was left of Washington lay in the center of a blanket of charred rat bodies. Smoke, silence and the god-awful smell of burned hair and flesh hung heavy in Sam's kitchen.

O'CONNOR WAS NOMINATED by default to remove the dead rats. It was what she was hired for, after all. She took one last drag from her cigar and jettisoned the smoke into the cage where it hung around her head like a halo. She rubbed out the cigar's ember on the back of a dead rat and threw the stub into an open garbage bag.

Bradley watched her go to work. She pulled scorched bodies off the cage and placed them into the bag. Most of the time, O'Connor was able to remove the rats with her gloved hands, but the odd rat required a garden trowel to dig it out of the wire mesh. It was a gruesome spectacle, and once Washington became more visible, Bradley had to look away. After an hour, O'Connor had filled four garbage bags with rat bodies.

"That's just the tip of the iceberg," O'Connor said. "From what we saw on the third floor, there's hundreds more. Maybe thousands."

"I think you're going to need a bigger cage." Sam looked at O'Connor, uncertain.

"Maybe." O'Connor looked at Washington in the cage, except to her it wasn't Washington anymore. It was just burned gore in human form. "I'm going to need your help getting Washington's body out of the cage. You up for it?"

"How do you do it?" Sam stared at O'Connor with a baffled look.

"What?"

"Just turn it off." Sam studied O'Connor. "It's like nothing happened. Washington is *dead*."

"This is a job. I'll grieve on my own time." O'Connor remained stoic. "So, are you gonna help me or not?"

"I guess I'm the only option left," Sam said. "I don't want Brad to do it, and I don't think you want Hope's help."

"Okay." O'Connor tossed Sam a pair of gloves. "It's you and me. You might want to throw on a pair of coveralls."

"Oh, so now you offer me coveralls."

O'Connor shook her head and shrugged indifference. "I didn't say I was supplying them."

"Fuck it," Sam said. "I'll throw away these clothes when we're done."

In the TV room, Bradley unhooked the television and unplugged it from the wall. Hope positioned herself on one side of the television and Bradley on the opposite. Together they lifted the old television up.

"This thing weighs a ton." Hope strained against the television's bulk.

Together they shuffled it out into the hallway, then into the bathroom. They placed it on top of the toilet seat, which creaked under the television's weight.

"Those rat fucks aren't getting in now." Bradley scowled and kicked the base of the toilet.

When Hope and Bradley returned to the kitchen, Sam and O'Connor had the remains of Washington's body halfway out of the cage. Sam carried his legs and O'Connor, still in the cage, lifted him up under his arms. Washington's charred body lolled like a rag doll. What was left of his right hand dragged along the bottom of the cage.

Sam nodded to the garbage bags full of rat carcasses. "Can you guys take those bags to the dumpster?"

Bradley and Hope didn't protest. They tried to grab two bags each, but the bags were too heavy. They settled on two trips with one bag each and headed out the door. Bradley led the way.

"A BAG FULL of rats is heavier than I thought it would be," Hope said. "This has got to be at least forty or fifty pounds."

Bradley was surprised by the weight as well, but remained silent and hid his struggle.

The mound of crumpled fire escape was a spectacle to see from the ground. Hope and Bradley gave it a wide berth.

"Hard to believe we were up there, moments ago." Hope followed the line of the downspout from the third to the second floor. "Shit, that's high up."

"Lots of things happened moments ago," Bradley said. Halfway to the dumpster, his bag developed a leak. An errant pair of incisors had poked a hole in the bag. Blood and guts began to trickle out.

"You got a rip," Hope said.

Bradley turned and flung the bag around. It left a trail of viscera on the alley pavement. "What?"

"Your bag. It's got a rip." Hope pointed at the pavement. "And it's leaking."

They both reached the dumpster and set their bags down.

"You better not throw it in," Hope said, "or the bag's going to break."

"Just shut up with your advice." Bradley swung his bag around and up toward the lip of the dumpster. It hit the edge and broke open, just as Hope had predicted. Most of the rats spilled into the dumpster, but about two dozen cascaded down onto the pavement. "FUCK!"

Bradley broke down, tears breaching his eyelids. He clenched his fists and paced back and forth. "Why'd he have to die?"

All Hope had to do was touch Bradley's shoulder. He turned and hugged her, much to her surprise. Hope knew right away that it wasn't a romantic hug, but one of sorrow and loss, so she hugged him back. "I don't know, Brad." Tears formed in her eyes as well. She hadn't needed to know Washington long to know he was a good man.

Bradley buried his sobs in her shirt. They stood in the alley and took comfort in each other, processing what had just happened. Hope waited until Bradley was done.

He sniffled and pulled away. "Sorry."

"You don't need to be sorry," Hope said. "I know you liked Washington. He was cool."

"Don't tell my dad." Bradley wiped his face. "You know, about me crying."

"Secret's safe with me." Hope smiled and wiped a tear from her cheek. "By the way, women like men who aren't afraid to show their emotions. Remember that. Now help me get this bag into the dumpster."

Hope grabbed the tied end and Bradley took the bottom and together they heaved the remaining bag of rats into the dumpster.

"I guess we got to clean up the rest," Hope said.

"Guess so." Bradley spotted some paper wrappers from Kingsley Fried Chicken beside the dumpster and grabbed them. He placed one over a rat carcass and picked it up. "If you don't look at it, it feels like a drumstick."

"New addition to the menu." Hope took the other paper wrapper. "Kingsley Fried Rat…"

"And pizza," Bradley looked at Hope. They both burst out laughing.

Working together, the spilled rat bodies were back in the dumpster in no time. They headed back to Sam's apartment for their second load. Bradley was more careful the second time.

SAM HELPED O'CONNOR shroud Washington's body in a bed sheet. They placed him against the wall in the hallway. Blood seeped through the sheets in spots and left the edges of the shroud peppered with crimson stains.

Bradley and Hope returned from the dumpster. They cast Sam and O'Connor a mournful glance before moving past the cage to the kitchen. Hope's stomach lurched at the odor of charred hair and coppery blood, still heavy in the air.

She pulled open a window and stuck her head out. Facing the alley, she got a noseful of the dumpster below, which wasn't any better.

Been there, done that.

Hope closed the window again.

O'Connor knelt in front of Washington's body. Sam placed his hand on O'Connor's shoulder and gave it a light squeeze, then stood and walked down the hallway to join Hope and Bradley in the kitchen.

O'Connor rested her hand on Washington's shrouded head. "You had to go and be a god damned hero, didn't yah?" She crossed herself, an automatic reaction. O'Connor didn't realize she was doing it until the gesture was done. "And here I am getting all fuckin' religious. You woulda laughed your ass off." O'Connor wanted to cry, but she was too angry. "It shoulda been me, god damn it. I'll get these motherfuckers if it's the last thing I do."

To her surprise, a tear did manage to squeeze out from the corner of one eye. "You have my word." O'Connor said.

The kitchen table was still pushed over to one side of the room. Hope and Bradley sat and stared at the Kill-O-Matic, their eyes vacant, but their brains busy trying to block unwanted memories they would hold for a lifetime.

Sam flipped a chair around and sat in it backward.

"You two okay?" Sam said. "Brad?"

Bradley nodded, his enthusiasm drained. He held Washington's pendant tight in his hands.

"That was the worst thing I have ever seen," Hope said.

O'Connor entered the kitchen. "I'd reserve judgment, if I were you."

"Don't you ever say anything positive?" Hope said.

"Just being realistic." O'Connor said.

"We should call an ambulance." Sam looked toward the hallway. "With Baxter on the third floor and now Washington—"

"That can wait. We need to act now." O'Connor spotted a dead rat she had missed still stuck inside the cage. "We don't have much time. For every rat we just fried, there's ten or more somewhere else. We need to bait the rest. They're hungry, so it should be easy."

Hope watched O'Connor climb into the cage. The dead rat was frozen in a death pose, stuck to one corner of the cage. She grabbed the tail and pulled. The fur and skin remained attached to the cage, as the body slipped out in a red, greasy clump.

"I think I'm going to be sick." Hope ran for the kitchen sink and vomited into it. She turned on the water to try and rinse her mouth, but its brief spray turned to a trickle almost instantly.

O'Connor worked at the fur and skin embedded in the cage with her trowel. "Everyone's got to toughen up, right fuckin' now, or we're not going to win this." She poked her head out of the cage door. "You hearing me?"

The old O'Connor was back. She was done with mourning. She wanted payback and she wanted it now.

CAMPFIRE

O'CONNOR LIFTED UP an unmarked plastic tub and placed it on the kitchen table. She looked at Bradley. "Hey, kid. Grab the little metal bucket from one of the duffels, will yah?"

Bradley looked straight at O'Connor and ignored her.

"What are you, deaf?" O'Connor said.

"No. I'm not deaf." Bradley stood his ground.

"Then move your ass."

Sam was about to react when Hope grabbed his arm. She shook her head.

"Let him go," Hope said into Sam's ear. "He's stronger than you think."

"I'm not a kid," Bradley said.

O'Connor cocked her head in condescension. "For fuck's sake, I'll get it my—"

"I'm NOT a kid." Bradley took a step towards O'Connor and grabbed her arm. "If you want my help, treat me with some respect. And you'll call me Brad."

O'Connor blinked, taken aback by Bradley's sudden outburst. She looked at Hope and Sam, but they offered no help. "When did yah grow balls, k… uh, Brad?"

Sam crossed his arms and smiled. "That's my son." He looked at Hope and bumped fists. "Thanks."

Hope nodded.

"Alright." O'Connor said. "Brad. Could you grab the little metal bucket from one of the duffels?"

"Was that so hard?" Bradley walked to the duffel bags and dug through them. It didn't take long to find the metal bucket and bring it back to the table.

O'Connor gritted her teeth. She didn't like being upstaged, but the alternative would have been worse. She peeled back the lid of the plastic tub to reveal a brownish-gray sludge.

To Sam, it looked like shit on a bad day. "What the hell is *that*?"

"Custom-made rat bait." O'Connor smiled as she scooped out the concoction and placed it in the metal bucket. "Peanut butter, scrambled egg and a bunch of other proprietary stuff. Nectar of the Gods, if you're a rat." Her smile faltered. "Washington was the brains behind it. Like a lot of the things you see around here."

"You should sell it on-line," Bradley said. "A website and some social media, and you'd be set."

"Maybe I will. Know any Internet gurus?" O'Connor smirked at Bradley.

"A few." Bradley smiled back.

O'Connor grabbed the bucket and placed it at the back wall of the cage. She unfolded a small ramp from the side of the bucket and positioned it leading to the bucket's rim. "Hey, Brad. A little help moving the cage?"

O'Connor had been hiding behind a shield of machismo for so long, she had forgotten how good it felt to be civil, towards Bradley, or anyone really. And civility bred camaraderie, something everyone needed now. Bradley trotted over to take one side of the cage. Together, they slid the cage's open door to face the underbelly of the kitchen sink.

"Is this O'Connor, version two?" Sam said.

O'Connor sent Sam a sly grin. "Maybe. Can I swear and be civil too? Not sure I can give it all up."

"Anything's possible," Sam said.

Hope looked at the cage. "Now what do we do?"

"We wait," O'Connor said.

"You know…" Hope smiled. "You promised to show me how to blow smoke rings."

"Fuck." O'Connor sighed. "Alright."

SAM PACED BACK and forth beside the cage. His eyes flitted back and forth from the bucket of "bait" to the entrance of the cage. Bradley, Hope and O'Connor sat around the kitchen table, some bottles of water between them. O'Connor took out her last cigar and ran it under her nose.

"Ahhh. Now that's a cigar. Smell it." O'Connor handed the cigar to Hope, who took a quick a sniff. "No, really take it in."

Hope sniffed along the length of the cigar. She didn't find it appealing, but went along with it. She didn't want to disappoint O'Connor now. Hope handed the cigar to Bradley, who sniffed the length of the cigar as well.

O'Connor looked at the two from across the table. "What do you smell?"

"An old barnyard," Hope said.

"Yeah," Bradley said, "with fresh dirt on top."

"Interesting." O'Connor closed her eyes and smelled the

cigar again, enjoying its aroma. "I smell freshly seeded fields after a rain. Everyone smells something a little different."

Sam stopped his pacing. "Why aren't they coming?"

O'Connor bit the end off the tip of the cigar and spat it across the kitchen. "Relax. Give it some time." She sparked her lighter into a broad flame and toasted the end of the cigar. She drew air through with quick puffs until the end of the cigar glowed its familiar orange.

"Okay." O'Connor jettisoned a thick, smoky cloud. "Number one rule. Don't inhale the smoke. Just hold it in your mouth, savor it and blow it out. If you inhale, you're probably going to blow chunks into the sink again. Or get nicotine poisoning. Or both." O'Connor punctuated with another puff. "Got it?"

Hope and Bradley nodded.

"And no drooling on the end," O'Connor said. "You wouldn't do that with a joint, so don't do it with a cigar." O'Connor held the cigar out to Hope. "Take a puff."

Hope took the cigar and placed it to her lips. She drew smoke into her mouth, then coughed it out again. "Sorry. Let me try again."

Bradley watched Hope's cheeks turn concave as she pulled smoke into her mouth. She held it for a second before blowing it out, coughing at the last moment.

O'Connor looked at Bradley. "Now you try."

Bradley took the cigar from Hope, placed it to his lips. Instead of holding the hot smoke in his mouth, Bradley inhaled. He dropped the cigar on the table and burst into a coughing fit.

"You corrupting my son?" Sam still paced.

"Guilty as charged." O'Connor grabbed the cigar and looked at Bradley. "Try again."

Bradley waved his hand. "No thanks. I'm done." He tried to clear his throat, as he sputtered and wheezed. "I don't know how you can smoke that. It tastes horrible." He grabbed a bottle of water and took a couple of gulps.

Hope looked at Bradley. His face looked a little green, like characters in the cartoons she had watched as a kid. "I dunno. It tasted a bit spicy to me."

"Yep. Lots of different flavors." O'Connor took a puff. "On to smoke rings. The first thing you gotta do is open your mouth like you're sucking cock."

Sam shot O'Connor a look. "Language."

O'Connor shrugged. "Sorry. Sue me. That's the best way to describe it. So open your mouth, like this." O'Connor opened her mouth in an "O" shape.

Hope mimicked O'Connor. Bradley looked at both of them. His mind raced places he didn't want it to go.

"I'll just watch." Bradley blushed.

"Oh, you're one of *those* types, huh?" O'Connor laughed.

"What types?"

"Never mind, Brad. Just bustin' your balls." O'Connor looked at Hope. "Now where were we?"

"Pretending to suck cock," Hope said.

"Oh yeah, sucking cock." O'Connor smirked at Brad. "That sound right to you?"

Bradley's cheeks were a rosy shade of red. "*Pretending* to…"

Sam stopped his pacing and stood at one end of the table. Hope and O'Connor looked at him watching them. "I'm one of *those* types… that likes to watch." Sam grinned.

"Figures. Okay. Mouth open, jaw down." O'Connor demonstrated for a second. "Then you stick your tongue up to the center of your mouth and hold it there." She repeated the action with her tongue. "To make a smoke ring, you jerk your jaw up. Pretty simple, really."

O'Connor drew in smoke from the cigar and demonstrated for real, mouth open, tongue up. When she jerked her chin up, a ring of rolling smoke tendrils sailed out into the kitchen.

"That's so fucking cool," Hope said. "Let me try."

O'Connor passed Hope the cigar. She filled her mouth with smoke, then copied O'Connor's instructions as close as she could remember. When Hope moved her chin up, a small, weak ring of smoke rolled out.

"I did it! Did you see that?" Hope's eyes twinkled. She took another puff and ejected another small ring. "That's awesome."

"Good. Consider yourself schooled." O'Connor took back the cigar. "Now, don't say I never did anything for you."

Sam walked back to the cage and crouched down to look at the bait bucket. "I thought you said this shit was irresistible?"

O'Connor threw Sam a bottle of water. "Sit down and relax. Let it do its magic."

Sam pulled the remaining chair from the table, reversed it and sat down. He cracked the seal on the water and took a sip. It was heaven, exactly what he needed. "So what's the deal with your leg?"

"Great," O'Connor said. "Tell everyone, why don't yah."

"What?" Sam looked surprised. "It's not a secret, is it?"

O'Connor blew cigar smoke in Sam's face. "I don't fuckin' advertise it."

Hope and Bradley looked at each other, then back at O'Connor, confused.

"I have a fake leg," O'Connor said.

"Okay." Bradley took a quick peek under the table. "Left or right?"

"Left."

"Looks real." Bradley was impressed.

"Doesn't feel real." O'Connor swung her leg against the leg of the table. A metallic *clang* rang out.

"How did it happen?" Hope said.

O'Connor heaved a sigh. "Twenty-five years ago. I remember it like it was yesterday. Surfing the north shore in Hawaii. I was lining up for my turn and a shark attacked me."

Ten seconds into O'Connor's story and Bradley was hooked. "What kind of shark?"

"A tiger." O'Connor puffed on her cigar. She blew smoke rings at Hope and winked at her. "They called it a 'hit and run'. The shark didn't get my leg, but it shredded it so bad it had to be amputated."

"Damn." Sam felt a shiver roll down his back.

"It's not too bad now," O'Connor said. "I don't notice it unless I've been on my feet for a while… like on this fuckin' job. But I still get phantom pain."

"What's that?" Bradley said.

"You're just full of damn questions, aren't yah?" O'Connor gave Bradley's chair a shove with her foot.

Bradley shrugged.

"Phantom pain is when my nerves still think I have a leg, even though I know it's gone. It's a mind fuck." O'Connor's words held the other three fascinated. "So every so often I get to relive that shark bite again. And that hurts like a son of a bitch."

O'Connor gulped some water. "That's probably why I'm such a bitch. What about you and that tail of yours?"

Bradley fell silent. He looked over to the hallway where he could see the head of Washington's shrouded body.

O'Connor followed Bradley's gaze. "What, did you see something?"

Bradley shook his head, and touched Washington's pendant hanging around his neck. O'Connor clued in to the connection. Bradley still mourned the loss of his new friend. It was too fresh. O'Connor knew she would feel it too, after this job was done. She would end the work day in an empty office, without her friend and colleague of ten years. Bradley was right to feel sorrow. O'Connor was not looking forward to facing her loss alone. But the job always came first.

"Washington was a good man," O'Connor said. "A mechanical genius, but a little too hocus pocus for my tastes."

"Believing in something isn't hocus pocus," Bradley said.

O'Connor shook her head. "Trust me, Brad. This isn't a conversation you want to have with me." She looked at Hope. "How about you? Anything profound to share?"

"Nope," Hope said. "I'm pretty much an open book. What you see is what you get."

"Not buying it." O'Connor blew smoke on the burning ember of her cigar, making it glow orange. Flecks of ash settled onto the table.

"Do you mind?" Sam said. "I eat off this table."

"Do you use fuckin' plates?" O'Connor swept the ash off the table with her hand. "Come on, Hope, sweetie-pie. No one leaves the table without sharing something."

"Well… I got a few piercings and some tattoos," Hope said.

"Now we're talking." O'Connor clapped her hands and rubbed them together. "What are you waiting for? Show us the goods."

"Most are private, but I can show you this." Hope stood up and faced away from everyone at the table. She pulled up the hem of her black t-shirt to just below her shoulder blades. A single tattoo of a rat spanned the entire length of her back. The rat's tail disappeared into her jeans, following the curve of her hips.

"Woah." Bradley fought against his eyes wanting to bug out as he traced the outline of the rat tattoo on Hope's back. And the subtle curve leading to her breasts under her raised t-shirt. According to his keen, sixteen year old eyes, she wasn't wearing a bra again. Ever since their first meeting on the fire escape, he suspected Hope had an aversion to bras. Bradley filed this image away in his "Holy shit I almost saw a grown woman naked" part of his brain.

Sam looked at Bradley and flashed his eyebrows and motioned at Hope's back.

"You can stop drooling now." Bradley smirked.

Sam gave Bradley a light punch to the shoulder. "Touché."

"Impressive," O'Connor said. "Now that's a *rat's ass* to get excited about."

"Haven't had any complaints so far." Hope dropped her shirt and sat down again. She looked at Bradley and scanned his arms, grinning. "You should get a tattoo, Brad."

Bradley felt heat rise up on his cheeks. He was lucky to be sitting because his knees had turned to jelly again and the bees in his stomach were back.

"No way," Sam said. "Absolutely not."

"Why? He's almost eighteen." Hope adjusted her t-shirt. "Soon he won't need your permission."

"You said it. He's *almost* eighteen."

"Come on," Hope said. "Just a small one wouldn't hurt."

"Not on my watch." Sam crossed his arms. "His mom would never go for it, either. Right Brad?"

"Yeah, probably," Bradley said. "If she knew what I've seen since I've been here, she'd shit."

"Sounds like a real tight-ass." O'Connor tapped Sam's shoulder. "What about you? Why are you so afraid of rats?"

"I got bitten by one when I was five," Sam said.

O'Connor looked at Sam, incredulous. "You buying this shit?" she said to Hope and Bradley. "You don't get *scarred for life* from a fuckin' rat bite. What a load of crap. What's the *real* story?"

All eyes were on Sam, especially Bradley's. He had wanted to know about Sam's time in prison ever since Claire had mentioned Sam was a convicted felon, but she had refused to share any details, if in fact she had details to share. He could never find the right time to ask Sam about it. Now Bradley was going to learn a piece of Sam's puzzle.

"Alright." Sam collected his thoughts. The silence in the kitchen was palpable.

Images of Sam's tattoos flashed through both Hope and Bradley's minds. Hope had only seen Sam's back, but Bradley had seen the whole deal.

Murderer. Motherfucker for Life.

He would never forget the image of those tattoos, sprawled across his dad's sinewy muscles.

Sam took a deep breath. "I spent some time in prison upstate. I got thrown into solitary confinement for a month for fighting… and spitting in a guard's face. Don't ever do that."

Hope's eyes widened. "A month?"

"Yeah. Unreasonable, I know. But it's prison." Sam noticed a slight tremble in his hands and clenched them to fists. "I had no bed, no toilet, no clothes. Just me, naked, in an eight by eight concrete cell. The lights were on twenty-four seven. The only time I saw people was when they brought my food. I won't even get into the food. That's a whole other story. The first thing I did was divide the space. You know, one corner for shit and piss. Opposite corner for sleeping. Even though I could see, I was lucky if I was aware which side was which by the end."

Sam took a sip from his water bottle. Bradley reached out and placed his left hand on Sam's right fist. Sam offered a weak smile, and a felt some relief wash over him.

Sam continued. "The guards, they had it in for me. Usually they'd slide my food through a slot in the door. About three weeks in, they brought my dinner tray on top of a cardboard box. They said it was a gift for good behavior."

Sam felt his heart jack-hammering in his chest and paused to breathe. "What they didn't tell me was the box was full of starving rats. First, those little fuckers ate my food, they even ate my shit… and it didn't take long for them to start biting. I tried to fight but even in the light I'd fall asleep. And when I was awake, I'd hallucinate. I was seeing and hearing all sorts of shit that wasn't there."

"Sounds kinda like *The Rapture*," Bradley said. "And I'm not talking about religion. People suffer from it when exploring caves. The isolation drives them insane." He gave a sideways smile. "I did a report on it at school."

Sam nodded, pleased about making a connection with Bradley. "Yeah, sounds right. And those fuckers kept biting me. I had to stand and walk around to keep them off my feet. Eventually, I'd pass out from exhaustion." Sam rubbed his arms. "All these scars are from rat bites. They put a stop to it after the third day, but the damage was done."

Sam rubbed his temple and tried to block the flood of memories. "I've had issues with rats ever since."

Bradley remembered planting his rubber rat in the pizza box earlier in the week. The gravity of his joke, which was originally Claire's idea, took on new meaning. Claire knew about Sam's time in solitary. Bradley found it hard to understand how Claire could be so cruel.

"How long were you in prison?" O'Connor said.

"Fifteen years." Sam shared a look with Bradley, but he couldn't hold on to it. Sam was barely keeping himself together as it was. "Missed out on a lot of things."

"What did you do, Dad?" Bradley said.

Sam released a heavy sigh. "Driving drunk. Killed two people." Sam gathered the courage to look at Bradley. "I almost killed you and your mom too. I was a fucked up mess. So the judge threw the book at me. I deserved it."

Silence consumed the kitchen and for a moment it felt like no one would be able to break it.

"I'm sorry." Hope reached out and touched Sam's hand.

"Want to know something else?" Sam looked around the table. He stood up, pointed at the cage and resumed his pacing. "That bucket of peanut butter sludge ain't getting it done. We need better bait."

Hope looked down at her hands and began to fidget. "A female rat would be the best bait. They're always in heat. And rats love sex."

Bradley's ears perked up. As a teenaged boy, if he hadn't responded to the word "sex," it would have been considered abnormal. And he responded by blushing again. Bradley's thoughts leaped back to Hope's bare back and her sprawling rat tattoo.

Hope continued. "If they're not eating or sleeping, they're having sex. Did you know that male rats will even fuck other males, even if they're dead?"

Bradley tried to deflect the heat blasting off his cheeks. "Talk about desperate."

"I don't know." O'Connor blew a cloud of smoke up into the smoky haze that had collected over their heads. "An existence of eating, sleeping and fucking sounds pretty good to me."

"Except when you're eating people," Bradley said.

"Yeah, there's that." O'Connor pointed at the rat in the cage on the kitchen counter. It still chewed the bars, determined to escape. "Besides, unless that rat is a female, which I don't think it is, we don't got shit."

Hope shared a glance with Sam, then with Bradley. It didn't take either of them long to clue in. "I don't see any other way."

"Am I missing something," O'Connor said. "What the fuck are you talking about?"

"Hope has a pet rat. A female." Sam looked at Hope. She nodded and offered a forced half-smile. "We can use her as bait."

O'Connor threw her hands up in the air. "For fuck's sake! Anything else I don't know?"

"Her name's Harriette," Hope said.

"Oh, that's just great." O'Connor stood up and joined

Sam pacing the kitchen. "We're all gonna be saved by Hatsy the rat."

"It's Harriette," Hope said. "You got a real problem with names, don't you?"

O'Connor leaned over the table towards Hope. "I got a problem with vital info being withheld."

Hope stood up to go nose to nose with O'Connor, and sent her chair flying backward. "I don't remember you asking!"

Hope and O'Connor stared at each other, each huffing and puffing.

Sam stepped in and placed a hand on each of their shoulders. "Are we done?"

O'Connor looked at Sam and pushed away from the table.

"Get back here," Sam said.

O'Connor's looked at Sam. Her eyes still held anger.

"Shake hands."

"What?" O'Connor and Hope said simultaneously.

"Do it," Sam said.

O'Connor and Hope eyed each other with scorn. Hope was the first to hold out her hand.

"You taught me to blow smoke rings," Hope said. "That's got to count for something."

O'Connor considered Hope's words, then jutted her hand forward. The two women shook hands.

"Okay," Hope said. "Let's get Harriette."

Harriette

The elevator opened onto to the third floor. Carny was out of the elevator like a shot, sniffing around. It didn't take the little dog long to zero in on Washington's blood on the carpet and begin licking it.

Melvin stepped out of the elevator and saw the blood. "Carny! Git outta there. Git!" Melvin crouched to touch the blood. It was still tacky and left the tip of his finger painted red.

Melvin's first thought: *What the hell happened here?* His second: *Why don't I know about it?*

He had heard suspicious sounds from the third floor, and he knew Sam wouldn't be offering any explanations.

"That damn Sam Shaw," Melvin said. "I could do a better job than that fuck-wit."

Carny ran down the hallway towards the fire escape and followed the scent of bloody footprints to the window. The dog left little red paw prints of his own behind.

Melvin tried to open the fire escape window, but it was jammed closed. With his head against the glass, he could just see that the fire escape was gone, crumpled to the ground at the base of the building.

"What the hell?"

Melvin walked back to the main hallway and headed

down toward Mrs. Baxter's and Hope's apartments. Carny followed and tracked more bloody paw prints into the carpet.

Mrs. Baxter's door stood ajar. Melvin saw the blood underneath. "What the fuck?"

He pushed the door until it stopped, half open. He peered around the leading edge and was met with the sight of Mrs. Baxter's ravaged body.

"Holy shit." Melvin took in the carnage, but instead of horror, he saw opportunity. He peeked out into the hallway. The coast was clear. He entered Mrs. Baxter's apartment, closed the door back to the way it had been when he entered, and began to search for valuables.

"Shouldn't we call the C.D.C. or something?"

"Why the fuck did you hire me, Sam?" O'Connor walked to the Detest-A-Pest's stockpile of supplies in the corner of the kitchen. "The publicity I'll get from this job could keep me in business for years."

"I didn't know it was going to be this bad." Sam shrugged. "I don't want anyone else to die."

"They've already killed a cat and a man... your words." O'Connor shook her head. "How bad did you think it was then?" She dug through a duffel bag and pulled out a fully charged taser rod. "Sam, you're a pussy."

"Look," Sam said. "I'm not a pussy, but I *am* afraid of those fucking rats."

O'Connor placed her hand on his shoulder and pulled herself up. "Look Sam, I'm sorry you went through that shit." She puffed on her cigar. "But you gotta face those fuckers head on." She raised her taser rod between their faces and pulled the trigger. A blue bolt of electricity arced between the electrodes, then disappeared. For a moment, the air smelled more of ozone than cigar smoke.

"You gotta send 'em back to hell where they came from," O'Connor said.

Sam nodded. "You're right, but I can't do it. You and Hope know the most about rats. You seem like the best choice."

"Nothing good is ever easy." O'Connor punched Sam in the shoulder.

Hope rummaged in one of the duffel bags and found a Bowie knife. "Knowing about rats hasn't helped us much so far."

"I'll go," Bradley said.

O'Connor shook her head. "Nope. You stay and that's non-negotiable."

"But I'm fast." Bradley looked at O'Connor's left leg. "A lot faster than you."

"If I didn't know you, I'd smack you." O'Connor said. "The last thing I want is the blood of a teenager on my hands."

Indignant heat rose on Bradley's cheeks. He pointed at Hope. "But she's practically a teenager, too."

Just as being called a *kid* drove Bradley crazy, labeling Hope a *teenager* had a similar effect, and Sam had a front row seat.

Hope's eyes narrowed as she attached the knife to one of her belt loops. She walked to face Bradley, nose to nose. She could feel Bradley's body heat and knew he could feel hers. Hope was a little taller than Bradley so she looked down on him a bit, too. She took a step forward, forcing Bradley back with her chest. "I'm no teenager. You know that better than anyone here."

Bradley's mouth had dried up. Everyone could hear the *clicking* of his throat as he tried to swallow. He had no words.

O'Connor tapped on the door frame. "You ready, Toots?"

"Bring 'em on." Hope stepped back and joined O'Connor, but kept a stony glare on Bradley as long as she could.

O'Connor cracked open the door to Sam's apartment and peered out. As Hope stood beside O'Connor, Sam noticed the difference in height between the two women for the first time. O'Connor was at least eight inches shorter than Hope, maybe a foot. Hope used her height advantage to look out over O'Connor's head.

"All clear." O'Connor looked back at Hope. "Elevator or stairs?"

Hope didn't like either choice, but remembered the state Washington was in after he had exited the stairwell on the third floor. *And all that blood.*

"Elevator," Hope said.

"You got balls, I'll give you that." O'Connor turned back to face Sam and Bradley. "You stay put, no matter what you hear. Got it?"

"Yes, Mom," Bradley said.

"I'm not fuckin' around." O'Connor locked gaze with Bradley. "Neither should you."

Bradley nodded.

"Okay. Let's go." O'Connor led the way, followed by Hope a step behind.

Sam and Bradley watched the two women walk down the hallway towards the elevator.

"You got to let your brain catch up to your mouth before you talk," Sam said.

"I could say the same about you."

"Touché." Sam held up his fist. Bradley considered it for a moment, then they both exchanged fist bumps.

HOPE AND O'CONNOR stood in the elevator and watched the floor indicator ascend to the second floor, then past the second floor.

"I guess if things go bad, this elevator could double as our coffin," O'Connor said.

Hope focused on the floor indicator. "You're not helping."

"Where do you think they got in?" O'Connor scanned the ceiling of the elevator for access holes.

"You know, it's okay not to talk every once in a while."

"I'll stop talking when I'm dead."

Hope looked at O'Connor. "After what we've seen? Careful what you wish for."

The elevator reached the third floor with a hitch. The floor indicator *dinged* and the doors scraped open.

They stepped into the hallway. To their left, they could see Washington's bloody footsteps leading to the fire escape window. Further down the hallway, Mrs. Baxter's door was still ajar, just as they had left it earlier in the day.

"Hey, look." Hope pointed at the floor. Little paw prints were scattered all over the hallway. They led to Mrs. Baxter's apartment. "Someone else has been here."

"We'll check it out later," O'Connor said. "Stay on target."

Hope fumbled with her keys, a visible shake in her hands.

O'Connor noticed it too. "Are you okay to—"

"I'm fine." Hope turned her key and slid the deadbolt back into the door with a *thunk*. She unlocked the door handle and twisted it open.

Hope hesitated for a second before opening her door. She half expected an ambush of rodents. But her apartment appeared to be clear.

O'Connor inhaled a deep breath through her nose. "Do you smell that?"

"I don't smell anything other than that cigar," Hope said.

"I smell… rat shit." O'Connor sampled the air again. "And something else I can't place. Maybe I'm smelling your beloved Harriette."

"Your schnoz is better than mine." Hope moved down the hallway. She rolled on the outer edges of her shoe treads to minimize the sound of her steps. "She's in the bedroom."

"You sleep with a rat." A shiver ran down O'Connor's back, a rare occurrence for her. Washington would have said the universe was trying to warn her. She didn't like it one bit. "Guess that makes sense, after seeing your tattoo."

"She does live in a cage," Hope said. "I'm not that hard core."

"Wait." O'Connor unholstered her taser rod and turned it on. The charging light flipped from red to green. Ready to rock. "Call it insurance."

She stepped in front of Hope and led the way, stopping at the bedroom door, slightly ajar.

O'Connor placed her hand on the door handle. "Does the door creak?"

Hope shrugged. "Haven't got a clue. Sorry."

"Don't apologize yet." O'Connor pushed open the door. It swung open silently and revealed Hope's bed, closet, and finally the rat city, covered in a thick blanket of squirming rats. Harriette's cage couldn't be seen.

The sound of muffled chewing, incisors on steel, filled the room. To Hope, the sound was like nails on a chalkboard. They fell back to the hallway and spoke in whispers.

"Shit," O'Connor said. "What if she's dead already? There's a lot of gnawing teeth in there."

"Harriette can't be dead," Hope said. "Her cage is top of the line."

"Okay. Assuming she's not dead…" O'Connor peeked back into the room. "Any suggestions?"

Hope blurted the first thing that came to her mind. "How about I scream as loud as I can, you grab the cage, then we run." As soon as the words were out, Hope cringed. To her surprise, O'Connor paused to consider the idea. In fact, O'Connor had been more than polite towards her so far, now that they had to work together.

"That's better than what I got," O'Connor said. "It's just crazy enough to work. You ready?"

Hope nodded.

"On three."

"Wait," Hope said. "Do you mean 'one, two, three, scream'? Or 'one, two, scream'?"

"You academics… does it really matter?"

"Yeah it does."

"The first one."

"Okay," Hope said. "Ready?"

O'Connor nodded and gripped the taser rod. Hope held her hand up and began to count off with her fingers.

One... two... three.

MELVIN'S POCKETS WERE already stuffed with jewelry. He was in the kitchen topping them up with silverware when he heard the elevator *ding*. Carny heard it too and trotted towards the door.

"Carny! Git!" Melvin hushed his voice. But it was going to take more than words to get Carny to stay. Melvin turned to the refrigerator. That did the trick.

Carny heard the refrigerator open and reversed direction, trotting over to see what his master had found. The dog was a whore when it came to food. Why Carny wasn't as plump as an Easter ham was anyone's guess.

Melvin was in luck. There was an open tin of Fancy Feast on the top shelf. He took it out with one hand and scooped up Carny with the other. The greedy little dog didn't discriminate and ate like there was no tomorrow.

Melvin walked toward Mrs. Baxter's apartment door and stood right beside the door frame.

He heard voices, ones he didn't recognize. Melvin waited until he heard the sound of keys unlocking the door across the hall. He peeked out to see Hope and O'Connor disappear into Hope's apartment.

"Perfect timing," Melvin said to himself. Carny didn't care what was happening as long as he had access to the can of Fancy Feast, his new favorite snack.

Melvin squeezed out of Mrs. Baxter's apartment and

skulked down the hallway towards the elevator, as silent as he could manage with pockets stuffed with precious metal. He pressed the elevator's call button.

Then Melvin heard the scream.

SAM COCKED HIS head to one side. "Did you hear that?"

"Was that a scream?" Bradley said.

They both paused and listened.

Another scream.

Sam opened the apartment door and headed into the hallway.

Bradley grabbed Sam's arm. "O'Connor said stay here."

"Do you always do what you're told?"

"No, but—"

"What if they're in trouble?"

"If they're in trouble, it's because of rats," Bradley said. "Lots of them."

Bradley was right. While Sam's rodent phobia was weakened, he was far from cured. He would be useless against a horde and would only slow them down.

"Okay, but I'm going to stand right here."

Bradley nodded and managed a small smile. "Me too."

HOPE SCREAMED AT the top of her lungs, but got no visible reaction. She looked at O'Connor, surprised.

"Apparently your Harriette's an irresistible sexpot." O'Connor shrugged. "Step it up a notch."

Hope screamed again and stomped on the floor for good

measure. That got results. Rats scattered off the miniature metropolis and into the corners, momentarily spooked. O'Connor zapped the few that remained on Harriette's cage, then grabbed the handle at the top. "Let's go!"

Hope and O'Connor ran for the door. The rats realized the object of their frenzy had taken flight. They reversed direction and charged after Harriette's intoxicating scent.

Hope stopped at the door, and dug into her pockets.

"What are you doing?" O'Connor said.

"I was going to lock—"

They both looked down the apartment hallway to see a wave of rats emerge from the bedroom, moving fast.

"Forget it!" O'Connor left Hope at the apartment door and headed down the main hallway towards the elevator. Hope tried to close the door but it was blocked by a rat already.

Hope screamed, this time real horror in her voice, and let go of the door knob. Rats filed out around her feet and past her. The rats wanted Harriette, up ahead in O'Connor's hand.

Hope ran after O'Connor. She caught up and overtook her in no time.

"Wait for me, you bitch!" O'Connor managed a steady lop-sided gallop, with the rats in hot pursuit. She zapped any that got too close. "Remember, I got your precious Harriette!"

Through the open elevator door, Melvin saw Hope and O'Connor's fast approach.

"What the hell?" He squinted at the hallway floor until he realized what he was seeing: a horde of rats closing in. Eyes wide with horror, Melvin pressed the button for the first floor over and over, as if the speed of his button pressing had any effect on the elevator doors closing (it didn't). Even Carny stopped his gorging on Fancy Feast and began barking.

"Wait!" Hope continued to run for her life. "Hold the door!" As she got closer, Hope noticed silver flashes poking out from Melvin's pockets.

Cutlery? What the fuck?

Melvin increased his efforts on the first floor button until the doors began to close. Carny barked like a little maniac and Melvin smiled, smug that he had won this little competition. The elevator doors slammed shut just before Hope reached them.

"Fucking asshole!" Hope said.

"Forget him!" O'Connor tried to avoid the blood in front of the stairwell door as best she could. "The stairs! Come on!"

Hope and O'Connor burst into the stairwell. The carnage of bloody rodent carcasses left behind by Washington littered the landing and stairs leading down. Hope grabbed the hand railing to steady herself as she flew down the stairs, followed by O'Connor.

On the landing between the second and third floor, Hope and O'Connor looked back up the stairs. The slow, self-closing fire door hadn't closed fast enough to stem the tide of rats that flowed down the third floor hallway.

Melvin stood in the elevator, holding Carny. He watched the floor indicator approach the second floor and move past it. He shifted from foot to foot with unease.

His plan to leave the building unraveled as he heard jangling in his pockets and remembered they were filled with stolen jewelry and silverware. And that bitch from across the hall had seen it. He was sure of it. Melvin hit the second floor call button, but he was too late. The elevator had moved past it and was on its way to the first floor.

Hope and O'Connor continued to bound down the steps two at a time, gaining time. Hope was amazed how spry O'Connor could be if she wanted to. They reached the first floor landing and exited into the hallway. The elevator hadn't arrived yet. The first floor stairwell door began its slow easing arc closed, just as it had on the third floor.

Sam and Bradley were in the hallway, standing next to the open apartment door.

"We heard a scream," Sam said.

Hope and O'Connor ran the length of the first floor hallway, past Sam and Bradley and into the apartment.

"Close it!" Hope said between breaths. "Quick!"

Bradley slammed the door and Sam plugged the gap under the door with a towel.

"They're on their way, boys and girls," O'Connor puffed smoke. Even through all the action and running, she had managed to keep her cigar lit and clamped between her teeth.

HOT ON THE trail of Harriette's scent, the rodent throng flowed through the slowly closing stairwell door to the first floor. The rats had gained momentum running down the stairs. They jumped steps and leap-frogged each other to lead the pack.

But halfway down the hallway the scent weakened once Harriette was safe inside Sam's apartment. The horde lost cohesion and almost scattered, until their dinner bell sounded.

Ding.

The elevator door opened.

Melvin and Carny stood facing the hallway and hundreds of rats. Carny leaped from Melvin's arms and attacked a straggler. He shook the life out of the rat and flung it against the wall. Feeling invincible, the little dog dispatched another rat in similar fashion.

Melvin was petrified and had already begun pressing the call button for the second floor. He didn't call out for Carny for fear of making too much noise. Carny was a diversion, his ticket to safety.

Denied their first prize, the rats settled for second and charged for Carny. Maybe in a past life Carny had been a champion rat terrier, but not in this one. But the little dog wasn't entirely stupid either. He turned tail, ran back into the elevator, and hid behind panic-stricken Melvin, who was pressing buttons in a frenzy.

It was a replay of the third floor moments ago, but this time Karma had come back to roost. The rats overtook Carny and Melvin, and ripped into their bodies. Melvin screamed and dug into his pocket. The first weapon he pulled out was a spoon, which proved to be useless against the mass of rats.

Carny howled in pain only once as the brown stains in his fur mixed with the fresh redness of his blood. The little bichon frise was dead in seconds, ripped to shreds by ravenous rats with white-tipped tails.

Melvin found a fork in his pocket and tried to use it to poke at the rats attacking him. One fork against hundreds of incisors was the pinnacle of bad ideas. He slipped in the slurry that used to be Carny and fell hard on the tiled floor of the elevator. One of Melvin's legs jutted out and prevented the elevator's doors from closing. The rats scrambled into his pants and tore into his calves. They burrowed into his socks and forced off his shoes.

Melvin couldn't see. His eyes had been torn out of their sockets. Rats fought each other for the pair of white orbs that rolled between their oily, furred bodies. He dropped the fork and his other hand searched the walls for a button, any button, leaving dirty blood streaks behind. His chewed fingers found the button labeled "Basement" just before his limbs stopped taking commands from his brain. Melvin's luck, and life, ran out.

The evisceration took on a life of its own, like piranhas in blood lust. The rats separated Melvin's leg at the knee, leaving his half-eaten calf and foot behind. The elevator door closed and began its journey to the second floor and ultimately the basement.

But Harriette's scent was strong. Once the elevator reached the basement, the horde locked onto it and zeroed in on the portal to Sam's apartment.

Bait

O'Connor placed Harriette's cage on the counter next to the other cage. The rat inside stopped, sniffed, and redirected its efforts to chewing through the cage wall adjacent to Harriette's.

"Your special rat has got the goods," O'Connor said. "Is she a virgin?"

"You're joking, right? You know female rats can breed as young as five weeks… so she's probably not a virgin." Hope leaned in close to Harriette's cage and kissed at her. "But she hasn't had a litter since I bought her on-line. Shipped by United Airlines."

"No wonder we got a problem," O'Connor said. "Flying rats in heat all over the god damned place."

A scream sounded from the hallway.

"What was that?" Sam said.

"Probably that asshole with the dog," Hope said.

"Melvin and Carny?" Sam looked at Bradley.

Hope shrugged. "He was on the third floor with his pockets filled with silverware. He didn't even hold the elevator door."

O'Connor nudged Hope's shoulder. "Taking the stairs probably saved our lives."

"Sounds like it," Bradley said.

"Stealing from Mrs. Baxter?" Sam said. "That's low, even for Melvin."

"He'll pay for it with his life." O'Connor dug out another small cage with a light mounted on top. The tightly spaced mesh walls were painted white, instead of the usual stainless steel. "If the rats that were after us got to him, he's dead as disco." She held the cage up to Hope. "Here. Transfer your little princess into this."

Hope took the cage and transferred Harriette into the new cage. Harriette scurried around inside this new environment, sniffing the corners. When Hope closed and locked the door, Harriette ran to it as if to ask "what's going on?" She sensed Hope's unease and it intensified her own.

O'Connor tied a thin rope to the top of the cage. "This is a new design, one of Washington's last prototypes."

"Has it been tested before?" Hope looked at O'Connor, worried.

"Maiden voyage," O'Connor said. "But trust Washington to come up with something brilliant." She looked to Sam, Bradley, then back to Hope. "We need to lower the cage into the access point under the sink. Any volunteers?"

Sam hesitated, and Bradley took a step forward, but Hope spoke before either could voice their intentions.

"I want to do it," she said. "Harriette's my girl."

O'Connor handed the rope to Hope. "Fill your boots."

Hope knelt down and crawled under the kitchen sink, the cage in her right hand. Harriette ran laps inside the small cage and under other circumstances, Hope would have described Harriette's activity as "having the rips", or excited play time. Today, the rat was scared. Hope knew it, too.

She poked the cage and her head through the access hole and looked down. The light above the cage wasn't especially bright and revealed nothing. Not a rat to be seen. "See you later, girl." Hope let out more rope and lowered Harriette into the darkness of the basement below.

Had Hope looked above her head, she would have seen the dozen rats perched on the criss-crossing overhead pipes. They watched her every move. One rat broke free from the group and leaped from one of the pipes and into Hope's hair.

Mad panic took over. "Fuck! Something's on me!" At that moment nothing else existed except the rat on Hope's head. She pulled her head out of the access hole, let go of the rope holding Harriette's cage and worked at her hair with her hands.

O'Connor saw the cage's rope speed across the floor but she was on the opposite side of the Kill-O-Matic and couldn't get to it in time. "The rope!"

Bradley leaped to grab it but missed. O'Connor ran around the Kill-O-Matic but was too slow and missed as well.

"Sam!" O'Connor pointed at the rope. "Grab it, for fuck's sake!"

Hope backed out from under the kitchen sink, still working to extricate the rat tangled in her hair. "Get it off! I can't see it!" She flailed at her face and head, but the rat bit Hope's fingers when they got too close.

Sam pushed the sight of vermin in Hope's hair out of his mind and leaped toward the access hole under the sink. Washington had had the forethought to tie a knot at the end of the rope, and just as Sam wrapped his fingers around the sliding rope, the knot at the end locked into his palm. He squeezed and held on.

O'Connor didn't have time to warn Hope. She took her taser rod and jammed it into the rat's fleshy body and pulled the trigger.

Zap!

The rat flew off Hope's head like it had been struck with a bat and landed on Sam's back. Its paws had been vaporized to twitching stumps and smoke rose in weak tendrils from its charred fur.

O'Connor looked at Hope. "You owe me."

Hope sat, catching her breath as she examined her bloody fingers. She had no words for O'Connor.

"Uh, guys…" Sam thought about asking what was on his back, but he knew already. The warmth on his spine was almost pleasant, except for the images of frenzied vermin running through his head. He worked to keep his voice calm. "Get that *thing* off me. *Please.*"

Below, in the darkness of the basement, the cage with Harriette inside dangled several inches from the floor. The drop had knocked out the bait cage's flashlight, but Harriette was very much alive.

And it was her essence that drew the rats out of the shadows. Melvin and Carny, their unrecognizable remains left in the elevator in a combined pool of blood and viscera, served only as a temporary distraction. The horde caught Harriette's scent and resumed their pursuit.

Bradley crouched next to Sam and pulled the dead rat off Sam's back. "Can you see it, Dad? The cage?"

Every time Sam heard Bradley address him as *Dad*, he felt a happy twinge in his heart. It was easy to get distracted by it. Sam maintained his grip on the rope and eased himself forward, toward the access hole.

"Look up as well as down," Hope said. "That was my mistake."

Sam rolled on his side to get a look above him. "All clear above," he said, "and I don't see anything below, either."

"Pull it up. Brad, give me a hand." O'Connor grabbed the knotted end of the rope from Sam and climbed into the Kill-O-Matic. She threaded the rope through a metal ring fastened to the top, then through a small hole in the cage wall opposite the door. "Take the rope and keep pulling."

"Got it," Bradley said.

O'Connor stepped out of the Kill-O-Matic. "Anything yet?"

Sam looked into the blackness of the shaft again. "Get me a flashlight."

Hope spotted a flashlight on the counter, grabbed it and handed it to Sam. He flicked the switch on and looked down. He followed the rope with the flashlight's beam until it… disappeared. The flashlight wasn't bright enough to penetrate the darkness more than several feet.

"Where's the cage?" Sam said to himself.

"You can't see the cage?" Hope knelt down and was about to crawl in next to Sam for a look when his arm shot back and stopped her.

"Wait." With every pull of the rope, a mass of fur and writhing white-tipped tails rose closer to the access hole, and within Sam's flashlight range.

Somehow, the horde of rats were flowing up toward him. The mass defied gravity like some kind of weightless interconnected rodent fluid, all surrounding Harriette's cage, trying to get in.

Sam retreated from the access hole under the sink and dropped the flashlight beside him. His breath came in rapid pants and his face was bathed in sweat. The rank odor of fear rose from him in waves and the whites of his eyes stood out between unblinking lids. Sam thought he was making progress, but the terror that gripped him now was complete.

"Shit," O'Connor said. "I know that look. Get ready, people."

The mass of rats reached the access hole before the cage. They writhed and scrambled at the cage tied to the rope. Sam's eyes remained locked forward as his nose captured the familiar smell of vermin, a smell forever burned into his memory.

These rats were smart, but not smart enough to chew through the rope. The scent of Harriette acted on them like an intoxicating perfume, and caused them to move as one, with one instinct driving them. The rats focused on Harriette in much the same way as Sam held himself frozen in horror.

The white cage burst through the top layer of rats like an onion being pulled from the ground. Rats spilled off the top of the cage next to Sam's face, and revealed Harriette alive inside.

"Pull it faster!" O'Connor said.

Bradley quickened his pace and tugged the rope through the hole in the cage. Harriette's cage dragged across the floor.

The rats followed Harriette into the Kill-O-Matic, where her cage swung from the center ring above. Rats swarmed, jumped and clambered over each other to get at her. Some rats were able to grab hold of Harriette's cage, but were knocked off by the next pursuer. As more rats entered the Kill-O-Matic, the rising tide of squirming bodies made it easier to latch onto the bait cage that hung about a foot from the mesh ceiling.

"That's good." O'Connor pointed to a hook near the bottom of the cage's back wall.

Bradley tied the rope to the hook. A steady stream of rats scurried out of the access hole under the sink, one on top of another, hot on Harriette's scent.

Sam managed to turn his head to one side enough to spy the exodus out of the corner of his eye. Beads of terrified sweat stung his eyes. The rats passed in front of the flashlight beside him, which caused the light to strobe his face. In an instant, his mind was back to his first encounter in the kitchen when his flashlight spun on the floor. He closed his eyes and tried to imagine himself surrounded by tall maples swaying in the breeze. Their large green leaves cut the sunlight into broken beams. But fear prevented him from forming the image. The rats could have made a meal out of him, but luck prevailed. Harriette was on the menu today.

"Close the cage!" Hope looked at O'Connor. "We can trap the rest."

O'Connor shook her head. "Wait."

The flow of rats from the access hole thinned to a trickle, then nothing. Thousands of rats wriggled and jumped over each other for a chance to get into Harriette's cage. It was a sight to behold.

"That's crazy." Bradley watched the mass of fur tumble and writhe inside the cage. "The ones underneath must hold their breath, just like when they were in the toilet."

"Something like that." O'Connor's eyes were on the

access hole, but there hadn't been any latecomers for several seconds. "Now, Sam!"

Sam flicked his eyes open and locked gaze with O'Connor, but he couldn't move. His brain wouldn't let him yet.

"Sam!" O'Connor said. "Close the fuckin' cage!"

Hope stepped toward the Kill-O-Matic. "I'll do it."

"No. Sam's got to do this." O'Connor unholstered her pellet gun and aimed at Hope. "Get any closer and you'll lose one of those pretty little eyes of yours."

Hope stopped in her tracks.

Bradley watched O'Connor shift her aim towards Sam. "What the hell are you doing?"

"Lighting a fire under your dad's ass." O'Connor squinted, aimed the gun, and pulled the trigger. The pellet hit Sam square in the upper thigh. "Bullseye."

"Jesus Christ!" The pain of the pellet striking his thigh overcame Sam's fear. On his back, he wriggled out from under the sink and kicked the cage door closed. He had to kick it a second time to close the door against the bulge of rats at the door.

"That's gonna leave a mark." O'Connor grinned, as Bradley came to terms with her decision to shoot his father.

"You could have killed him," Bradley said.

"With this?" O'Connor raised the pellet gun. "Not a chance."

As soon as the rats realized that they were trapped, many began to shift their focus from Harriette to gnawing the cage in order to escape.

"Light it up, damn it!" Sam said.

"Now we're talkin'." O'Connor grabbed the power cord

and went to plug it in where she had plugged it in before, but it came up a foot short. "Oh shit."

The distance to the electrical outlet was too far now that the Kill-O-Matic had been moved from the hallway to the kitchen.

O'Connor leaned her weight into the cage. She tried her best to avoid gnawing incisors that poked through the cage mesh. "Help me push it!"

Hope and Bradley joined O'Connor and pushed with all their weight, but the cage refused to budge.

"It's too heavy," Hope said.

"What about there?" Bradley pointed to an outlet next to the sink, where the coffee machine was plugged in. He grabbed the power cord from O'Connor and ran toward the outlet.

From under the sink, the alpha rat leapt from the access hole, latched onto Bradley's leg, and took a bite. Bradley screamed. The plug in his hand dropped to the floor, instantly forgotten.

"Brad!" Dealing with his own fear was one thing. To see that vermin mutation attack his son was quite another. Now past being afraid, Sam kicked the alpha rat off Bradley's leg. It rolled in front of the refrigerator and shook off the blow. The alpha rat remembered Sam and charged at him instead. It was an inevitable response, but one he wasn't completely prepared for. He grabbed the flashlight on the floor beside him, stood up, and prepared himself as best he could for the next attack.

Sensing the alpha rat in trouble, more rats switched gears and began to gnaw the metal mesh of the Kill-O-Matic. Some made enough progress to force their greasy, stained snouts and whiskers through small chewed openings in the cage.

The alpha rat leapt and slammed into Sam like a football dropping out of a long bomb. He smashed the alpha rat's head with the flashlight and sent it flying on its back. But it righted itself and charged Sam again.

"O'Connor!" Bradley held out his hand. "Your taser!"

O'Connor pulled the taser rod from her back and threw it to Bradley. He caught it and ran to where Sam stood struggling with the alpha rat. Bradley jammed the taser into the soft back of the rat, impaling it on the dual pronged ends of the taser rod.

"Take that, you fucker." Bradley pulled the trigger and zapped the alpha rat long enough for Sam to kick it against the side of the cage and hold it there with his boots.

Sam anchored his back against the counter and continued to pin the alpha rat to the exterior of the cage. He slid to a sitting position on the floor. To both his and Bradley's amazement, the alpha rat began to squirm again.

"The plug!" Sam said.

Bradley grabbed the end of the power cord and jammed it into the outlet next to the coffee maker.

Sam looked at O'Connor. "Do it! Light it up!"

"This one's for Washington, you sons of bitches!" O'Connor grabbed the remote and turned on the Kill-O-Matic.

The solitary light in the kitchen dimmed. A combination of sizzling and electrical sounds emanated from within the cage, followed by smoke and the stomach-churning smell of burning fur.

Sam held the squealing and squirming alpha rat against

the cage wall as its fur began to smolder. The combined cries of a thousand rats sent shivers down Sam's spine.

The wailing inside the Kill-O-Matic began to subside just as the lights went out. The kitchen fell into darkness, except for the light from Sam's flashlight and the late afternoon light from the solitary kitchen window.

Rats on the exterior of the cage were burned to a crisp. The luckier ones near the center of the cage had escaped most of the electrical charge and fought to get out through the fried carcasses against the cage wall.

"The fuse box." O'Connor pulled her flashlight from a leather loop on her belt and turned it on. "Where is it?"

"It's not going to matter," Sam said from his spot on the floor. "It's too old. And I don't have any replacement fuses."

Bradley got an idea and disappeared into the darkness behind the cage.

The alpha rat wriggled under Sam's boots like a stuck pig. The short jolt of electric current had done nothing except aggravate the monstrous rodent more.

"Someone zap this bastard," Sam said. "He's getting free."

O'Connor grabbed the taser rod from Bradley, jammed it into the side of the alpha rat, and pulled the trigger. "Eat this, you rat fuck." The shock did about as much good as poking a rhinoceros with a chopstick. O'Connor pulled the trigger again and got the same result.

"It's not working." Sam pointed at the LED light on the handle, glowing a solid red. "It's lost its charge."

"You think?" O'Connor threw the taser rod onto the floor. The alpha rat continued its struggle, pinned under Sam's boot.

Dozens of rats had begun to poke their heads out of

chewed holes in the cage mesh. The only obstacles slowing them down were the jagged edges of the chewed mesh. It wouldn't slow them down for long.

"Hey, I remember that thing." Hope watched Bradley roll the arc welding unit into the kitchen.

"We can use this," Bradley said. "Right Dad?"

Sam nodded. "Brad, you're brilliant! Get it over here, fast!"

Bradley navigated the arc welding unit around to the right side of the Kill-O-Matic and plugged the cage's power cord into one of the welding unit's auxiliary power outlets. He flipped the unit's big red 'ON' switch.

The Kill-O-Matic hummed back to life. New rats on the edges of the cage squealed in pain as their bodies hissed, popped and smoked. The rats with their heads partially through the cage wall had their eyes vaporized and their little brains cooked by the electricity. Their whiskers curled to charred stubs.

O'Connor dug a couple extra flashlights out of a duffel bag and tossed them to Hope and Bradley. "All lights on the cage. We don't want survivors."

The flashlight beams criss-crossed in the rising smoke. It took all of Hope's will to keep herself from vomiting again.

The rope that held the bait cage with Harriette inside burned through. The cage fell into the center of the dying rodent mass.

"Harriette!" Hope ran toward the cage, but O'Connor stopped her.

"No," O'Connor said. "You can't touch the cage." She leaned in against Hope, preventing her from getting close to the cage. "It'll kill you."

"Harriette!" Hope wanted to save her girl, but O'Connor stood her ground.

Even with the electrical current coursing through the Kill-O-Matic's walls and through the rats inside, several still managed to jump on top of the bait cage, trying to get inside.

"No." Hope watched Harriette and the bait cage sink out of sight into an undulating horde of dying, frying rats.

Sam looked at the alpha rat under his boots. All indications of struggle were gone. The alpha rat was dead. He pulled his boots off the rat. A layer of skin and fur had fused with the tread of his boots. It peeled off the alpha rat like the thickened surface of cold pudding.

The rest of the alpha rat, all eight pounds of it, remained fused to the side of the cage door. Soon, all movement inside the cage stopped.

"Are we done?" Sam said.

"You got it, bub." O'Connor walked around the Kill-O-Matic, looking for life inside the cage. "I could go for a bucket of Kingsley Fried Chicken. Extra crispy recipe."

Bradley turned off the arc welding unit and pulled the plug to the Kill-O-Matic.

"Ugh." Hope ran to the cage door and opened it. "How can you think of food right now?" She fought the urge to puke as she threw open the door to the Kill-O-Matic and waded into a sea of smoking rat bodies. Hope grabbed the burned end of the rope that was tied to the bait cage. She pulled it and extracted the cage through a cracking crust of burned rodent skin and bones.

Hope scraped residue off the side of the bait cage. She shone her flashlight into the openings between the bars, frantic to locate Harriette's body.

A pink nose appeared, whiskers twitching briskly.

"Harriette!" Hope peeled more rat remains off the side of the bait cage. "She's alive." A tear of joy dripped down one cheek.

"Here's to Harriette the Invincible." Sam gave Hope a thumbs up.

Hope trudged through the deep rodent muck and climbed out of the Kill-O-Matic. She looked at O'Connor, puzzled. "But how?"

"Wouldn't you like to know." O'Connor smiled.

"And you're going to tell me."

O'Connor sucked back on her Cohiba and blew smoke rings back toward Hope, all the while grinning. "I don't got to tell you shit."

"It's porcelain, isn't it?" Bradley crossed his arms on his chest. O'Connor glared at him, exasperated.

Hope looked back at Bradley, then began to nod. "Porcelain's an insulator, right? It doesn't conduct electricity?"

"Bingo." Bradley nodded at Hope. "It could have been plastic but those rats would have chewed through it in no time."

"Brad," O'Connor said. "You're too damn smart for your own good."

As far as compliments went, that was as good as it got from O'Connor. "Thanks," Bradley said.

"Well, you could have told me." Hope carried the bait cage to the kitchen table and set it down. Harriette scrambled around in circles inside the cage. "You're such an asshole."

O'Connor placed her right arm across her abdomen and took a bow. "At your service, my dear. Besides, that cage was a prototype. I couldn't promise that Harriette would survive."

Bradley knelt down beside Sam at the kitchen counter. "Dad? You okay?"

"Doing great," Sam said, "except for getting shot in the ass!" He rolled to one side and felt for frayed fabric. "Ruined a good pair of jeans, too."

"If that's your ass, I got a bridge to sell yah," O'Connor said.

Sam found the hole in his jeans and the welt on his thigh to go with it. He started to chuckle, then broke into a hearty laugh. O'Connor joined him. Bradley and Hope exchanged glances and began to laugh as well.

Bradley imagined what Claire would have thought about all this: four people laughing with a mountain of charred rodents between them. "Hey, Dad. Do you think Mom would approve?"

Sam shook his head, laughing harder. Tears streamed down his face. "Take a selfie just in case."

"Hey Sam," O'Connor said between guffaws. "I got a job for you if you want it."

Sam shook his head. "Tempting, but no thanks."

O'Connor spotted the lone remaining rat on the counter. The rodent continued to chew at the sides of the collapsible cage as if the century's biggest rat barbecue hadn't just happened. She grabbed the cage and brought it down to Sam's eye level. "Still afraid of rats?"

Sam saw the cage and the rat inside, but didn't flinch this time. Instead, he raised his middle finger towards O'Connor. "Fuck you very much."

Washington's taser rod still lay in the hallway. O'Connor

picked it up and held both the taser and the cage out to Sam. "The last spike. Want to do the honors?"

Sam shook his head.

"Suit yourself." O'Connor set the collapsible cage on the counter again and jammed the taser rod in through the bars. She pulled the trigger and the rat inside let out a short squeal before it jettisoned off the taser's prongs, smoldering and dead.

Hope cocked her head and narrowed her eyes at O'Connor. "I think you enjoyed that a little too much."

O'Connor shrugged. "I do what it takes to get the job done." She stuck her hand out towards Sam. He took it and O'Connor helped him up off the floor, then shook his hand. "And I think I'm done here." She looked at Washington's shrouded body in the hallway. "You can call the police now."

Sam looked over his shoulder. "Brad, could you—"

"Already on it." Bradley dialed 9-1-1.

"Who's gonna help me clean this mess up?" O'Connor looked at Hope, Bradley and Sam.

All three burst into laughter at the same time.

Terminus

IF YAH SEE *one rat, there's ten yah can't*. Sam never forgot those words. And Captain Hook at Hunts Point Hardware repeated those words to everyone who bought anything rat-related whether they cared to listen or not. Sam had heard O'Connor and Hope relay that information on more than one occasion, too. For Sam and Bradley, it became their mantra. Restocking trips weren't complete until they heard the words. *If yah see one rat…*

"We're the reason you're still in business," Sam had said once to Captain Hook.

"Nah. The rats are the reason." Captain Hook had grinned. "Long live the rat."

The Gambian invasion had left a lot of vacant apartments, and with the exception of Mrs. Baxter, it presented a happy problem for Sam. He oversaw all the new tenants that moved into the building and made sure they weren't belligerent assholes like Gustavo or Melvin. New tenants were told that they might see the odd rat or two, because New York City goes with rats like peanut butter goes with strawberry jam.

After the white-tails were exterminated (that's the name Bradley gave the Gambian hybrids), the summer proceeded as Sam had hoped. Sam and Bradley got to know each other better, and Bradley helped Sam work on his fear of rodents by dealing with the stragglers. There were always stragglers, but they never saw any the size of the alpha rat again. There weren't any hordes either. For those that made an appearance, either Bradley or Sam would catch and dispatch the dead rodents without delay. If the numbers ever got too great, O'Connor and her new crew were just a phone call away.

THE PLASTIC MAT that used to be next to Sam's apartment door had been replaced with a wooden free-standing cabinet. The double doors opened to reveal a coat rack on steroids. It looked like Sam had brought all of Hunts Point Hardware home with him. He had it all. Snap traps hung on the door in a chain. Boxes of poison sat on shelves beside peanut butter, rubber gloves, and small white garbage bags. On another shelf sat glue traps, smaller mouse traps, and sonic and electric traps (to appease Bradley's fascination with gadgets).

Sam used poison as a last resort. Rats would die and rot in the walls, and release an ungodly odor that would last for months. For the tenant, it was a choice between enduring the smell or ripping open the walls. And extraction of dead rat bodies from the old walls was both expensive and time consuming. Occasionally, it led to more complicated issues, like when Sam cut into a decayed water supply pipe by accident, and flooded the unit below. The water damage would have been much worse if he hadn't known where the main water shut-off valve was.

On one side of the cabinet hung a taser rod. It had been

Washington's before he died, and O'Connor had presented it to Bradley after the Gambian invasion. Bradley, in turn, added it to Sam's burgeoning stock of weapons. Sam was ready for anything now.

SAM DROPPED A pizza box from Kingsley's on the kitchen table. On the top of the box lay a dead rat caught in the jaws of a snap trap. He opened the cabinet and pulled out a garbage bag.

Back at the table, Sam picked up the snap trap and raised the dead rat up to his face, something he wouldn't have been able to do two months ago. He stared at the rat's dulled black eyes.

"Sorry," Sam said. "Either you go or I go, and I got nowhere else."

Sam pulled back the kill arm and dropped the rat, stiff with rigor mortis, into the garbage bag. He peeled off his disposable gloves, dropped them on top, and secured the bag with a knot. He placed the bag on the kitchen counter.

"Get it while it's hot!" Sam said.

Sounds of the television clicked off. Bradley entered the kitchen and spotted the white garbage bag on the counter before he sat at the table.

"Is that from the Dobbies in 201?"

"Yup, but I think there's more."

"There's always more, Dad."

Sam pulled open the pizza box to uncover a steaming pepperoni and mushroom pie, sliced into twelve haphazard pieces. "Their pug's been going ape shit, scratching at the walls at all hours of the day and night. I left another trap and reminded them to keep their dog away from it."

Sam and Bradley each grabbed a slice of pizza.

"So, what do you think?" Sam said. "Same time next year?"

"Sure, Dad," Bradley said between chews. "It's been cool. But it doesn't have to be just summers."

"You think your mom would go for that?"

"If she doesn't, she's going to have a moody teenager on her hands." Bradley smiled.

"You've been planning this, haven't you?"

Bradley's smile melted into a wide grin.

"I like the way you think," Sam said. He looked to the table for beverages to salute with. "Shit. Just a sec."

Sam went to the refrigerator and grabbed two Cokes. The refrigerator door, bare two months ago, was now covered in notes and photos. One stood out from the rest, a selfie of Sam and Bradley holding up a dead rat by the tail. They both were gasping in feigned horror. Sam loved the photo. It represented everything they had accomplished in two months.

He returned to the table and handed one Coke to Bradley. Sam cracked the seal on his can and raised it up.

"To my son, Bradley," Sam said. "A better exterminator of vermin than I'll ever be."

"Thanks, Dad."

They clinked cans and each took a sip.

A knock sounded. Hope popped her head in before Sam had a chance to open the door. Bradley swallowed his bite like a stone. Hope would always be his Kryptonite.

"Hey guys," she said. "Something smells good."

"Pepperoni and mushroom." Sam held up the box. "Want some?"

"Rain check," Hope said, "but I need a couple of bulbs replaced."

"I'll put it on our list for tomorrow." Sam bit into his slice of pizza. "I'm sure Brad can handle that for you."

"Yup." Bradley straightened himself in his chair. "No problem."

"How's Harriette?" Sam said.

"Still in her cage."

"Good."

Hope stepped into the apartment. "Brad, how's your shoulder?"

Bradley shot Hope a glare, but Sam caught it as it went past. Silence hung heavy in the apartment for a moment.

Sam looked at Hope, then at Bradley.

"Alright." Sam pointed at Hope. "You. Sit."

Hope tiptoed to the kitchen table. "I thought you told him," she said, under her breath.

"Told me what?" Sam eyed Hope and Bradley. They both looked as guilty as two dogs next to a half-eaten Christmas turkey. "Okay, guys. Spill it."

"Just show him," Hope said.

Bradley looked at Sam. "It wasn't my idea."

"Bullshit it wasn't." Hope crossed her arms. "Show him."

Sam looked at Bradley. "Show me."

Bradley drew a deep breath, grabbed the right cuff of his t-shirt sleeve, and rolled it up his biceps. A tattoo of a stylized black rat with a red circle-backslash symbol over top appeared on Bradley's shoulder, a half inch at a time.

Sam stared at the tattoo. The first thought that went

through his mind was how he was going to explain it to Claire. But he squashed the thought. "Do you like it?"

Bradley smiled at Sam's reaction, which was the opposite to what he had expected. He looked at the tattoo. "Yeah."

"Your mom's not going to like it."

"That's between me and her," Bradley said. "Don't worry. I'll keep you out if it."

"Thanks, but I'm sure she'll find some reason to tear a strip off me." Sam nodded at Bradley. "I guess you're a man, now."

Bradley shrugged. "Guess so."

Sam turned to Hope. "You did this?"

"There's a place with a good rep a few blocks away." Hope grinned and thumbed at Bradley. "The design was Brad's idea."

"Nicer than prison tats, which I don't recommend." Sam leaned in for a closer look, then examined his own heavily tattooed arms, looking for free space. "I want one, too. If I can find the room, that is."

"On second thought…" Hope grabbed a slice of pizza. "I'm starving." She took a bite, chewing hungrily. She shifted her gaze back and forth between Sam and Bradley. "So Brad, what's your next tattoo going to be?"

"I don't know," Bradley said. "What do you think, Dad?"

"How about a heart with 'Mom' written inside?" Sam winked at Bradley. "It could go right in the center of your chest."

Bradley laughed. "Shit, no."

"How about 'Kingsley's Fried Chicken & Pizza?'" Hope said. "You'd probably get a discount for life."

"So I could buy more of this." Bradley held up a slice of pizza that drooped like a wet flag. "I'll get right on that."

All three were laughing now.

"Did you see that story about the woman who tattooed her boyfriend's name on her face?" Hope shook her head. "Not a good look. Stay away from the face."

"Trust me. One's enough." Sam said. "But on the odd chance that you feel compelled to get another, just don't get it in prison."

"You got it." Bradley bumped fists with Sam.

"I'll be right back." Sam stood up and grabbed the garbage bag on the counter with the dead rat in it. "Got to get rid of this."

Sam walked down the hallway to the garbage chute. He pulled open the spring-loaded door and looked down its dark gullet.

A wide smile crept across his face as he dropped the bag into the chute, swallowed up by darkness.

"Have a nice ride, you little bastard." The rat in the bag bounced against the metal walls of the garbage chute, echoing all the way down.

Sam closed the door to the chute and walked back to his apartment, his thoughts already on his next slice of pizza and his next tattoo.

April 7, 2016 - March 20, 2017
Victoria, BC

Titles by Lee Gabel

Detest-A-Pest Series
Molerat 2.0
Arachnid 2.0
Vermin 2.0

Standalone
Snipped
David's Summer
Tied

Afterword

Like it? Rate it. Share it.

If you enjoyed *Vermin 2.0*, please rate and review it. With your rating, you take part in this book's success. If you're interested in joining Lee's Reader Group for updates and advance notice of upcoming releases, please sign up by going to LeeGabel.com.

Note from the author

Thank you for reading my second novel. The genesis of the idea came from having to become a rodent exterminator on my own property in 2008. In the space of a few months, I caught more rats than I care to admit. A few properties down from me, a dirty, run-down house stood vacant, and had been that way for years. It was the neighborhood eyesore and affected property values of the surrounding homes. The owner of the property was given an ultimatum: clean up and renovate the place, or demolish it. The owner chose to raze the house, but before that could be done, the community's health authority needed to inspect the home's interior for asbestos, lead, and anything else harmful to the environment. That's when the colony of rats were discovered. Hundreds of them. The air was so bad inside the house that inspectors had to go in wearing hazmat suits and breathing apparatuses. They didn't use electricity to kill the rats, but in the end the colony was decimated, and the house was bulldozed soon after. I didn't see many rats on my property after that, but the idea of a rat-infested living area stuck with me. Since I had hands-on experience as exterminator, the ideas and images were forefront in my mind. I wrote a screenplay first (which placed highly in a couple of competitions), then used the screenplay as the basis of this novel. As with both of my books so far, I have used real street names, but have altered addresses and made up all locations and businesses.

I would like to thank my Advance Reader Team for their insightful comments before this book was published. As they say, more critical eyes are better. Many thanks go to my wife Sheila for editing my many drafts. I couldn't do this without you. As always, I owe a debt of gratitude to David Hoselton for helping me workshop and refine the screenplay that this novel is based on. To my family and friends who supported my decision to quit my job to write full time (the scariest decision I've ever made), you were right. I am *your* number one fan now.

About the author

Why does Lee write? In his own words: "Writing is magic. I'll never understand how it works the way it does, but I do know if I put energy into writing, it rewards me in strange and wonderful ways. Even if I know where I'm going in a story, often I'll end up being pulled in directions by my characters that I least expect. What ends up on the page never ceases to surprise me, and that's super cool.

Writing continues to be one of the most difficult and most rewarding aspects of my life."

Lee has spent most of his life living on an island in the Pacific Northwest and has worked within the visual and dramatic arts landscape as a graphic designer, illustrator, visual effects artist, animator, screenwriter and author.

Find Lee on the Internet:

Want to join Lee's Reader Group or find out more about Lee and the books he writes? Please go to:

LeeGabel.com

Facebook.com/Lee.Gabel.Author

Twitter.com/LeeFGabel

Or follow Lee on BookBub

* 9 7 8 0 9 9 9 1 8 4 9 8 4 0 *